DRUMLINE

STACY KESTWICK

Copyright @2017 by Stacy Kestwick

ISBN-13: 978-1975961206
ISBN-10: 197596120X

All rights reserved.

No part of this book may be reproduced in any form or by any electronic or mechanical means, including information storage and retrieval systems, without written permission from the author, except for the use of brief quotations in a book review.

Cover by Hang Le
Editing by Erin Noelle and JaVa Editing
Proofreading by Kata Cuic, Julie Deaton, and Ellie McLove
Formatting by Champagne Book Design

DEDICATION

For all the band geeks.

CHAPTER 1

Laird

"**I**S THIS ALL OF THEM?" MARCO STUDIED THE CROWD of lanky drummers milling around the undersized room we'd been assigned and then checked the time on his phone. A quick glance at the standard school clock on the wall confirmed it was four past eight in the morning. The shitty acoustics and incessant, discordant sound of thirty pairs of drumsticks tapping away on whatever surface was handy – the cinderblock walls, cheap plastic chairs, the thin carpet whose original color was no longer discernable – grated on my last nerve. Combined with the stink of so many guys trapped in subpar air-conditioning and Marco's surly attitude, I couldn't help but feel like a popcorn kernel in the microwave. Annoyed and hot, with a temper ready to explode.

Normally, I loved this.

Auditions. The beginning of band camp. That easy

month before the fall semester actually started, when the only ones on campus were the über-nerds who took summer classes, the football team, and the marching band.

But not today.

Today, I was fucking cranky. Tired from last night's bullshit with my dad and his unreasonable expectations, hungry since my fridge was empty except for some hot sauce and half a bottle of mustard, and frustrated because I hadn't been laid in the last month and my balls were aching to empty themselves somewhere other than down the shower drain. And the damn gas station had been out of coffee. Eight was considered the asscrack of dawn in a college town. How the hell had they already run out of coffee?

I shot Marco a warning look and yanked the plastic clipboard from his loose grip. Ignoring his scowl, I scanned down the list of names and reviewed today's schedule. An hour of admin stuff and then PT.

Great. It was already over eighty-five degrees in the shade.

Trying to summon up some iota of motivation, I chugged the rest of my nasty energy drink that was not even remotely a substitute for coffee and crushed the aluminum can in my fist before tossing it in the trashcan. The harsh metallic rattle caused heads to swivel our direction and the chatter to die down.

I took a deep breath and let it sit in my lungs for a few seconds before I exhaled. It probably wasn't cool to admit it, but drumline was generally the highlight of my year. The transition time at the beginning for the new crew to gel into a cohesive unit was always a bitch, but after that, things were golden.

And this was my year. As snare captain, it was my rules to follow, my ass on the line. Rodner University had the reputation of having the best snare line in Alabama—argu-ably the whole Southeast—and upholding that standard would fall on the shoulders of the ten best drummers this side of the Mason-Dixon.

But mostly mine.

Good thing I had some big fucking shoulders.

Marco glared menacingly at the motley bunch of wan-nabes mixed in with last year's guys. He took his role as lieu-tenant way too seriously. His thin lips twisted into a sneer as he flicked his gaze over the newbies who thought they had the skills to hang in the Shark Tank—the affectionate name we gave our football stadium.

He opened his mouth to speak, but I noticed the move-ment and rushed to cut him off. I liked the guy, but he loved nothing more than stealing my thunder and my patience was wearing thin. "Welcome!" Ugh, the saccharine in my voice had even me wincing.

"If you're in this room, you should be auditioning for the snare line. If you're not auditioning, time to get your ass out of here." My eyes drifted from face to face before settling on a chick in the corner, waiting for her to rise and kiss her boyfriend goodbye and skedaddle.

Nothing against her, but I wanted to get started already. By tradition, Rodner's snare line had always been an exclu-sively male domain. It wasn't so much that girls weren't al-lowed, just that none had ever been good enough, and over the years, they'd simply stopped trying out.

She met my gaze steadily, her shoulders relaxed and her full mouth set in an unimpressed line. I paused a beat, then tipped my head toward the door, signaling to her. Her dark eyes flicked that direction, then returned to me, her expres-sion unchanged. She blew a pink gum bubble languidly and crossed her toned arms below her chest, and my attention automatically dipped to assess her small, but perky rack outlined by a tight gray tank top. Her tits weren't that big, but she was wearing a sports bra, so they were probably fuller without it. And they looked real. Lord knows that small hint of cleavage was the first good thing I'd come across all week.

My lonely dick stirred behind my thin nylon shorts, and I casually moved the clipboard in my hand to waist-height to conceal the evidence.

The bubble popped and she sighed like she was bored.

"Hey, girl, that means you." Marco wasn't big on subtlety.

"Pretty sure I'm right where I'm supposed to be." Her voice was light, unconcerned, and she lifted one shoulder in a shrug, as if his comment wasn't even worth the effort of moving them both. It was like waving a red flag at a pawing bull. Marco stiffened, his hand already rising to point at her, when she continued. "Reese Holland. Check the list. I signed in earlier." She looked down at her fingernails and it was then I noticed the pair of drumsticks held loosely in her grasp.

Well, fuck me.

Marco tore the clipboard from my hand, then dragged his finger down the column of names, and I shifted my stance to look over his shoulder. And hide my burgeoning erection.

Sure enough, number nineteen on the list was none other than a Reese Holland from Morgantown, West Virginia. Freshman. Eighteen years old. He stabbed at the paper, wrinkling it with the motion.

"But, you're a girl." Marco's snarl of indignation had me cringing at his delivery.

She tipped her head to the side, her dark ponytail

spilling over one smooth shoulder as she considered him. "Pretty astute there."

Snickers from some of the other guys in the room had him turning to glare at me, as if her gender was my fault. I bit back a grin. Very few guys had the balls to go up against Marco, and to see this chick giving him shit right back was kind of doing it for me. It was a dumb move on her part, because the guy held a grudge against me for beating him out for lead snare since middle school, but I couldn't deny that I enjoyed it just the same.

Too bad she probably wouldn't last the day. Again, it wasn't personal. Most of the freshmen auditioning would be cut—and soon. The math didn't stack up in her favor. But still, it was a shame. I could get used to the view.

"Right." I nodded like an idiot, trying to regain control of the situation. "So. It's the first day of auditions. I'm Laird Bronson, this year's captain, and I'll be running the camp for the next two weeks. To get this far, you've already submitted a video to the faculty, proving you at least know the difference between a triple and a flam, and now it's time for the real testing to begin. But before you all go getting hard-ons about making the line, know this. There are thirty-seven names on this list, and we only have ten spots on the field. Seven of those belong to returning drummers."

While everyone technically had to tryout, it was an unspoken rule that once you made the line, you had a guaranteed spot. Assuming you weren't a total fuckwad the year before and we needed an excuse to get rid of you. And since what remained of last year's crew was solid, that left another seven spots to fill between those who made the cut to march on the field and a couple of alternates for back up.

Time for the motivational part of my welcome speech.

"You can do the math yourself, but the bottom line is,

most of y'all are going to wind up getting cut. I expect about half of you will be gone by the end of the day. Definitely by the end of the week."

I let that sink in as I looked at the overconfident faces hanging on my every word. Yeah, they all thought they were special, special snowflakes. The one that would beat the odds. Only the top ten percent of them would spend any time under the floodlights of the stadium on game day, playing for forty-thousand screaming fans.

"Drumline is the heartbeat of any marching band, but more than that, *this* snare line is unrivaled. We're the starting quarterbacks. Sure, as a whole, the band is great, but let's be honest, the drumline is what people are really coming to see. And if we don't hold up our end, the entire performance falls apart. So we're not just looking for someone who can keep time and bang out some rhythms and throw in some fancy stick work. We're looking for those of you who can perform." I paused to emphasize my next words. "Reliably. With distractions. And under pressure."

A proud smirk stretched my lips. "We're looking for the drummers who can take it all the way to the end zone."

"Damn straight!" The hoot came from Bubba, the only returning senior besides Marco and myself.

I nodded at him and the other veterans grouped together in the corner, knowing they understood exactly what I meant.

We were the main attraction that drew the crowds. Yeah, okay, they were there to watch some pretty fucking intense football too, but at Rodner, no one left their seats at halftime until we were done. Only then would they swarm the over-priced concessions for BBQ nachos and slushies.

We ran the show all right, on and off the field. And making the line meant surviving not just auditions, but drumline hazing.

These NADs—our purposefully raunchy nickname for the Newly Acquired Drummers—had no idea what they were getting themselves into. Hours of practice. Mandatory parties. Stupid pranks. Dumb objectives to achieve and tight deadlines to reach them in. It's how we bonded, learned to read each other's movements and play perfectly in sync.

But first things first. Weeding out the weak and pathetic. The bottom-feeders.

Because snare line was the very top of the food chain.

"To start with this morning, we have a five-mile jog. This one's pretty straight forward. You'll have backpacks with twenty-five pounds of sand bags inside, which you'll wear on your chests to mimic the weight of the snare. You have an hour to complete the laps around the track in the heat, or you're out. Later today, we'll move onto stick work, some sight-reading, and begin going through the first song of the show." I ticked off the rules. "Stay hydrated. Don't bitch. Help each other out. If a vet asks you to do something, do it. Don't ask questions. All the vets are wearing red shirts to make it easy on you idiots. If you're asked to leave, exit without making a scene. Most of you will be gone in the next two weeks and that's just reality. No need to throw a fucking tantrum like a girl."

After the last sentence left my mouth, I froze, my eyes automatically sliding to Reese.

Okay, yeah, poor word choice there. Reese's face twisted like she'd just tasted something sour and she looked… was that disappointment she was aiming my way? A wedge of discomfort poked at my ribs and I found myself wanting to say something more, to fix my gaffe, but I held my tongue.

The captain didn't cater to anyone, least of all a NAD. In fact, the only special treatment they got was to work longer and harder to earn that field spot.

But, damn, if I didn't want to erase that look in her eyes. Replace it with something else. Something hotter. I bet she looked incredible when she was aroused. Those lips swollen and slightly parted, wet from earlier kisses. Eyes dilated and half closed. A flush painting those high cheekbones. Pulse throbbing at the base of her throat. Dark hair mussed from where my hands had been buried—*wait a second.*

My hands?

I forced my gaze to the toes of my Nike's, where the rubber on the right one was starting to curl away from the leather, and counted to ten to calm myself down, but couldn't stop my eyes from seeking hers out again. This time, amusement brightened her gaze and, fuck, if she didn't have a dimple on one side where her lip had pulled up in a smirk, as if she knew what I was thinking and found it laughable.

I wanted to lick it, that dimple.

"Be trackside in twenty minutes to suit up and check in," I barked. "Grab a folder with the paperwork and release forms, fill that shit out, take a piss, make sure you have a water bottle, whatever the fuck else you need to do. The weights will be down at the starting line and the clock starts at nine, sharp. Questions?"

Two guys raised their hands and I stared right through them, not acknowledging either one. Behind them, Reese stretched her arms over her head, her hands gripping both ends of her drumsticks, and I would've given my right nut for the AC to choose that minute to turn on, to get a glimpse of her hardened nipples against the fabric straining at her tits as she arched her back. I must've bargained with the wrong deity though, because she relaxed back into her seat without the telltale rattle kicking in.

Beside me, Marco made a small noise of appreciation

and a quick glance confirmed his eyes were planted where mine had been just a moment before. Anger swelled my chest and my fingers curled into a fist I wanted to bury in his gut for noticing her body. I didn't want his eyes—or any other part of him—anywhere near her.

"No? Great. See you there." Cursing under my breath, I turned and left the room. If there were additional things to discuss, questions to answer, shit to deal with—Marco could have at it. As long as he stayed away from her.

Fuck, what was wrong with me this morning? Was that damned energy drink laced with Viagra or something? Was the passionfruit flavor an indicator of some side effects I hadn't anticipated?

I needed to splash a bucketful of cold water on my face and pull myself together. But my feet walked right by the water fountain, took me out the heavy steel double doors, and across the grassy courtyard dotted with picnic tables to the white stucco English building.

Burton Hall was guaranteed to be empty this time of day, the men's bathroom on the second floor deserted.

I had twenty minutes to relieve the ache.

Turned out, I only needed eight.

CHAPTER 2

Reese

MARCO ALL BUT BARED HIS TEETH WHEN HE DROPPED the backpack on my shoulders. He'd held the nylon straps away from my body, so when he let go, the sandbags in the bottom whooshed down and nailed me in the stomach, pushing a surprised grunt past my lips. If possible, his mouth stretched further, until he resembled the Big Bad Wolf.

But he was way off the mark if he thought I could be chased away as easily as Little Red. I'd battled much tougher enemies in my life than an insecure man-child. Marco seemed like the type of guy who liked his women soft-spoken and subservient. Where he could be the one to beat his chest in all his imagined alpha glory and shine in the public eye, while she stayed tucked away in the library, writing his term paper for him, hidden from the glow of the sun. In my mind, I renamed him Scrotum Breath, since his head was so far up his own ass.

"How's that? Too much?" He attempted to look down his nose at me, but the fact that we were the same height—five foot ten—ruined the effect because he had to tip his head back so far.

"I doubt anything about you would be considered *too much*—but thanks for the concern." I dropped my chin, and glanced pointedly at his crotch. He was still sputtering his outrage as I walked away, my eyes firmly on the rubber track so he wouldn't see the satisfaction painted across my face.

Reese 2, Scrotum Breath 0.

After tucking a water bottle in the mesh side pocket of the bag for easy access, I lined up with the rest of the guys, adjusting the straps to a slightly more comfortable position. The two drummers standing closest on my right took a step back, distancing themselves from me, and I raised an eyebrow in disbelief. Turning to confront them directly, I wiggled my fingers at them and whispered, "Cooties!" They scooted farther away, and I rolled my eyes at their lack of balls.

So far, this drumline's reputation was not living up to the reality.

Well, except for maybe the captain. My fingers were crossed that he wasn't a turd sandwich beneath all his admittedly pretty packaging.

A soft chuckle came from behind me and I whipped around, ready to dish out more, but when I faced the tall, caramel-skinned smirk hiding behind mirrored-aviator sunglasses, I got the sense he was laughing with me rather than at me. He came closer and bumped his shoulder against mine. "You know," he grinned as he tipped his head in Marco's direction, "nothing good is going to come from antagonizing him. You're just making yourself an even bigger target than you already are."

I pursed my lips as I thought about it for a minute, respecting the fact that he was probably right. "I know. But I can't help it. I'm allergic to assholes."

He threw his head back and laughed, a full-on belly laugh, not caring about the stares we generated. I smiled, liking him already. But then he sobered and caught my eye. "I hear you. But you're poking a hornet's nest with that one from what I've heard, so just don't be surprised if you wind up getting stung."

His warning rolled right off my back. I'd been dealing with overly sensitive male egos since I'd picked up my first pair of sticks. It wasn't anything I couldn't handle. Inclining my head in acknowledgement, I stuck my hand out in his direction. "I'm Reese."

"I think we *all* know your name after this morning." He shook my hand without hesitation, his palm swallowing mine. "And I'm Smith. Smith Whitmore. Need a running buddy this morning?"

Trying to feel out the sincerity of his offer, I searched his face. Smith was just a smidgeon taller than me, with close-cropped dark hair and a smile that radiated nothing but honesty. My stomach was calm, his presence not setting off any ripples of unease, and if there was one thing I'd learned to trust over the years, it was my gut. Smith was one of the good guys.

I leaned closer as if divulging a secret. "Think you can keep up?"

"With you? Girl, you're out of my league, there's no denying that. But you could take pity on me anyway."

"Damn, I'm fresh out of pity this morning." I held up my empty palms as evidence. "The only thing I brought with me today was some attitude and a metric fuckton of badassness." My wide eyes and the innocent tone of my voice earned me another one of his fabulous laughs.

"Alright, alright. I see how it is. But you're talking a big game, so if you can't back it up when the time comes, this is gonna have a really bad ending."

I flipped my sunglasses on top of my head and cocked my hip. "Are you doubting me, Smith?"

"Just don't make me look like a fool. That's all I'm asking." His inflection was light, almost mocking, but the slight tensing of his jaw hinted at a seriousness to the request. He glanced around at the noticeable distance the rest of the guys were giving us.

I softened. He was the first one to seem genuinely willing to give me a chance, to literally stand by me, and, Lord knows, I needed an ally. "Trust me." I nodded. "I've got this."

He rocked on the balls of his feet as he studied me, then a half smile cracked his face when he registered my candor. "You set the pace, and I'll stick with you. But you better know how to use those long ass legs of yours." Smith held his fist up between us and I tapped it with my own.

"You have no idea." I winked.

I turned toward the starting line, where the nervous prattle of the others was getting louder, and found my nose two inches from Laird's chin, the bookbag strapped to my chest digging into his solid abdomen. Sucking in a surprised breath while I regained my balance did nothing but bring his scent—peppermint gum and something woodsy—deep into my lungs, where I held it close for a few pounding heartbeats, unwilling to release it so easily. But when I flicked my gaze a bit higher to his eyes, I let it all out in a whoosh.

His eyes.

Dear sweet little baby Jesus, they were beautiful. His irises were a green so pure, it made me picture a field of shamrocks. In Ireland. On St. Patrick's Day. Tiny flecks of gold were sprinkled near the center, adding a depth and richness, and his lashes rivaled mine, although I used Benefit's mascara for assistance. The strong slash of his eyebrows made me itch to trace their shape with my finger, just to see if the line would bend, to discover if they felt soft or rough against my skin.

I licked my dry lips, swaying slightly as I fell further into my inspection. High cheekbones rose above a chiseled jawline tempered only by a day's worth of stubble. I bet it would be scratchy in the best way when it rubbed against a girl's neck. Or her inner thighs. I swallowed. His full mouth parted and his chest rose from a sharp inhale. I found myself wanting to lean forward, to let him hold my weight and not flinch from the extra burden. His nostrils flared and the heat from his fingers seared my hips as he reached out to steady me.

My eyelids drooped at the contact and I fought the instinct to rub against him and purr my pleasure. Mark him as mine. It was like his pheromones were custom designed to have the impact of a sucker-punch, stealing my breath and turning me into a junkie after just one hit.

Until he opened his mouth and ruined it.

"You sure you can handle this? Five miles?" The concern in his voice snapped my spine straight. His arms dropped back to his sides. "There's no shame in quitting now. No sense in putting yourself through it for no reason."

"Do you ask the guys that question too?" I squinted at him.

"No." He locked eyes with me, not shying away from the question. "Just you."

I stretched one calf and then the other, ignoring the way his gaze drifted over my face, lingering on my pursed lips. The heat that settled low in my belly, it was irritation. Definitely not some stupid, misplaced attraction. I reminded myself that some chocolates looked perfect on the outside too, all shiny and glossy and flawless—until you took a bite and realized it was the nasty raspberry one. I smiled, a brittle, superficial smile that I hoped he recognized for what it was.

"Don't you worry 'bout little ol' me," I cooed around a clenched jaw. "I'll see you at the finish line. But that guy over there looks like he might need your help." I nodded at a pale kid on the edge of the track, sucking desperately on an inhaler. Whether or not he caught my emphasis on the word *guy* was hard to tell.

With a muttered curse and one last lingering look that promised this conversation wasn't over, he turned and left, off to play hero to someone who actually needed it.

But he'd distracted me. When the air horn blast threatened to burst my eardrums a few minutes later, I was still bent over on the track, retying my shoes. The rest of the guys shot off, leaving Smith and me behind. Marco joined the two of us as we trailed the pack around the first bend. He was both shirtless and unencumbered by a backpack.

"Reese. Not surprised at all to find you in the back. But, Smith, I expected more from you." He jogged so close to me his elbow jabbed me with every swing of his arm. A real fucking gentleman.

Smith smiled widely, but didn't change his pace. "You been thinking about me, Marco?"

"What? No!" Marco's step faltered next to me, and I capitalized on his distraction by surging forward, eager to escape his unwelcome company. Smith followed me easily and we passed three guys who were already gasping for breath at the end of the first straightaway.

"Do you know him?" I regulated my breathing, settling into a tempo I knew I could maintain over the distance. Inhale for two steps, exhale for one.

"Marco? Kinda. I know *of* him more than I *know* him. We went to the same high school, but just like now, he was a senior when I was a freshman." He laughed softly. "He was a pretty big deal there, but not as big as he thought he was. Looks like some things haven't changed."

"You mean he's always been this much of an asshole casserole? Today isn't a special occasion or something?"

Smith looked at me reproachfully. "Asshole or not, he's the lieutenant and he can still make our lives miserable if we piss him off. Or, hell, even keep us from making the line."

My lip curled. "He had it out for me before he knew a thing about me except that I had tits instead of a dick."

Smith sighed. "You always this prickly? There a cactus somewhere in your family tree?"

It took half a dozen steps for me to process his dig. "Smith, we're gonna get along just fine, me and you. And because I like you, I'll even try to tone it down around Marco." I smiled slowly. "Unless he starts it. Then all bets are off. If he can't take it, he better be smart enough not serve it up in the first place."

Smith grunted and we switched over to comparing our upcoming class schedules. Turns out we had the same evil eight AM biology class.

By the end of the third mile, four guys had dropped out, their bookbags abandoned by the starting line. Smith and I had lapsed into a comfortable silence, and, because we were drummers, our steps pounded out a matching rhythm as we circled the track. We were solidly in the middle of the remaining pack at this point, with runners spread out pretty evenly around the oval, most in pairs or small groups.

Footsteps thudded behind us, signaling someone's approach.

I glanced over my shoulder, ready to cede the inside lane when they got close enough.

It was Laird.

Unlike Marco, he was wearing a pack, not pulling any punches on himself just because he was the captain. I peeked again, unable to help myself.

His arm muscles were shiny with sweat, and I couldn't resist taking a second to appreciate the way his biceps gleamed in the Alabama humidity. He was bulkier than the average drummer. And his shoulders. Damn, I had a weakness for a nice set of shoulders.

When I stole a third look, Smith turned his head too. I was totally caught. It didn't stop me from noticing, though, where Laird's focus was. Squarely on me.

My cheeks burned from more than just the exertion, and I became acutely aware of the way my running shorts had worked their way up between my thighs, balling up just below my lady bits. Bits that might have been clenching knowing he was back there watching my ass jiggle with every stride.

"You okay there, Reese?" Smith was all but laughing at me.

"Shut up, okay? Just keep moving."

He slanted an assessing eye over me. "I don't think he's out to get you. At least, not the same way Marco is."

"What's that supposed to mean?"

"Nothing. But he's been following us the last two laps, and he seems quite happy with the view from there."

My ears would catch fire if they got any hotter. I hadn't

realized he'd been back there so long. "He has?" I cursed my voice for squeaking.

"Think he's admiring all this milk chocolate I've got going on?" He waved his hand down his body.

"Milk… wait. What?"

"I see you. You're assuming he's feasting those gorgeous green eyes of his on you, aren't you? And you accuse Marco of being sexist." He lowered his chin for a moment. "You wound me, considering you're all about being equal opportunity and shit. Because my ass is looking damn good this morning too."

My eyes widened and I think my jaw dropped a little. I scrabbled for words. "I… no. You're right. I mean, he could be. I don't know." I hesitated. "So you're—"

"I'd like to believe I'm pretty equal opportunity myself, if you get my meaning." He winked and then laughed his great laugh at the shock on my face.

"Girl, you should see yourself. And, don't you worry. His eyes haven't once bothered to enjoy everything I have to offer. I even tried shaking it a little extra." He frowned, an exaggerated look of defeat furrowing his brows. "Nah, he seems pretty damn fixated on you. It's too bad. I bet I could rock his world."

"Smith, I don't doubt you could." My eyes crinkled in amusement.

He nudged me, but not enough to knock me off balance or upset our synchronized rhythm. "Well, if I can't have him, no reason one of us shouldn't get a shot at all that. Don't disappointment me, ya hear?"

I reached for my water bottle, using that as an excuse to look back again. Laird grinned at me, and I whipped my head back around.

Busted.

"So... this equal opportunity stuff? Is it common knowledge? Or... a secret?" I tried to focus on Smith. Not on Laird. Definitely not on Laird, with those shoulders. And those eyes. And those—

"—see what they want to see." Smith's voice brought me back to the present. "And most people don't really look too hard for something like that, ya know? And don't get me wrong, I got all kinds of thoughts about those legs of yours. But I got the feeling you've already got me friend-zoned, so I'm just making the best of it."

I blinked stupidly. My legs? I tried to give Smith a sur-reptitious once-over but he was on to me. "Nah, girl. Don't even try. If I didn't wow you right off the bat, it ain't gonna happen for us." He chuckled. "And it's all good. I could use a friend here too. You can be my sidekick."

I huffed. "Excuse me? What happened to equal oppor-tunity? You can be *my* sidekick."

"Oh, yeah?" He slanted me a challenging look. "Race you for it. Winner gets to be Batman. The cool Batman, not the Val Kilmer version."

I shoved his shoulder, just hard enough to make him stumble two lanes to the right when his backpack slipped down his arm. I waited until he shot a glare at me, smiled not-so-apologetically, then hightailed it down the track. "Enjoy the view, Robin!"

CHAPTER 3

Reese

WHEN MY PHONE DINGED LATE THAT AFTERNOON, I eased up with a wince from my bed, where I'd been laying with ice packs under my shoulder blades. That fucking run. It'd felt good to finish with more than six minutes to spare, edging out Smith in the process, but now, *fuck*, I was paying for it. I would've accused him of letting me win, but Marco had joined him for two laps and from what I could tell from my furtive glimpses, they'd been deep in discussion the whole time. That distraction was probably the real reason I beat him. I punched in the passcode on my phone and squinted at the screen.

Drumline party. Mandatory. 8pm.

The text from an unknown number was immediately followed by another one with an address two blocks from campus.

I groaned, collapsing back on the ice. I wouldn't lie. I

hurt. And the last thing I felt like doing was dressing up and pasting a fake smile on my face.

Laird had been right. They cut a lot of people today. Thirteen out of the thirty NADs were already gone.

But still… I'd already beaten thirteen guys at a game they didn't think I could play. That was a victory of sorts, right? One worth celebrating at a mandatory party?

Two hours, four ibuprofen, and a hot shower later, I examined myself in the mirror hanging on the back of my dorm room door. I'd given it my best, and tonight, my best was gray skinny jeans, a loose black tank with a strappy watermelon-pink bra peeking out from the racerback, and sexy sandals. Heels were just asking too much. My chestnut hair was slicked back in a high ponytail, and I'd doubled my normal amount of eye makeup, going for a dramatic look without tipping over into caked-on territory. My lip gloss and my toenails matched my bra.

Behind me, the empty twin bed on the other side of the room was littered with my discarded outfits. I hoped whatever poor girl showed up in two weeks to be my roommate wasn't a stickler for tidiness. Shrugging my shoulder at my reflection, because, really, I had no intention of changing my ways even if she was, I snagged my phone off my desk and headed out the door.

By the time I trudged my way up two flights of stairs to the designated apartment, it was half past eight. I figured attendance was the mandatory part, not punctuality.

But I was wrong.

Before I was allowed entrance into the thumping, crowded space, I had to do three penalty shots of something clear that I highly suspected was bottom-shelf vodka. One for every ten minutes of tardiness. Thank fuck I wasn't any later than I was.

Trying not to make a face at the lingering burn in my throat, I spotted Smith on the other side of a faded red couch and worked my way over to him.

"I should've given you a head's up not to be late, but, *damn,* girl, if that's what you needed the extra time for, it was worth it." He eyed me up and down, and then leaned back and unapologetically checked out my ass.

Rolling my eyes, I popped it out and gave it a little shake for him. "Yeah? You knew that would happen, Robin? Some sidekick you are." He acted like he was going to smack it and I whipped back around to face him. "Uh-uh. You left me high and dry and think you have a shot at touching this? Hell, no."

He handed over a small bowl of Goldfish crackers he had tucked against his abs. "Here, Batman. Peace offering to help soak up some of the alcohol." He surveyed me again. "For real. Eat some. You don't have a ton of meat on your bones, and trust me when I say there's more alcohol to come tonight."

"You have insider information or something?" I crunched on a trio of fish. Man, I'd forgotten how good these things were. I was probably a kid the last time I had some.

He glanced around before answering, putting his hands on my forearms and leaning close to my ear before speaking. "I got a cousin who was on the line two years ago. He told me some things I'd get in trouble for knowing ahead of time. Hazing shit. But I'll do my best to look after you." I pulled back and narrowed my eyes at him, and he bit back a grin. "Not that you need it, of course."

I nodded. As long as we were clear about the state of my independence. I tossed a few more fish in my mouth. "Who're all these other people?"

"The rest of the line. Cymbals, bass drum, quints. I don't think the pit got the invite, though." He referred to the percussion instruments that didn't march. The group that handled the xylophones, gong, and other unwieldy apparatuses hung out on the fringes of the action, both on the field and off, even though they were technically a part of the drumline. He tipped his head toward the makeshift bar on the kitchen counter. "I think a few of the especially bouncy ones over there are majorettes."

The pitch of their giggles confirmed his guess, as did the length of their skirts. I didn't blame them for showing up though. Drummers were hot and were known for their talented fingers. "Is there anyone here you've—"

An arm flung around my shoulder and a red plastic cup was shoved in my face, the liquid inside sloshing dangerously close to the rim. Marco's face was uncomfortably close to mine as I rescued the drink before he dumped it down my shirt. I schooled my expression as his beer breath bathed my face. My shoulders were still aching and him leaning on me wasn't helping matters.

"What's this?" I held up the cup and used the motion to force some more space between us. "I wouldn't have expected you to come bearing gifts."

He laughed, a loud, grating sound that gave me a pretty good indication how many drinks he'd already had himself. "It's the official drumline drink. NAD juice."

I swirled the thick, syrupy red concoction. It smelled both sweet and strong at the same time.

"Drink up, babe." The challenge in his voice was unmistakable.

After the three shots at the door, I was feeling loose as I lifted it to my lips and chugged the whole thing in one go, maintaining eye contact with him the whole time. Finished, I smacked my lips and handed him the empty cup. "Delicious." And, in truth, it wasn't bad. I wouldn't have been surprised at all to find out NAD juice was cheap Hawaiian punch mixed with something like Everclear.

"Damn…" Smith nodded his respect, and the corner of his lip twitched like it wanted to smile, but he was trying to contain it.

Marco snorted. "Looks like someone's had a lot of practice swallowing."

I looked him over slowly, taking in his untucked button-up shirt with the rolled-up sleeves and predictable distressed jeans paired with pristine-white classic Adidas. Flicking my eyes back up, I arched an eyebrow. "Jealous?"

Smith coughed, holding a fist up to his mouth, and I turned to pat his back. "You okay there, buddy?"

"Yeah, thanks. Something kinda burned all the sudden, ya know?" He cleared his throat a few more times, no longer trying to hide his grin.

Marco slung his arm out, but it collided with a leggy redhead before he could open his mouth to respond. She caught his wrist on her admittedly impressive chest, entwined their fingers, and scooted over until she was plastered to his side. I blinked. The girl moved *fast*.

"Marco," she cooed, batting her fake lashes at him. "I was hoping to run into you tonight."

"What?" I mouthed at Smith. This chick *wanted* to spend time with him?

The redhead twisted briefly in our direction. "Hi. I'm Amber. And this is Willa." She tipped her head at the petite blonde next to her. "We both play cymbals." Her and Marco's joined hands rubbed back and forth along the fly of his jeans. "We do our best to keep our snare players happy."

Marco's eyelids drooped, and he seemed to zero in on her candy-red lacquered lips. No doubt he was picturing how that gloss would look circling the base of his dick. "If you'll excuse us..." Without another word, he pulled her through the crowd until they disappeared through a door. Presumably to a bedroom, but I wouldn't put it past him to hog the bathroom instead.

Willa shook her head, her sleek hair swaying gently around her shoulders. "Please, don't judge all of us cymbal girls based on her."

Smith laughed and introduced himself, and then pointed his thumb at me. "And this is Reese. We're both trying out for snare."

"Wait," she peered at me more closely, "you're *both* trying for snare?"

"Yup," I answered. Her reaction would let me know if she fell into the friend or foe category.

"How's that going?" Respect, not derision, colored her tone. Friend it was.

"I'm still here."

She smiled and her whole face lit up, and I thought Marco was an idiot for going for someone like Amber over someone like Willa. "For the record, I hope you make it. I'd love to see things around here shook up a little." She squeezed my arm and whispered conspiratorially, "Plus, you get to work with Laird Bronson all day? How fucking lucky are you!"

"I wouldn't really know." I rubbed my sore shoulder absently, but at the mention of his name, my eyes automatically scanned the crowd, seeking him out. "I've barely talked to him." And it was true. After the run, they'd kept us pretty busy, and while I'd felt the weight of his eyes on me from time to time, we hadn't spoken again.

It took me a minute to spot him in the kitchen next to Bubba and some other guys I hadn't met yet, gathered around a keg while one of them tapped out a rhythm on the side of it with a pair of drumsticks. But what stole my breath was the way he was looking across the room—right at me. His green eyes captured mine boldly, and I fidgeted under the intensity of his gaze, my fingers tugging on the hem of my tank top, smoothing it over the waistband of my jeans.

And I wasn't the only one to notice. Willa squealed, then whispered, "He's looking this way!" She jutted out her curvy hip and twisted toward me and Smith, presenting Laird with an excellent view of her ass. Then she peeked over her shoulder again, working her hair flip like a pro. Even I was impressed.

I shifted my weight to see past her and was oddly disappointed to find him edging around the small bistro table wedged in the corner, our connection broken. But when he climbed up on a cheap, folding kitchen chair, I didn't pass up the opportunity to scope out the way his worn jeans hung from his lean hips and hugged his thighs.

Next to him, Bubba put his fingers to his mouth and let out an ear-splitting whistle. "Y'all. Shut your traps for a minute and listen to the captain!"

The background noise fizzled out and the packed room swung their collective attention his way. Was it just me, or was he blushing slightly under the sudden scrutiny? Our eyes met again, and his gaze lingered for a long moment before roving over the rest of the gathered crowd.

"I want to thank all of you who are still here after the first day for coming out tonight and enjoying some NAD juice with us. We're excited for the upcoming season and to see which of you will make the final cut."

"And for some fresh pussy!" a voice called out.

He laughed. "New faces are always a good thing." Laird held up his cup in agreement and a chorus of hoots rang out. I cringed, wondering if that's all they saw me as—a pair of thighs to be spread, conquered, and discarded. "And so are drumline traditions. The first of which starts tonight. In the effort to mingle and make some new friends, it's expected that all you NADs at least reach first base tonight. Enjoy some drinks, introduce yourselves, and have a good time."

"Condoms are in a bowl by the front door!" another voice shouted. "Be safe!"

"If you don't understand how to hit a single, find a vet to instruct you, or, better yet, go ahead and cut yourself. This is the motherfucking Rodner drumline!" He hopped off the chair as catcalls and howls rang out. I guess that was the official welcome speech.

The buzz rose as everyone shuffled about, groups dispersing and reforming as they lined up their potential partners. While I might have been the only girl auditioning for the snare line, most of the cymbal players were female.

Willa bounced on her toes and dug some lipstick out of her pocket. She smeared on a quick layer of dark pink and smacked her lips. "This was my favorite part last year!" she confided, offering me the tube.

I declined, and scrunched my nose up at her. "Really? It didn't bother you that it was just for some dumb challenge?"

"What? Hell, no. Have you looked around? These are some of the hottest guys at Rodner. Why would I be upset?" She glanced over my shoulder. "Oh, look, Laird is headed this way! I thought we'd kind of had a connection last year, but I didn't hear from him over the summer, so I wasn't sure what to expect." She lifted her arms and fluffed her hair as if trying to decide on which pose she should strike. "I held hi-hat for him for the show, and, you know..."

I didn't, but I wasn't sure I wanted to.

Smith elbowed me, and I swiveled his direction. "What do you think? You want to do this the easy way and get it over with or the hard way?"

"There's an easy way?"

He smiled, slow and confident. "There's always an easy way."

I paused for a beat. "I like easy."

"I was hoping you'd say that. Just remember, I was a gentleman and asked first."

With that, he swooped. One arm caught me around my waist while the other circled my shoulders, then the whole room tipped as I was bent over backward. I reflexively grabbed ahold of his neck for balance. "Nice touch," he murmured.

And then his lips were on mine.

CHAPTER 4

Laird

THE STAB OF WHITE-HOT JEALOUSY WAS SO SHARP AND unexpected, I found myself frozen in the middle of my own fucking party. All around me, people were flirting, laughing, drinking.

And I was stuck, my legs and feet useless beneath me, my heart slamming against my ribcage.

Topher, the drumline's resident hipster, bumped into my side and I shifted to the right a step, unable to tear my eyes away from Smith and Reese. From her lips moving under his, and her arms wrapped tight around his neck.

I ripped the bottle of beer from Topher's hand, ignoring his protest, and chugged it without tasting a drop as I plowed my way through the room. Halfway there, a palm landed on my elbow and I blankly registered a girl calling my name, but I didn't stop.

Couldn't stop.

Why the fuck were they still kissing?

Would I be out of line if I cut Smith from the auditions on the spot?

I was three steps away when they finally broke apart—although the bastard still had his hands on her waist. My lips pinched in annoyance. As if that little display was enough to truly knock her off balance.

"Woah, Smith." She wiped her mouth on the back of her hand, and I couldn't suppress the surge of satisfaction that gave me. "What have you been drinking tonight?" She licked her lips. "It actually tastes pretty good."

He would die.

"Grape lollipop on the way over here. I'm kind of an addict." Smith must've had some tiny measure of self-preservation, because his eyes flickered to me briefly and he dropped his hands. "Better watch out…"

"For what?" Reese laughed, and I couldn't look away from her long enough to glare a warning at Smith to keep his damn hands to himself or he'd find it mighty fucking hard to play the drums tomorrow.

He glanced at me again warily, but held his stance next to her, close enough their arms were still brushing. "Or else you'll get addicted too."

"Bring me one tomorrow. I gotta see what the fuss is all about."

Nothing. There was absolutely nothing about him to fuss over whatsoever.

I joined their circle and thrust my empty bottle at Smith, catching him solidly in the gut. To his credit, he barely flinched. "Here, NAD. Get rid of this and bring me another cold one." I purposefully didn't use his name.

"Sure," he said slowly, studying the hard set of my jaw. "Reese, Willa, can I get you two anything?"

Willa requested something fruity. Reese declined a drink, but called his name as he started for the kitchen. "Can you find me some more of those Goldfish? I think I accidentally spilled the last few when you—"

"Is your shoulder bothering you?" I interrupted.

She turned and tilted her head at me quizzically.

"You're rubbing it." Reese looked down and seemed surprised to find her hand massaging the spot where her neck curved into the slope of her left shoulder.

"Yeah, a little," she admitted, lowering her arm. "But I'm fine. I took a few Motrin, and I'll be good as new tomorrow."

"Want me to take a look at it?" I was already reaching out, my fingers itching for any excuse, no matter how lame, to touch her skin, to see if it felt as soft as I imagined.

She tipped her chin up at me, her expression wary. "Do you ask all the guys that?"

"What?" I screwed up my face. "Fuck, no."

She stepped back, my fingers denied their goal. And, honestly, I was surprised. Not to sound like a dick, but I didn't typically have trouble attracting a girl. Usually the issue was dodging the ones I wasn't interested in.

"Look," she waited a beat until our eyes connected before continuing, "I don't want any special treatment from you. I'm just another drummer trying out for the line, like all the other guys."

Fuck that shit.

On the field, yeah, I was gonna hold her to the same high standard I would any drummer. Hell, I honestly wouldn't be surprised if she still got cut, just because the odds weren't in her favor. But off? She was nuts if she thought the way she looked in those jeans made her blend into the crowd.

No, tonight, she was anything but ordinary. I didn't get a chance earlier today to study the stubborn angle of her jaw, or the delicate way the tip of her nose turned up just a smidge. With her dark hair out of the way, the creaminess of her neck called to me, begging me to trace its curve with my fingers, my mouth, my tongue. And for the first time, I got a good view of her eyes. She didn't need all the makeup she was wearing. No way they could ever look anything but stunning. Her big, coffee brown irises, dark enough to swallow me whole, flashed with irritation as I stepped closer, edging her in front of me until her back was to my chest.

"But you're not," I whispered, dipping my head and deliberately letting my lips graze the shell of her ear.

She shivered, and my cock stirred.

I cupped her shoulders with my palms, my thumbs drifting down between the multitude of bright pink bra straps. I pressed just inside the ridges of her shoulder blades and dug in where I knew she was most likely to have knots from today.

She groaned and tried to jerk away, but I held her in place. *Bullseye.* "Stay still." My voice brooked no argument. Using deep, meticulous strokes, I rubbed the tension out of her upper back, gratified when her muscles slowly relaxed beneath me. Her skin was like warm silk under my hands, and when she arched her back like a cat, lolling her head from side to side, a soft moan escaped from her mouth, and I had to stop myself from pressing against the swell of her ass.

I studied the pink bands crossing her back as I worked, wondering how in the hell it came off. I was jumping ahead several steps in my mind, but this feisty girl was making me crazy. She smelled like cherries and I wasn't sure if it was from her, or the fruity drink I'd seen her gulp down when Marco had joined her. The pads of my thumbs smoothed their way up the tight cords of her neck, and I felt more than heard the hum of satisfaction vibrate through her.

I couldn't help it. I eased closer, rationalizing it was a crowded room and I was conserving space. She was the perfect height for me, tall for a girl, but still several inches below my six foot three. Kissing her would be easy, her tilting up and me tipping down. No awkward crouching required while she balanced on her toes.

"You know," Willa said, rolling her shoulders, "those cymbals get damn heavy." She sidled my direction and motioned to her own back. "Last year, I always got the worst pain right there—remember?"

No, I didn't.

In front of me, Reese stiffened, her spine straightening until her ponytail tickled my chin. I tightened my fingers, not ready to let her go yet. I aimed a noncommittal noise at Willa. "It always takes a few weeks to strengthen up."

Reese pulled away from me, one foot sliding forward to break our connection. "I think I'm good now, thanks," she murmured. Pink tinged those high cheekbones of hers. "How much do your cymbals weigh?" She directed the question at Willa.

"God, who knows, but it feels like a hundred pounds by the end of the day."

I pressed my lips together as Reese scooted away, a full two feet of emptiness between us. Who fucking cared about her cymbals?

"Yeah," Reese said. "I know what you mean. The drum seems like it gets heavier and heavier sometimes."

Great. They were bonding.

Then Smith showed back up, drinks and crackers in hand, and I knew it was a lost cause. I huffed out my irritation as I accepted the beer he'd retrieved for me. "Thanks," I acknowledged, the word clipped. I took a quick swallow and then held the bottle loosely in front of me, using it to camouflage what was left of my erection.

Reese took the cup filled to the brim with Goldfish and sent Smith a blinding smile. Over some fucking crackers. I scowled. She stepped aside, and Smith settled into the open space between us.

Willa touched my shoulder and asked me something about the schedule tomorrow, but I barely heard her, muttering a quick reply about checking her email, my eyes repeatedly drawn back to Reese.

I might not have been standing next to her, but she was aware of me. It was in the way her eyes flicked to mine, and then quickly away, her tongue slipping out to wet her full lower lip. The way she sucked in a quick breath when I continued to watch her, ignoring Willa's blathering next to me. Hell, it was even in the way her shoulders and hips faced me, despite placing her at an awkward angle within our little circle.

Smith distracted me, asking me a technical question about stick height during the opening number. "Nine inches to start," I answered without ever looking at him. It was rude, but I didn't care. I was thoroughly preoccupied by the sight of Reese chasing an errant fish out of the loose neckline of her shirt, her fingers disappearing into her cleavage.

"That's what she said," Marco jeered as he shoved his way next to me, dragging a redhead with him. April? Amy? Her name was something like that.

"Right," I deadpanned, in no mood for his company tonight. The beer tasted like shit when I took a long swallow, but it was cold and wet and made Marco infinitely more bearable.

Smith tipped his head toward Marco. "That piece for sight-reading this afternoon was pretty wicked. Any chance we'll get to play something like that for the drum break?"

"Ooh." Willa clapped. "I'd be happy to be your part-ner for that again this year, Laird." *Okay, whatever.* I smiled weakly when she grabbed my bicep and squeezed.

"Not likely," Marco snorted. "Unless you guys do a hell of a lot of practicing between now and then. Most of you NADs fell apart on that exercise."

Reese hadn't. In fact, she'd had one of the cleaner ex-ecutions of it. She lifted her chin, her shoulders rigid, but she didn't say anything. I started to speak up, then stopped when I caught the way her eyes narrowed in warning at me. *No special treatment...* And, shit, I wouldn't normally de-fend another snare—because they would've fucking done it themselves.

"Nah, man. Me and Reese were playing around with it later, tweaking the intro a little. We could show it to you to-morrow if you want." Reese shot Smith a grateful smile.

What the fuck? It was fine for him to speak up, but not me?

"Yeah, not gonna happen, man. You're NADs. You don't change the music around, and you definitely don't help de-cide the drum break. Shit, you're not even on the line yet."

Smith kept his face neutral, but his fingers tapped a quick, agitated rhythm against his thigh. "Right. Of course," he bit out, his voice walking the fine line of apology and sarcasm.

Reese's jaw was set and she stared at Marco flatly, no doubt holding back that sharp tongue of hers.

"Anyway, kids," Marco continued, oblivious to the ten-sion in the air, "Amber and I"—ah, right her name was *Amber*—"are headed out for a little private practice session."

"I thought you already took care of that," Reese snorted. I grinned, not sure why I loved the way she gave him shit, but I did.

Marco assessed her coolly. "Just a warm up, babe. Just a little warm up. Don't be all jealous now. You want to join us?"

Oh, hell fucking no. Not in this lifetime. If she left with anyone in this room, it damn better sure be *me*. My chest swelled, and my fingers tightened into fists.

"Here's the thing." Reese spoke softly, stopping me in my tracks, and Marco was forced to lean in closer to hear her. "When I sleep with someone, I don't want him to still need *practice* at it. I prefer my men to already know what the fuck they're doing in the bedroom."

Silence descended on our group as her words hung in the air.

I might have fallen in love with her. Just like that.

Smith pressed a fist to his mouth, eyes crinkled with barely hidden mirth, and Willa muttered an impressed, "Damn." Her deep Southern accent stretched the word into two long syllables.

Marco's face transformed, twisting into an ugly sneer, and I automatically took a step closer to Reese, a telling action that Marco registered. Snapping his tight gaze between us, the tendons in his neck bulging, he raised his hand and pointed his finger at her. "You better be ready for tomorrow, little girl. You're gonna pay for that on the field."

Then Marco snatched up Amber's hand and yanked her behind him as he stalked to the front door, slamming it behind them hard enough to rattle the frame.

At the commotion, Bubba wandered out of the kitchen, two full plastic cups in hand. He looked at me inquisitively, and I gave my head a slight shake, signaling him not to make a big deal out of it. Bubba kept his path toward us though, delivering the cups to Reese and Smith upon arrival.

"Drink up, children. The night's still young!"

Smith tapped his cup against Reese's. "To surviving day one!"

"I'll drink to that." She smiled, her whole face lighter, as if the last five minutes never happened. "Race you, Robin."

Robin? I didn't like that she had a stupid little nickname for him. Something hot twisted in my gut.

With that, they both lifted the cups to their mouths, guzzling the punch like a couple of frat brothers. Smith lowered his arm slightly ahead of her, crumpling the cup in his hand as he finished. "Batman loses. You're going to need to hand over that cape."

Swaying on her feet slightly, Reese giggled. "I don't think you understand how this whole sidekick business works." I wrapped my fingers around her hip to steady her, but she swatted my hand away. "Stop it. I'm fine." She sounded like Willa, the way she drew the word out into a caricature of its original form.

She jerked her head to face me, her ponytail whipping out and landing over one shoulder in a silky waterfall. I had a brief vision of it spread out across my bare chest, her head nestled on my shoulder as she caught her breath post-orgasm, our skin hot and sticky from our combined sweat. *Fuck.* I wanted to feel it in all its iterations. Coiled around my fist while she was on her knees. Tangled in my fingers while I held her mouth to mine. Bouncing wildly around her face as she rode me hard and fast. Mussed and rumpled first thing in the morning, when she woke up in my bed.

I murmured to her, keeping my voice low to avoid causing a scene, "You sure you know what you're doing?"

CHAPTER 5

Reese

I HAD NO IDEA WHAT I WAS DOING. LAIRD'S WORDS FROM last night came back to me, and even as my head pounded louder than the snare drum I was tapping out a warm-up cadence on, I loved every second of it. Not the headache part, the not having a plan part.

I'd moved here from West Virginia precisely because I didn't know anybody—and they didn't know me. None of my baggage had followed me across state lines.

My plan was simple. Whatever I pursued, I'd do it wholeheartedly. No half-assed bullshit.

Although, after last night, I probably needed to take it easier on the alcohol next time. I hadn't puked when I woke up, but I'd come damn close. The drumbeats echoed in my aching skull, a slow roll with a sharp accent on the third beat that sped up steadily every eight counts until it was just noise punctuated with other noise, my hands a blur as I struggled to keep up.

With a stinging slap to his drumhead, Marco ended the exercise and began tapping out the rhythm to the next one, starting out slow. Warm ups always went slow to fast, with the goal to keep the precision, regardless of the tempo.

I groaned silently and closed my eyes. The Alabama sun was fucking bright on Tuesday mornings.

Prying my eyes open to slits, I glared at Marco. He was way too chipper, bordering on downright fucking gleeful at nine in the godforsaken morning. He hadn't even said anything rude to me yet. I guess Amber had emptied his balls good after the party.

Maybe she could practice with him every night.

Smith stood very still behind his aviators next to me, moving only the bare necessity required, but he looked like he was in better shape than most of the NADs clustered in a semi-circle on the practice football field. Bubba appeared largely unaffected. Probably from his sheer bulk.

And Laird... I wasn't sure about him yet. His movements were brittle, and when he bothered to glance my way, which wasn't often so far, it was as if he couldn't decide if he was pissed off or liked what he saw.

My eyes drifted shut again. Sight wasn't technically needed for this part of the practice, just rhythm and coordination, and it was nice and dark behind my eyelids. My sunglasses hopefully hid my outward show of weakness.

Thwap!

My eyes shot open to find Laird in front of me, reaching forward to play on my drum in tandem with me. I automatically adjusted my hands to make room for his sticks. Breaking rhythm briefly, he shoved his sunglasses on top of his head, purposefully exposing his eyes to me, before seamlessly resuming the cadence.

Confused, I studied his face. He stared right at me while we played, neither of us looking down. Was this a test? Was he trying to send me a message—either personal or professional?

With no shield to block them, I could see smudges of purple under his eyes, the way the slight grooves around the outside corners seemed deeper this morning. His brow sagged and his back wasn't as ramrod straight as it should've been.

I tipped my head to the side almost imperceptibly in silent question.

His answer was a clenching of his jaw and tightening of his fingers around his drumsticks, his rhythm shifting to a slightly more staccato execution of the triplet pattern.

So… tired? And pissed? At me?

His green eyes bore into mine and when I couldn't take it any longer, I mouthed a silent, "Sorry," apologizing for whatever I'd done to upset him. He raised his chin a smidgeon in acknowledgement, but that shamrock gaze promised we'd be having a discussion later.

What had I done?

The question rattled around my throbbing head as we transitioned to the next round of torture.

We had to drink a full glass of cold milk before we started a five-mile run, this time thankfully without weighted backpacks. If you puked, you had to drink another glass. Based on the almost two-hour time limit, this was more an exercise in survival and stamina than speed.

Scrunching up my nose in distaste, I chugged mine down in three long swallows. Milk wasn't really my thing. It was alright in cereal, or in ice cream form, but just drinking it for the sake of drinking it was something I'd stopped doing years ago.

Laird and Marco stripped off their shirts, tossing them to the side of the rubberized track. Some of the other guys followed suit. When Marco glanced my way, his eyes full of challenge, I shrugged off my tank top as well, making a point of stretching my arms overhead and twisting at the waist. They weren't the only ones with flat abs.

I hoped his dick swelled and hurt like hell when he tried to run with a stiffy. It'd serve him right.

"You showing off for Marco or Laird?" Smith teased from beside me, flexing his bared pecs and making them dance. "Or is it for me?"

I made a face. "It could be that it's just fucking hot out here and my thick blood isn't used to it yet."

"Batman, there ain't nothing thick about you."

I let his compliment roll off me. My body was fine, strong and capable, but nothing to get all that excited about. Average boobs, average ass, good abs, thighs that almost had a gap if I stood just right. I had curves but they weren't as exaggerated as what the guys tended to drool over. I was just… me.

"Bet you ten bucks Laird runs behind you again."

I shot him a warning look, blaming the heat blooming across my cheeks on the weather. "And I bet you twenty that Marco finds a way to talk to you while we're out there. You never did tell me, what was that about last time anyway?"

He waved me off, but his lips twisted in annoyance. "He just wanted to talk about old high school bullshit. Asking if the line there had gone to hell after he left."

All around us, NADs and vets alike surged forward. I must have missed the start signal while we were talking.

We fell into the pack near the end, our pace easy. I could feel the milk sloshing in my belly as we ran. The banana and ibuprofen I'd had for breakfast did nothing to absorb the liquid and I regretted not getting a stack of pancakes in the dining hall instead.

On lap two, a NAD jetted to the edge of the track, vomiting into the grass. Another one joined him on lap three. By lap six, they'd both quit, the second glass of milk not going down any easier than the first.

As we ran, I tried to recall last night. I honestly didn't remember much after that last cup of NAD juice Marco gave me. I woke up in my own bed, in my locked dorm room, so I'd gotten home somehow. I'd even washed my face and changed into an oversized Rodner University t-shirt before crashing. I frowned as we rounded a curve. The details were fuzzy, dancing just out of my reach. Had Smith helped me out? Or Willa? I had a vague memory of her saying she lived in the dorm building next to mine.

At the end of the run, Marco looked pleased as he watched the quitters pack their stuff and walk away, and I'd lost both bets to Smith. Laird had brought up the rear of the group, whether because he felt it was his spot as a leader or, as Smith predicted as he held out his hand for payment, to watch me jiggle. And Scrotum Breath had kept his distance the whole time, which somehow struck me as more suspicious than if he'd taunted us during the event.

As we both used our shirts to wipe down our sweaty upper bodies, I stole furtive glances at Laird. He was talking with a skinny guy named Topher I'd been introduced to briefly last night, his hands bracketing his narrow hips, making no effort to cover himself up yet.

My throat was dry and my tongue stuck to the roof of my mouth as I watched him. Laird's chest was carved perfection, with a star inked high on his left pec and something else small tattooed on the other one. A letter, maybe? I was too far away to tell for sure.

Laird laughed at something Topher said and his abs rippled, framed by a pair of delicious obliques that arrowed down to his groin.

Dear sweet Jesus in the garden, I wanted to smell him. Covered in sweat and sunshine with a smile on his face. Maybe lick his neck for good measure.

Smith handed me a bottle of water, and I forced myself to turn away from my all too tempting half-naked captain before I did something stupid to gain his attention, like dump the water all over my chest instead of drinking it.

"Hot today, isn't it?" I said dumbly, sipping at the water.

Smith chuckled and elbowed me, his knowing gaze touching briefly on Laird. "It damn sure is."

I scowled. It's not like I could call dibs. He was the fucking captain.

Nothing could happen between us, no matter how much I might want it. If I made the line—no, scratch that—*when* I made the line, I didn't want there to be any doubt how I earned my spot.

And it'd be with my drumsticks, not on my knees.

But that didn't mean I couldn't daydream.

Marco clapped his hands, effectively calling our attention to him, and we dutifully gathered around. He stood up on a bench, and I swore he flexed his biceps as he spoke. "Two more down. C'mon NADs, suck it up. You're making this too easy for us. You get an hour break, which I highly suggest using to shower so I don't have to smell y'all the rest of the day, and then we're meeting back in East Hall for more sight-reading. I need to get rid of a few more of you ball-lickers today."

Smith choked on his water next to me as Marco finished dismissing us.

"You okay there, Robin?"

"I'm fine." He waved me off. "Just went down the wrong side. C'mon, let's get out of here and get some caffeine before the afternoon session."

We gathered up our stuff and headed out. A few of the other guys actually talked to me as we trekked across campus back to the dorms. I met Cade and his older brother Charlie, who was a junior on the line. While Cade seemed like a nice guy, his presence at auditions worried me. There were only a few spots available, and I'd bet anything his brother would be able to guarantee him one of them. Van, the other junior besides Topher and Charlie, rounded out our group, and I tripped over my feet when he complimented me on playing.

Holy shit, was it happening? Were they finally starting to accept me as a fellow drummer?

But then Marco drove by, honking the horn of his shiny black, jacked-up Ford pickup that was no doubt compensating for inches he was lacking elsewhere, the bass thumping so loud I could feel it in my chest, and I remembered that Van wasn't the one I needed to worry about impressing.

He was.

I was in the last group for sight-reading, and had been killing time in the holding room for over two hours waiting for my turn. My earbuds were in and I was tapping away to a Spotify playlist using my thighs as a makeshift drum to quietly pound out the percussion line. Three NADs had already walked out with their heads down, shoulders drooping, and avoiding eye contact. They didn't say it, but I knew. They'd been cut.

Smith had gone in the first group and come out beaming. He'd given me a high five before slipping out of here for the day. The only guy left besides me was Heath, who wouldn't look at me, let alone talk to me. In this case though, I wasn't taking it personally. I hadn't seen him speak to anyone so far unless absolutely necessary.

Marco and Laird appeared in the doorway.

"Holland," Laird said without inflection, waiting impassively for me to reach the doorway and follow him into the next room. Heath followed Marco farther down the hall.

In the room, Laird was stoic. No smiles, no jokes. All business.

I worked my way through five pieces, each time waiting anxiously as he jotted down notes without providing me any feedback. Not so much as a flicker of expression budged his carved jawline and I found myself smiling bigger at him, raising my eyebrows, cocking my head to the side, every nonverbal cue I could think of to try to trigger a reaction.

After the last piece, I grabbed my sticks and my bag and headed for the door, not waiting for him to finish writing down whatever it was he was noting about me, fed up with his lack of response. I knew I should wait to see if he wanted to discuss whatever it was that had him scowling so hard during warm-ups, but if he'd wanted to talk, he'd had more than enough opportunities. I was done.

I wrenched the door open, then flinched when his hand circled my left wrist and he kicked the door closed again.

He studied me, his eyes roving over every inch of my face as if memorizing the contours. I puffed out a breath, the loose tendrils that'd escaped my messy ponytail resettling around me.

"What?" I demanded finally.

"Why are you doing this? Trying out for drumline?"

I stared at him in disbelief. "I'm a drummer."

"But why drumline? Why not a garage band or

something else?"

"Look," I started, annoyance threading its way into my tone. "Do you ask all the guys this too?"

He lifted a hand, and brushed a lock of hair behind my ear. Time stretched as the pads of his fingers hesitated for a moment on the side of my neck. "No. Just you."

Laird stood close enough that I could smell the coffee lingering on his breath, and I wondered if he could feel my pulse kick up where his hand still held my wrist.

His gaze drifted lower, then he paused, his eyes narrowing. Tilting his head to the left slightly, he let go of my wrist, raising his hand to trace the faint scar that was just barely peeking out from the neckline of my scoop neck shirt.

Goose bumps sprouted on my arms, and my nipples pebbled at the feel of his skin grazing mine so gently, so carefully.

He sucked in a breath, and raised his eyes to me. Neither of us moved, his one fingertip the only thing connecting us. The tenderness was unexpected, and it was a sensation I wasn't used to. My past physical experiences with guys had shown them to be impulsive, hasty, and too distracted by the final destination to enjoy the journey getting there. The softness nearly undid me. I sensed if Laird were to ever touch me, *really* touch me, it'd be completely different.

I peered up at him, wondering if he felt it too, the heady awareness that seemed to permeate the air between us, making it heavy and thick with possibility. Emotion warred in his eyes. Concern, heat, frustration, indecision.

"It's nothing," I said finally, and twisted my shoulders until his hand fell away. "Car accident when I was a kid."

"Reese." His mouth opened but no more words came out. Between us, his hand curled into a fist, as if holding onto the memory of the way I felt, not quite ready to let it go.

The intensity of the moment was too much for me, and I forced a mocking smirk to my face. "Do you touch all the guys' chests too? Or just mine?"

This time, there was no mistaking the flare of hunger in his green gaze, and he leaned closer, his hot breath fanning my cheek, his answer a whispered promise in my ear. "Trust me, if I were touching your chest, you'd know it."

CHAPTER 6

Laird

"**V**IDEO GAME DESIGN? REALLY?**" ELI'S GLASSES framed huge green eyes that squinted at me in disbelief. Or maybe they looked so big because he was twenty pounds underweight for an eight-year-old. Or maybe because the hospital bed we were sitting on seemed like an island, an oasis of blankets and pillows surrounded by an ocean of machines and monitors and equipment that no kid his age should even know existed.

"Yeah, Tuesdays and Thursdays at," I exaggerated my wince for his benefit, "nine in the morning. Ugh." I clutched my chest and fell back at the horror of such an early hour.

He didn't so much as blink at my theatrics. "What else?"

"Human Centered Computing, Data Mining and Analysis, Medical Psychology, and the second Anatomy and Physiology. I think I get to dissect a pig or something this semester. Want me to bring pictures?"

His smile stretched from ear to ear. "Hell, yeah."

I glanced quickly at the door for any sign of his parents. "Watch it, buddy."

"Yeah, yeah, yeah, whatever." He rolled his eyes. "I'm old enough to have cancer, but not old enough to cuss. Which is bullshit if you ask me."

I silently agreed.

"But, seriously, why video game design? That one doesn't seem to fit with everything else."

"Little man, are you doubting me? I can totally make a kickass video game."

"Look, Laird, I don't know how to break it to you, but you're kind of a nerd. Like, too nerdy for video games, even."

"I am not!" I was genuinely offended. "I'm totally cool. Need I remind you I'm the *captain* of the Rodner University Drumline?" I said the last three words slowly, because if there was one thing Eli lived for, it was Rodner football and anything associated with it. "If that doesn't give me legit cool points, then you're out of your mind."

"More like out of my white cells," he joked, collapsing onto his pillow in laughter.

This kid. He was the best part of my week—even better than the performance high of a halftime show during a home game—and I always spent most of my time in his room during my visits. Other guys probably wouldn't consider hanging out on the pediatric cancer ward their idea of a fun afternoon, but it'd been part of my life for so long, I hadn't been able to stop coming when it was no longer necessary.

"Alright, so tell me the good stuff. You got a chick yet?"

"Ha!" I scoffed. "Why tie myself down like that?" But it didn't stop my mind from wandering back to the drumline party a few nights ago. How I'd helped Reese back to her dorm room. How I'd found a washcloth and cleaned off her face the best I could. How I'd somehow managed to get that crazy strappy bra off her from behind, without once giving into temptation and sneaking a peek—or a handful—of her tits, because the first time I saw them—and it would happen—I wanted it to be because she wanted it too.

So maybe I'd stayed with her a few hours, making sure she didn't puke or need anything. Maybe I'd snuck out of her room at 4:30 in the morning, finally convinced she'd be okay, but wished I could've stayed longer just to watch her sleep. And maybe she didn't seem to remember any of it the next day, staring at me blankly during warm-ups. No softening in her expression, no mouthed *thank you*, no pulling me aside to acknowledge my help.

Yeah, that realization had burned and festered in my gut, but I wouldn't have changed a moment of it. Because, for the first time in a long time, I'd *liked* the responsibility of looking after someone other than myself. But more than anything, I'd liked looking after *her*.

"Because," Eli drew out the word like I was an idiot for not understanding the obvious, "Dad said you can't get any action with a girl until she's your girlfriend."

Well. Not technically true, but also not a point I wanted to disagree with his dad on in front of Eli, either. "What do you know about 'getting some action?'" I arched an eyebrow at him. "You got your sights set on a babe somewhere?"

He blushed all the way to the top of his bald head, and looked around to make sure the room was empty. "There's this new girl on the floor, osteosarcoma, and, Laird… she sets off my heart monitor. It starts going really fast and I watched it the other day, the line jumped funny and Mom got scared, but the nurse said it was just a skipped beat." He paused, his eyes unfocused behind the thick blue plastic frames. "I want her to make it skip more."

I wrapped an arm around him and tugged him gently to my side, careful of his wires and tubes, to hide the way he was breaking my damn heart. *This kid. This fucking kid.* I think he knew more about love and life at age eight than I did at twenty-two. "What's her name, bud?"

"Amelia. Isn't that the best name ever?"

I nodded, although he couldn't see it with his head against my chest. "It is. It really is."

He pushed me away, his thin shoulders set with determination. "So you gotta teach me. She's a year older than me, and I need some game so I can get her. I think Jaxon across the hall has his eyes on her too." He scowled. "He's only Stage II, so he gets more time in the game room with her."

My forehead wrinkled like I was heavy in thought. But, really, what was I supposed to tell him? The kid was eight and trapped in a hospital for the foreseeable future.

A flash of yellow passing the open doorway—the ripple of a dress over textbook perfect curves—caught my attention and we both craned our necks for a longer look.

"Damn, Laird," Eli whispered. "Did you see those legs?"

I raised my eyebrows, although I had to agree with his assessment of the glimpse of thigh I'd seen. "What happened to Amelia?"

"Amelia's a babe. But her legs don't look like that." He said it matter-of-factly, giving me a shove toward the door. "Go look. Maybe take a pic on your phone. Quick, before she's gone!"

Humoring him, I ambled toward the doorway, making a show of pulling my phone out of my back pocket and wiggling it at him. "Be right back."

"I call dibs!"

I stepped out into the hall and looked to the right, the direction the legs had been headed.

At the nurses' station in the middle of the floor, five doors down from where I hovered in the doorway, were the sexiest legs I'd seen all summer, peeking out from beneath a yellow sundress.

But what the fuck was Reese doing *here*, on the pediatric cancer wing?

I eased down the hall, both Eli and the phone in my hand forgotten. Her dark hair was pulled back in some kind of loose braid, and her bare arms were tan from all our practices in the sun this week. Eavesdropping shamelessly, I caught the tail end of her conversation with Martha, my favorite nurse.

"… so, Wednesday mornings would be good?" Reese asked, glancing down to check something on her phone. "I could do that. At least this semester."

Martha smiled and reached out to squeeze Reese's hand, happiness smoothing the multitude of wrinkles etched into her face. Fuck knows, Martha didn't have a lot to smile about on this floor, but she was always quick to share a grin with the patients and crack a joke. Cancer humor was dark, and it took a special person to embrace it, to understand why it was so desperately needed sometimes.

"And you said something about music?"

Reese nodded. "It worked out well for me back home. Bringing in drumsticks and letting them beat their pillows—or the side rails of the beds, if y'all don't mind the noise."

Martha winked. "Depends whose shift it is. I wouldn't mind though."

"Do y'all have a group activity room? Or do you prefer one-on-one in the patient rooms? I'm comfortable doing either." She paused, set down her phone, and rubbed her upper arms. She was probably cold in that dress. The hospital was always freezing. "To be honest, I feel like I get better results doing it one-on-one, but I'm flexible to whatever works best for you guys."

"Honey, if you're offering to help, we'll take it any way we can get it. If one day, you want to do a group activity, do that. If you want to meet them and have solo time, that's great too. I'm just pleased as punch you want to be here." Martha caught sight of me over Reese's shoulder, and her coffee-colored eyes twinkled at me. "In fact, here's just the young man to show you around. Do you mind, Laird?"

At the mention of my name, Reese's spine straightened until I worried it would snap. She turned around slowly, almost suspiciously, as if she was hoping it wasn't really me standing there.

No lie… that hurt.

But I pushed it away. I was more interested in the *why* behind her visit today. Did she know I came here? Was she somehow following me?

Snagging her elbow in a loose grip, I pulled her to my side, and then tossed my arm around her shoulders. "No worries, Martha. I got it from here." I tipped my chin at her, and not-so-calmly guided Reese down the hall to a vacant alcove near Eli's room.

Irritation and morbid curiosity warred inside me. While I was flattered she put in the effort to locate me here, of all the places in Rodner she could track me down, this was *my* thing. The part of my weekly routine that had actual meaning. And as hot as I found her sexy little body, and as much as her smart mouth seduced me, *nobody* followed me to my place.

Dropping my arm, I spun her to face me none too

gently. "What are you doing here, Reese Holland?" I demanded bluntly.

She rubbed her arms again, and, sure enough, there were goose bumps. I nudged her a foot to the left, so she wasn't standing directly under the chill of the vent, ignoring the instinct to take her in my arms and warm her up. Glowering at her, I waited impatiently for her response.

"What are *you* doing here?" She threw my own words back at me.

"I come here every week to spend time with the kids," I answered steadily. "You?"

Reese shivered, and looked down the hall both directions, then at her feet. Anywhere but me. Biting back a growl of frustration, I took her chin in my thumb and forefinger and lifted it until she had no choice but to meet my eyes.

And I paused.

Her coffee-colored gaze was wary, not triumphant. Shadowed with hidden secrets, not blazing with righteous indignation.

This was not the Reese I was used to.

I stepped closer, crowding her back against the wall. Softening my voice, I asked again, "Why are you here, Reese?"

Wrenching her chin from my grasp, she stood tall and squared her shoulders, her breasts brushing my chest with the action.

"I'm sorry," she clipped out, "but I didn't know I had to explain myself to you. Hell, I certainly didn't expect to find *you* at the children's hospital." She slipped out past me, her body rubbing against mine in the process, and put several steps between us. I burned where she'd touched me. "Now, do you have time to show me the activity room? If not, I'm sure I can find it myself."

"Laird!" It was Eli, his voice carrying down the hall. "Who's the hottie? Remember, I have dibs!"

Reese cocked her head, eyebrows raised, a questioning smile teasing the corner of her full lips. Her whole countenance changed, morphing from annoyance to intrigued. "He called dibs, huh? Sounds like I better go meet him."

Before I could stop her, she'd waltzed right into his room, and by the time I followed, she was already perched on his bed, in my spot, rubbing the sanitizing foam on her hands.

I leaned against the doorway, frowning, unwilling for some reason to leave her alone with my favorite patient. Or maybe I was just unwilling to leave her alone, period.

"Hi. I'm Reese. What's your name, hot stuff?"

"Eli." Oh fuck. He was already blushing.

"Hey, Eli. What's a handsome guy like you doing in a place like this?"

"Leukemia. Stage III."

"How's that going for you?" She asked it in the same way she'd asked someone what day it was, instead of the syrupy, sad puppy dog way I expected. Reese held her body loosely, at ease with herself, the exact opposite of most visitors to these sterile hallways, the ones whose hesitant, awkward movements always reminded me of giraffes learning to walk for the first time.

He shrugged. "Better this month than last." He leaned in closer to whisper in her ear. "There's a cute new girl down the hall. Can you help me make her my girlfriend?" Less than five minutes and I was already being replaced.

"I can try." Reese nodded slowly. "What have you already tried?"

"Nothing."

"Doing nothing is generally not the best way to get the girl."

"It works for Laird." Eli pointed at me. "He said he doesn't have to do anything. Girls are just always there."

Reese's eyes pinned me on the spot and her voice was flat. "Does he now?"

Was it wishful thinking, or was there jealousy heating her brown eyes? I had the good sense to look away, pretend I didn't know what he was talking about.

"Right, Laird?" Eli's voice rose with his enthusiasm. "You said you just have to look a little bit scruffy, because girls like bad boys, and smell good, and that's all there really is to it. *Bam*! Instant girl magnet!"

I didn't remember saying it quite like that, but he was in the ballpark of the conversation from one of my last visits.

Reese's gaze flitted over the monitors, studying the numbers, and I wondered if any of them made sense to her. Beyond the obvious things, like pulse and blood pressure, I couldn't usually make sense of what they all did.

"Well," Reese mused. "I was going to suggest maybe writing her a poem, but if Laird's the expert, how can we make you look like a bad boy instead?"

Eli snickered. "If I go to her room, my ass will be hanging out of my gown. Does that count?"

Her wide eyes ping-ponged between us, and I grinned. "Eli is a bit of a rebel if you couldn't tell yet."

"What about if I brought you some temporary tattoos? Girls love ink. And Laird has a tattoo, you could be like him."

Eli stared at me like I was his hero. I was nobody's hero. "You do?" The awe in his voice had me wincing.

"Yeah, buddy. I have two."

"And the girls like it?"

I started to nod my agreement, but paused, a devious smile edging up the corner of my lips. "I don't know. Why don't you ask Reese?"

"Reese, do you like his tattoos?"

If looks could kill, I'd be six feet under from the withering glare she shot me. Turning back to Eli, she shrugged indifferently. "They're okay."

"Where are they?"

"On his chest," she replied before I could speak up.

He thought about it for a second, his mind working overtime on her answer, and I knew he was smart enough to figure it out. "You've seen his chest?"

I loved this kid.

The blush started at the top of her dress and crept up her neck, all the way to her cheeks. Something about her neck made me crazy. I wanted to nibble her there. Learn what kind of noise she would make if I kissed the tender spot on the edge of her jawline. If I licked a slow path to her ear. If I sucked hard and plunged deep inside her wet core at the same time. I wanted to leave a mark there, purpling her flesh, marking her as mine for the world to see.

"What about if I bring some tattoos in next week when I visit again? Will your girl still be here?"

Eli nodded, his smile stretching as wide as I'd ever seen it.

She was good with him, I hated to admit.

"Alright, handsome. I have to go right now, but I'll be back on Wednesday morning, okay? It's a date." She tapped the tip of his nose and headed out the door, ignoring me altogether.

I muttered a hasty goodbye to Eli, and chased after her. By the time I caught her, the elevator doors were parting, ready to whisk her away from me.

"Why are you really here?" I just couldn't let it go.

She stepped on and I copied her, refusing to let her put any significant distance between us. "Is it a problem with drumline? I'm doing this on my own time, and I won't let it interfere." She crossed her arms over her chest, and I couldn't help but notice the way it emphasized her boobs.

From where I stood, I could just see the tiniest bit of cleavage down the top of her dress. I followed the edge of the yellow cotton with my eyes, until I got to where that pale pink scar of hers peeked out.

I frowned. I didn't like the idea that she'd been hurt, even if it was a long time ago. I rubbed the same spot on my chest, and my breath stopped in realization.

She wasn't here because of me.

The elevator doors opened. I didn't move. Neither did she. They closed again, and we started rising.

My mind was racing, trying desperately to come up with any other explanation than the one I feared.

But I *knew.* Deep down, I knew. Her comfort level in this environment. The way she hadn't blinked at his diagnosis. And that scar. That fucking scar that gave her away if you knew what to look for. Going with my gut, I asked her softly, "Is it because you had cancer?"

"What?" Her hand flew to her chest, to her scar, rubbing it almost absentmindedly. A dead giveaway to my knowing eye. "Why would you think that?"

I put my hand on top of hers, linking our fingers, tracing the raised mark with her. "It's from a chemo port, not a car accident." I swallowed hard. "Isn't it?"

Her eyes clenched tightly and her hand curled beneath mine. I wanted her to tell me I was wrong, that I was seeing things that weren't really there, that she had never suffered like all those kids upstairs. She took a long breath, exhaled just as slowly, then braced her feet as if readying herself for a battle. When she opened her eyes, they glimmered with resolve and determination. "That was a long time ago. I'm *fine* now." She dropped her hand and mine fell away. I felt oddly bereft at the loss of her touch.

And then her words hit like a sledgehammer, almost knocking me down.

She'd had cancer.

If I'd been wearing one of those heart monitors like Eli, alarms would be flashing and nurses would be running. I ran my frantic gaze over every inch of her body as if I could detect any lingering malignancy with my eyes alone. My words were rushed, tumbling over each other in their hurry to get out. "Are you sure drumline is a good idea? All the hours? The heat? The workouts? *Fuck*, the drinking…?"

I reached for her, but she pushed me away, pushed past me and stabbed the button that would take her back to the parking lot.

"Laird. Listen to me, because I'm only going to say this once." The steel in her voice forced my attention back to her face. "If cancer didn't kill me, do you really think drumline will?"

The elevator doors closed before I could answer.

CHAPTER 7

Reese

MARCO CAUGHT MY ARM AS I WALKED INTO BOLDT Auditorium, stopping me from following Smith down the hall to the storage room where we kept the marching snares. I tugged sharply at my elbow to free it, but he held on tight, his fingers digging into my bicep almost hard enough to leave a bruise.

"Woah there, hotshot. Practice doesn't start for another ten minutes, and I need to have a quick word with you."

I stared at his hand pointedly until, after one last harsh squeeze, he released it. When it fell back to my side, I didn't give him the satisfaction of rubbing it or even looking to see if his handprint remained behind, reddening my tanned skin. *Asshole.* I fixed a blank expression on my face and waited impatiently for whatever it was he needed.

"I'm not sure if they told you NADs yet, but one of the things you're expected to do for the upper classmen is clean their rooms once a week. I'm talking dusting, vacuuming, taking the trash out, changing the sheets—everything. We drew names last night, and I ended up with you."

He paused as if expecting a reaction. I refused to give him that pleasure. "Okay," I said evenly. "You have my contact info in triplicate on all those forms we filled out last week. Text me your schedule sometime, and I'll handle it."

Slipping his hand in the back pocket of his skinny jeans that failed to give him any kind of rock star credibility, he withdrew a dull silver key and pressed it into my palm. "It better be spotless, Reese. Or you'll be on the bench or off the line before your classes even start."

"Oh, Marco." I smiled sweetly and patted him on the cheek, ignoring the throbbing in my arm from his manhandling. "Don't you worry. I'm not going anywhere." Unzipping my gym bag a few inches, I tossed his key inside and let it slide to the bottom, where I'd worry about finding it later beneath the crumpled receipts and old gum wrappers. "Is that all, lieutenant?"

Indecision flattened into annoyance on his scowling face. Without another word, Marco shouldered past me and continued down the corridor, then ignored my existence when I slipped into the room after him.

Smith looked at me quizzically as he adjusted his harness and checked his drumsticks. "You okay?" he asked. His eyes narrowed a bit and he touched my arm lightly, skimming his thumb across the lingering redness below my sleeve.

I twisted the other direction, so my arm wasn't as visible, and forced a shrug. "Bumped into something. It was no big deal."

He opened his mouth to respond, but then shook his head instead. "Right." He left it at that and handed me my stick bag. "I already checked it for you. And your rig."

"Thanks, Robin." I flashed him a quick smile as Laird entered the room and the assembled group quieted, his commanding presence demanding it without him having to ask.

Laird huddled with Marco over a clipboard in the corner while I finished double-checking my gear. Then I assumed the default drummer position, arms crossed over my chest with a pair of drumsticks in one fist.

When he turned to face us, shifting to take the same stance as the rest of us, his eyes trekked across the room restlessly, as if he was searching for something.

Until they landed on me.

And stopped.

I sucked in a breath as shamrock green eyes held mine captive, and when his gaze wandered down my body, like he couldn't help himself from taking a longer look, a tingle zipped down my spine and took up residence low in my belly, warming me.

Self-consciously, I lifted my hand to rub at my cheek, that small action seeming to jerk him back to the present, and his attention dipped briefly back down to the clipboard in his hand before focusing on a spot somewhere to my left.

"Right. NADs, if you'll look around, you'll notice there's only seven of you left. And, for those of you who aren't math majors, there are seven vets. This is the part of the audition process where you get assigned to a vet who will be in charge of making sure you know what the fuck is going on and that you don't embarrass us. If he asks you to do something, you do it. If he asks you to do something not related to drumline, you do it. It's really that simple."

Marco took half a step forward, his shoulders loose, and sighed. "I'll sacrifice myself and take Hotshot over there."

The wink he shot at me was anything but reassuring, and distaste rose like bile in my throat.

"Actually," Laird responded before I could do more than flick my eyes at Smith, who was frowning, "as captain, I'll go first. And, Marco, since I know how much you're threatened by Reese's dick being bigger than yours, I'll take her."

I froze. He did not just say that. Around me, the new guys coughed and turned away, while the vets hooted and took turns punching Marco and Laird on the shoulders in glee. Nobody looked at me but Marco, and his eyes burned with a fire that promised retribution.

But what the fuck? Shouldn't he be glaring at *Laird*? I damn sure was, because this was all his fucking fault. Or maybe this was part of some kind of twisted plan to make my life so miserable I quit, because there's no way Marco was going to back down after that declaration.

"Holy shit," Smith breathed next to me. "I'm not sure whether you should be scared of what's coming your way as a result of that, or flattered as hell by the compliment he just paid you."

"Yeah. I'll let you know when I decide." I ducked my head and shuffled over a few steps, until Smith's lean back formed a buffer from being in Marco's direct line of sight.

"I don't think hiding is going to help disguise your giant cock, Batman." He flashed me a sympathetic look. "I'm not sure what his strategy was with that little move, but if you didn't already have a target painted on your back, you sure as fuck do now." He took a giant step to the side, blowing my cover. "If there was ever a time to grow some lady balls, now would be good."

No special treatment, I reminded myself, painting a bored look on my face and slouching in a show of indifference. *He's nothing I can't handle.*

Marco shrugged off Bubba, who was still hanging on his shoulder, and cast one last murderous look my direction. I blew him an insouciant kiss, and I swore steam came out his ears. "Whatever. She's Laird's problem now." He huffed out a short laugh. "I'll take Smith instead. Bubba, your turn."

The rest of the NADs were claimed by the other vets, with Charlie pairing off with his brother, Cade, a move I was surprised they allowed. It reinforced my opinion that Cade was probably getting one of the field positions, regardless of talent. Not that Cade was bad. He wasn't. But I was better.

After we finished our warm-up, we started working on the two opening songs. The first show we were doing this year was a medley of Bon Jovi's greatest hits. Once we'd worked out the major kinks, we headed down to the practice field to begin blocking out the choreography.

I was lagging a bit behind because the women's restroom was on the other side of the building and I'd had to make a quick pit stop. Quickening my pace, I jogged down the sidewalk to catch up, the snare harness thudding against me with every step, when Marco stepped out from around a corner abruptly, his giant foot landing in front of mine. It was too sudden and I couldn't stop my forward momentum, but all I could think was, *protect the snare*. I twisted as I fell, landing half on the sidewalk, half off the curb on the blacktop parking lot that skirted the field.

Stars danced around the edges of my vision as I struggled to pull air into my lungs, the snare resting heavy on top of me. My left hip throbbed where it'd landed right on the edge of the curb, taking the brunt of my weight. I sucked in a ragged breath, pinching my eyes closed to hold back the tears that threatened to fall. I refused to let him see any sliver of weakness, no matter what the cost.

When I cracked my lids open again, Marco's face

hovered above me, his expression impassive. "I hope you didn't fuck up the drum. Being careless with the equipment is a pretty good way to get cut."

I climbed to my feet, biting the inside of my cheek when my knee buckled on my first attempt to straighten up. It didn't escape my attention that he didn't offer to help me rise, instead standing there with his arms crossed and his own rig safely on the grass a few feet away. Snatching a pair of sticks from my bag, I played a quick four measure solo, proving the drumhead was still tight.

My lips twisted in an ugly imitation of a smile while my fingers flexed against the lip of the drum. "Guess I didn't notice you there. I'll have to watch out for you better next time." I forced out the strangled apology for him purpose-fully knocking me down, distaste curling my stomach, and a look of dark satisfaction stretched across his face. I wouldn't have been surprised if it was the same expression he had when he came. *Fuck, this was the kind of bullshit he got off on.* There was no mistaking it now, and I'd literally fallen right into his trap. *Reese 1, Scrotum Breath 1.*

He held my gaze, and I couldn't suppress the shiver of unease that slid down my spine. "Yeah. You'd do good to stay out of my way."

I moved ahead of him, my left side throbbing with every step. It didn't help that the snare rested along my hips, so that every movement I made prodded the point of impact. But I kept my pace steady, my gait even, because I could feel his eyes burning into me as I continued down the sidewalk, and I refused to let him see me struggle.

Guys like Marco preyed on the weak, if for no other reason than to make themselves feel better, bigger. Being lieutenant of a college drumline was probably going to be the pinnacle of his musical career, and no doubt he was trying to squeeze every ounce of power he could from the position. The fact that a freshman girl threatened him so much reflected his own insecurities, I reminded myself, as I hurried to the far side of the field away from him. If I wasn't good, he wouldn't care.

But I was good. And we both knew it.

I compartmentalized the pain, learned the maneuvers, and made it through the rest of the day. Smith tried to stall me when we put away our equipment after practice, concern evident in the angle of his eyebrows and the tilt of his lips, but I waved him off. "Girl stuff," I muttered, pressing a palm to my lower abdomen. When he backed off, I made a stealthy escape, knowing I was nearing my breaking point.

The only detour I made was to Sammy's, the popular deli on the edge of campus. Nothing made me feel better than a hot turkey-and-cranberry sub, and if there was ever a time for comfort food, it was tonight. The line wasn't bad, only half a dozen students deep, but by the time I'd collected my sandwich and filled the largest Styrofoam cup they had with Cherry Coke Zero, I was having to bite my lip with every step.

Stopping to poke a straw through the lid and add a handful of napkins to my tray, I tensed when I heard my name spoken from right behind me. I whirled around too fast and my hip protested the sudden motion, my knee partially giving way beneath me.

Laird's arms shot out, his hands catching my hips to steady me and I couldn't stop the yelp that tore from my throat. "Careful there, Reese, mind if I join—"

His words cut off abruptly, his attention focused on where the fabric of my shirt was bunched up beneath his hand. Below it, the purple bloom of a fresh bruise darkened most of my side. Swallowing back a groan, I tried to back up, but he tightened his fist, and the cotton-blend material digging into my skin stopped any further movement.

"What. Happened?" He spat out the words like they tasted bad.

I licked my dry lips, heat rushing to my face. "I tripped earlier at practice, and—"

"And why the fuck didn't you say something then?" he finished for me.

I sucked in a sharp breath and lied again. "I didn't think it was that bad."

He yanked my shirt higher and tugged the waistband of my shorts down an inch. The discoloration was larger than the span of his oversized hand.

"Hey, Palmer?" Laird didn't look away as he called out to the guy behind the sandwich counter. "I'm gonna need you to repackage her order to go, and get me one of whatever she ordered as well."

"What? Stop. It's fine," I gritted out, swatting his hand away and readjusting my clothing.

"Were you not listening at practice earlier?"

I paused. "When?"

"When I told you that if your vet tells you to do something, you fucking do it." His forced smile was tight, but his eyes spoke volumes. Those shamrock green irises warned me away and promised me everything at the same time.

A skinny guy with freckles, whose name was apparently Palmer, took my tray from me and disappeared into the back.

"And what are you telling me to do exactly?"

"You're coming home with me."

CHAPTER 8

Laird

S HE WAS SO FUCKING STUBBORN. I BOTH HATED AND
loved that about her. When I offered Reese my hand
to help her climb into my Wrangler, she pretended she
didn't see it, the same way she tried to cover her wince of
pain when she tucked her tall frame into my gray leather
seat with an awkward laugh.

But after watching her bite her lip every time I hit a dip
in the road on the six-minute drive to my townhouse, I'd
had enough. The idea that she'd been in pain all day while
I'd been blindly unaware infuriated me. I should've known.
After I put the car in park, I raced around to open the door
for her and lifted her down before she could say a word to
stop me, careful not to touch her left hip in the process.

"Why didn't you tell me?" I demanded as I unlocked the
door to my two-story home. I had an end unit. It was nice
because I only had to listen to one neighbor's bed frame

slamming against the wall when he had sex, which was way more often than me these days.

Before she could answer though, Oscar came flying around the corner, his short legs scrabbling for purchase on the tile floor of the kitchen as he howled out a welcome. He rejected me completely in favor of sniffing every inch of Reese's legs he could reach.

Predictably, she cooed and stooped down to stroke the sleek, speckled fur of my piebald dachshund. *At least one of the wieners here tonight is seeing some action.* Yeah, I'd reached a new low. Jealous of my own damn dog. And despite her injury and the fact that she was only here because I hadn't given her a choice, I couldn't stop my eyes from appreciating the way her shorts clung to her tight ass in that position. That sweet curve would fit perfectly in my palms.

"Aren't you handsome?" Reese asked my dog, who thumped his tail enthusiastically in answer.

"Oscar," I scolded, using my foot to herd him gently back inside the door, "quit humping her long enough for us to come in."

"His name's Oscar?"

My lips twitched. "Oscar Meyer. What else would I call him?"

She didn't even hesitate. "I mean, you could've gone with Frank."

I scoffed as I skirted around the end of the galley kitchen and retrieved a bag of frozen peas from the freezer. The cool air felt good against my overheated skin. "Frank is far too plebian for a wiener that good looking, c'mon now. Oscar has a certain amount of class."

She stood just inside the doorway where I'd left her, studying my downstairs living area with blatant curiosity. I wondered how it looked through her eyes. A matched pair of navy blue couches, a square coffee table I'd stained driftwood gray on top of a blue-and-green striped rug. A kitchen table with two wooden benches in the same stain. The flat-screen on my wall played Animal Planet on low volume. Some show about sloths was on, one of Oscar's favorites. Yes, he had favorites.

"So, you live here... alone?"

I snagged a blue-striped towel from a drawer in the kitchen and headed back her way. "Just me and my giant wiener." Oscar was a standard-sized dachshund, not a mini. But the other interpretation was accurate too.

"Right..." Reese rolled her eyes.

"C'mon. It's time to play doctor." I held up the peas. "And you're gonna tell me what the fuck happened."

"This really isn't necessary, I can—"

"—sit your sweet ass on the bench so I can check you out better? That'd be perfect."

She glared at me, but carried the bags containing our subs to the table and sat down. Ignoring me altogether, she pulled out the sandwiches and placed the one I assumed was mine on the opposite side of the table. I picked it up and dropped down on the bench right next to her instead, close enough my thigh brushed hers. Oscar situated himself at her feet, panting with excitement. I didn't blame him. He had the best view in the house.

I covered the peas in the towel, then tucked the veggies in the waistband of her shorts, pulling her fitted shirt over the top to hold it in place. She hissed in a breath, but refused to look at me, her focus completely on unwrapping her dinner and taking a giant bite.

"First, we eat. And then, we're going to talk."

I tore the paper off my sandwich with a lot less finesse than her and chowed down. "What is this?" I asked, taking a second to study the food after I'd swallowed my first mouthful.

"Turkey and cranberry."

"Damn. It's really good." I took another bite. It was like fucking Thanksgiving dinner in sandwich form.

She paused to suck down some soda and the way her lips looked wrapped around the black straw had me holding back a groan. "Yeah, it's my favorite. I didn't expect to find it down here in Alabama." She licked her lips, her pink tongue slipping out to catch a smear of cranberry on the corner of her mouth.

My cock jumped and I hunched over the table a little more to hide it. Gym shorts weren't exactly discreet.

Oscar whined beneath us, and I automatically ripped him off a piece of bread and tossed it to him under the table.

"That dog has you whipped," she teased.

I shrugged. "It's important to take good care of your wiener. Keep it happy."

She struggled to keep a straight face. I saw her grin fighting to break through but it never quite appeared, denying me a glimpse of her dimple. "Is there a story there? How the drumline captain ended up with a dachshund of all breeds?"

"There's always a story. This one's pretty tame as far as stories go, but I really shouldn't be telling it to you. Not yet anyway."

"Why's that?"

"The competition. It hasn't happened yet this year."

She looked intrigued, her sandwich forgotten as she turned her whole upper body toward me. "Tell me anyway."

I pretended to contemplate whether or not I should, and was rewarded for my ploy when her smile grew wide, that dimple on full display.

"There's always a contest at one of the parties, and my vet had given me the heads up about it my freshman year—kinda like I'm telling you now, even though he wasn't supposed to."

"What contest?"

"The dick measuring contest."

She choked on the Coke she had been drinking, her hand going to her mouth. "The *what*?"

I was enjoying this way too much. "It's one of the drumline rituals. One of the girls, usually a cymbal player or whoever the captain thinks is the hottest, lines up the snares by dick size. And I wanted to win. I mean," I shrugged modestly, "I probably would've won anyway, but I wasn't taking any chances. So, I went down to the animal shelter the day before the party and found Oscar. I brought him with me, and no one could deny I had the biggest wiener."

Her laughter floated between us and I wanted to capture it somehow, record it so I could listen to it again whenever I wanted. "You're crazy."

I made a sound of agreement. "It was worth it. And Oscar's a great dog. He's my second favorite wiener."

She nibbled on another bite, and when she glanced down at Oscar again, I saw her head tilt a little and check out my lap too. Yeah, busted.

Her chin snapped up, her brown eyes not quite meeting mine. "Is it… normally this hot in here?"

"I—" Frowning, I noticed for the first time I didn't hear the normal hum of the air conditioner. I carried my sub with me to the thermostat on the wall, where the digital display read eighty-two degrees. *What the fuck?*

I flicked the switch to off, waited a few seconds, and flipped it back to cool again. Silence.

"I don't think the AC is working."

"You're a smart one, Sherlock. What did you say your major was again?"

"Computer science," I answered, distracted. I punched some of the other buttons, lowering the temperature and turning the fan from auto to on. Still nothing.

Damn it.

As I finished off my sandwich, I texted the building superintendent to see when someone could come out to check on my unit. *First thing tomorrow* was the response I got. I swore under my breath.

Great. Just fucking great. Sweat beaded on my forehead and gathered along the top of my back.

"It's still broken?" She fed a piece of turkey to Oscar, who licked her calf in appreciation.

"Yeah, they can't come out and check on it until tomorrow." I moved around the room, closing the blinds to try to minimize the heat. The space was dim now, but still muggy.

I slipped my shirt off to combat the humidity, and double checked that Oscar had plenty of water in his dish before adding a scoop of kibble to his empty bowl. "Here, buddy, dinner time for you too." While I was in the kitchen, I grabbed a bottle of ibuprofen from the cupboard.

When I reclaimed my spot on the bench next to Reese, she was finishing the last bite of her sandwich. She brushed the crumbs from her hands onto the wrapper, but a smudge of cranberry sauce was still smeared just below her mouth. "Hang on," I said, giving into the impulse. I rubbed my thumb along her bottom lip, and a surge of lust shot through me when her mouth parted at my touch. Her pupils dilated as I brushed that full lower curve again, slower this time.

Her exhale was shaky, and she curled her hand around my wrist as if to hold me there longer. *Fuck, this girl.* The tip of her tongue met my skin, and the heat from the small point of contact made the room seem like an igloo in comparison. Those perfect lips closed around my thumb for a second, and all I could think about was what my cock would look like circled by that pink mouth, her hair wrapped in my fist. I groaned.

She turned her head, breaking the contact, but her fingers still held my arm while I brought my hand to my own mouth and licked the remaining cranberry sauce off my thumb. I murmured her name, and waited until my eyes captured hers. "I bet you taste better." Her gaze darted to my mouth, and I swelled in response. "Less tart, more sweet."

She sucked in a breath, and I leaned forward, ready to find out right then. But when I got close, when her exhale became my inhale, she turned away, my lips feathering over hers to land near her ear instead. I changed directions, sampling the spot just beneath her lobe, unable to stop my shit-eating grin when she shivered.

My lips followed the line of her neck when she spoke. "I fell."

I stopped, felt her body tense beside me where a second ago she'd been soft and pliable, and knew she was lying.

Reluctantly, I pulled back. "How did you fall?" I'd play along with her story for now.

"When we headed out to the field for choreography. I was a few minutes behind y'all, so I was running to catch up, and I... tripped." She touched the ice pack on her side, releasing my arm in the process. "My hip landed on the edge of the curb because I twisted to save the snare."

"Fuck the snare," I bit out, reaching between us to pull her shirt up. She tried to push it back down, but let go of the fabric when she looked at my face. Like hell she was going to stop me from checking out her injury. Unsatisfied with what I could see with her shirt bunched along her ribs, I pulled the whole damn thing over her head, ignoring her gasp of surprise. She was wearing a sports bra, and considering she'd paraded herself around without a shirt half a dozen times since auditions started, I wasn't worried about her modesty.

"Jesus, Reese." The peas had fallen to the floor along with her tank, and the purple outline of the bruise was stark against her tan skin, even in the shadows of the room. I traced the edges, wishing like hell I could absorb her pain, transfer the injury to my own flank. I popped open the Motrin and shook two pills into her palm. "Take these."

She obeyed me without an argument for once. My fingers slid to the waistband of her shorts again, because I needed to see for myself the full extent of the bruise. I lowered it past her hip, and the scrap of black lace I found had me cursing for a whole different reason.

"You should've fucking told me." My glare would've wilted most men.

"And then what?" Her eyes burned bright. "You would've taken it easier on me? Told me to march without the drum? Sent me home? Cut me on the spot?"

"I—" Yeah. Probably. Not cut her, but one of those other options she mentioned.

"No special treatment, Laird." Fuck, her voice saying my name. My fingers still gripped her shorts, the heat of her upper thigh warming my skin, and I itched to tug them the rest of the way off, to explore what those panties looked like beneath the nylon. To taste her through the lace.

I wrenched my hand away, wincing when she flinched from the snap of the elastic. Her words echoed in my head. It was one thing on the field, but off...

Beads of sweat gathered along her cleavage where her chest heaved in agitation. Her nipples pressed against the tight spandex, little points begging for my attention.

"You feel this." I pointed between us. "It's basic. Call it hormones, call it chemistry, whatever. There's something there when I look at you. When I touch you. Your body reacts, just like mine does." I didn't even try to hide my erection at that point.

"It's just because I'm the only girl you're around during the day. It's natural that—"

I laughed harshly, cutting her off. "You think this is some proximity thing? Reese, I don't mean to sound like an asshole, but getting laid is not a problem for me."

She flushed, the telltale redness spreading from her chest upwards. "I can't do this with you, Laird." My name again. I wanted to hear her yell it, scream it over and over as she came from my fingers, my tongue, my cock. "I can't have the rest of the guys thinking I earned my spot on the field by spreading my legs for the captain." She looked up at me from beneath those long, sexy lashes of hers. "I deserve better than that. I am better than that."

I didn't have an immediate answer to her challenge. She was right. Everything she said was true. But that didn't negate my desire for her, my all-consuming need to claim her for myself.

"We can't do this."

Fuck that. I carved my hand through my hair and gripped the back of my neck. "We'll be careful," I countered.

"What *we*?" she cried. "There is no *we*. You barely know me."

She was wrong. I didn't know her details. Her specifics. But she'd already shown me the broad outline of who she was. Strong. Tough. Stubborn. Funny. Sarcastic. Quick. Smart. A flash of her with Eli popped into my head, that single interaction with him telling me so much about her, and I added more words to the list. Compassionate. Giving. A fighter. A survivor.

I rubbed my chest, the spot where the small Gaelic G was inked on my right pec. I knew enough to know I wanted to know more.

I wanted to know her everything.

I wanted to fucking *be* her everything.

"Try me." I tipped my chin at her in challenge. "You're right. I don't know the little stuff. But the big stuff? I think you've shown your hand more than you realize."

CHAPTER 9

Reese

"**A**RE YOU SERIOUS RIGHT NOW?" I STARED AT HIM IN utter disbelief, my eyebrows practically touching they were pinched so hard together. I picked up the bag of peas again and pressed it back against my side. They were starting to thaw, the bag slippery with condensation, and tiny rivulets of water ran down my hip before falling on the floor, where Oscar happily licked up the small puddles. "How do you think this works? You pass some test on *What Makes Reese Holland Tick* and we're suddenly a thing on the down low?"

His jaw worked side to side, and he stared at me mutinously. *Okaaay*, maybe he did think that's exactly how this was going to happen. I huffed out a laugh. This was crazy talk. His eyes shone at me like gemstones, his fingers clenching and unclenching by his muscular thighs. Like I was some weird fucking prize he'd set his eye on, and now I was denying him.

"Laird," I started, but his eyes closed and his whole body relaxed. "I—"

"Say it again," he interrupted.

"Say what again?"

"My name," he growled. "Say my fucking name."

I licked my lips. They were somehow dry despite the pervasive Alabama humidity that had followed us inside and the heat emanating between us.

Us.

I swallowed hard and took advantage of his closed eyes to appreciate all the masculine beauty in front of me. The tattoos on his pecs begged to be traced by my fingers, my tongue, and his abs would've made any Hollywood heartthrob jealous. I followed the narrowing of his hips, the thin line of hair at his navel that led beneath his shorts, where a substantial bulge tented the black fabric.

He was gorgeous. And he wanted me to say his fucking name.

"Laird," I repeated, my voice huskier this time.

Goose bumps rose along his arms, tightened his flat nipples, and a shudder worked its way down his body. Irish green eyes flew open and met my wide chocolate gaze.

"Yes." Two strides brought him to my side, and from his position above me, he wrapped my ponytail around his fist, tipping my head back and arching my throat. He leaned down and ran his nose along its curve, nuzzled behind my ear, and inhaled deeply.

I forgot how to breathe.

He spoke against my sensitive skin, his lips brushing the shell of my ear with every word. "Ask me your questions. Then I'm going to make you say my name over and over again until I know every version of it coming from your lips by memory."

If he hadn't been fisting my hair and holding me captive with his words, I would've melted to the floor along with my makeshift ice-pack.

I turned my head instinctively, lips parted, seeking him, but he released my hair suddenly and took a step back. I wobbled and almost fell off the bench, catching myself just in time. Every nerve ending from every hair on my head still tingled from his touch.

"Your questions." He watched me hungrily, like I was all the desserts he'd ever denied himself to get a body that looked like his.

"I—" Disoriented, I blindly patted the table behind me for my phone, trying to rein in my scattered thoughts. Questions. I needed to ask him questions. "Okay. One second."

I pulled up my search screen, because I couldn't think clearly and Google knew everything. HOW WELL DOES HE KNOW YOU, I typed in the box.

The first result was a Cosmo quiz. I clicked on it.

Right. Here goes.

"Question one," I read aloud. "Her idea of a perfect date is A. Getting dressed up and going to a party. B. An afternoon hike with a picnic. C. Netflix and chill. D. Volunteering at an animal shelter."

He stared at me intently, as if he was trying to read my mind. "B."

"Nope." *C*, if I was being honest. I didn't need a guy in my life to do the other items on that list. "Question two. She hates it when her man A. Orders dinner for her. B. Won't get off his phone. C. Goes out with the guys on Friday instead of her. D. Skips foreplay."

"D." His answer was instant, confident.

But still wrong. I couldn't help but think—with the right guy—there were times when foreplay would be completely unnecessary. *Like right now.* "Wrong." Creases formed between his eyes as his brow furrowed. It was B. When I was with a guy, I wanted to know that I was enough to keep his attention, that nothing on social media was more important than me.

"Number three. When it comes to your friends, she prefers A. To always be there when you're hanging with them. B. You have the exact same circle of friends. C. You each hang out with your respective crowds solo, but still make time for each other. D. Friends, what friends? You can't stand to spend a minute apart."

He closed his eyes and looked at the ceiling. "This is ridiculous. B. We'd have the same friends."

Ugh, that was so smothering, C was a much better choice. I shook my head and dodged his glare. Oscar followed him as he started pacing from the front door to the stairs. "What's next?"

"Four. You want to go to the big party on Saturday but she isn't feeling well. You A. Skip the party to take care of her. B. Go. You don't want to both be sick. C. Make an appearance at the party, but leave early to drop some soup off at her place. D. Facetime with her the whole event, so she can still be there with you."

"A. Easy decision." He nodded once sharply and narrowed his eyes at me, like he dared me to disagree.

I smiled. "You got that one right. You're one for four."

But his streak ended there and he missed the next trio of questions about my preferences for living together, my ideal anniversary gift, and when to meet the parents.

A string of curse words flew from him and he stopped right in front of me, pointing at my phone. "This doesn't mean anything. The fact that I'm getting these wrong."

I lifted my shoulders insouciantly. "Hey, don't get mad at me. This was your idea."

"Yeah, I gotta couple of other ideas I'd rather try out on you," he muttered, picking up all the trash from our meal and stomping to the kitchen.

I hid my smile until he was around the corner, then I let it stretch wide. There was something endearing about seeing him get so worked up over this stupid quiz. I really should cut him a break, but what was the fun in that? "C'mon, big guy. You can handle it. Only three questions left. Eight. What is she most insecure about? A. Her looks. B. Her crazy parents. C. Her childhood photos. D. What insecurities?"

"D. I've never met someone more confident than you." And the way he said it made me wish it were true.

I swallowed hard, thinking back to those years as a kid, when I was swollen from the steroids and chemo and my hair was patchy at best. Yeah, I was good now. I'd made the decision years ago that fear was the lamest reason for not reaching my goals, because I refused to do anything except live my life to the fullest. But getting to this point was a journey I wouldn't wish on anyone. And choice B? Overprotective didn't even begin to describe it. There was a reason I chose to attend a college hundreds of miles from home, in a different time zone. Two reasons, in fact. Mom and Dad.

"Nope." I didn't hesitate, didn't give him time to react to my answer. I rushed right into reading number nine, reciting the words on my phone, but my mind was back in West Virginia, looking out the window of the children's hospital as my veins were pumped full of poison while people outside the hospital were busy with the task of *living*. Of doing. Of running and playing and going places without thinking first about the potential germ level and whether their white cell counts could handle the risk.

No, I was never going to be that person again.

Laird shifted in front of me, leaning against the wall two feet away, arms crossed over his chest. My eyes blinked away the past and he came back into focus. "Yup. You got that one right." I had no idea what the question was. Or his answer. He could have the stupid point.

I cleared my throat, swallowing back the memories. "Last one. When you look at her, you picture A. Later that night, in your bed. Or hers. Wherever you end up. B. The wicked cool weekend away you two have scheduled for next month and the new things you'll try together. C. That big event at the end of the season, the one you still need to rent a tux for. D. Whether your kids will have your eyes or hers."

Oh.

Oh.

It was asking where he saw the relationship going. How long he thought this would last. I blinked, caught off guard. "Look, this quiz is stupid, you don't have to ans—"

"All of them."

"What do you mean, all of them?" My voice crept up with each word, ending in a near shriek.

His voice was rough, his eyes hooded as he repeated himself. "All. Of. Them."

I laughed awkwardly, surely he didn't mean—

"Reese. I can't count the number of times I've thought of you in my bed, under me, on top of me, tangled around me, in every fucking position you can imagine. In my shower. On the couch. The bench you're sitting on right now, knees bent, ass in the air, tits pressed against the table with your fingers curled around the edges."

He took a step closer. My pulse skyrocketed.

"I've imagined you in a tiny little bikini on the Gulf Shore, me rubbing sunscreen on your back, your legs wrapped tight around my waist while I held you in the ocean, us fishing for our dinner on my cousin's boat."

Another step. I bit my lip.

"Did you know the band is invited to the football banquet in January? I don't normally go, but I wouldn't pass up a chance to see you in some killer heels and a long dress with a slit up the side, teasing me with flashes of those thighs all night. I wouldn't let anyone else dance with you." He paused. "You'd be all mine."

His arms caged me against the table he'd just talked about fucking me on from behind, and my vision went a little hazy.

"And kids? If we got to that point, I'd want a boy first. One who'd grow up big like me. And then a little girl, one just as gorgeous as you. But a boy first, so she'd always have a brother to watch out for her. To keep her safe when I wasn't there to do it myself."

There was a flicker in his eyes at the end, something dark and turbulent. It was gone before I could analyze it though, try to figure him out. He sucked in a breath. When he exhaled, he was inches away from me, his muscular chest bent over mine, forcing me backward at an angle.

His words came millimeters from my lips.

"Any other questions?"

Yes.

When, where, and how fast could we start?

My eyes drifted shut.

And I waited.

And waited.

I lifted my chin a bit, hoping it was enough to close the distance between us.

Nothing.

I peeked. His lips hovered just out of reach, his expression both soft and hungry at the same time. "Give me the words, Reese. Tell me off the field, I can have you. That you're mine."

Off the field.

It was like being doused with a bucketful of ice-cold reality.

My pride dueled with my wet panties.

And damn it all to hell, I had a vibrator in my dorm to handle my clit, but nothing to replace my self-respect and dignity if the guys on the line found out, if they treated me differently as a result. School hadn't even started yet. Gaining a reputation as a slut who failed to make the cut before the first day wasn't a risk I was willing to take.

"I can't." The words were faint. I could hardly force them past my lips.

He growled dangerously. "Can't? Or won't?"

"Right now, both."

I barely knew him, I reminded myself. He was beautiful and said things that made me want to spontaneously combust, but I barely knew him. If this turned out to be a mistake, a short fling—or worse, a one-night stand—how would the rest of the season play out?

Would I be around long enough to find out?

He pushed off the table. Blinked at me as if in utter disbelief, then turned away and rubbed his jaw. His voice was flat with disappointment. "Right. Let me grab a quick shower, a cold one, and I'll take you home. There are more veggies in the freezer for your side while you wait." He didn't look at me, just disappeared through the door to my left, slamming it behind him.

I shivered, despite the heat of the townhouse.

Oscar poked me with his nose, then jumped onto the bench beside me and laid his head in my lap, as if offering himself as a consolation prize. I rubbed his soft, speckled ears and smiled sadly at him.

"Thanks, buddy."

The sound of another door slamming and then running water broke the silence. Minutes passed. I didn't want to put my sweaty shirt back on, but I didn't want to be out here half-naked when he reappeared either.

He probably hated me now, I reasoned, as I rose from the bench and crossed to the door he'd gone through, the one I assumed led to his bedroom.

I cracked it open a tiny bit.

It was empty.

With as much quiet stealth as I could, I opened a random drawer on the dresser against the wall. Socks. I tried the one next to it and paused. Evidently, Laird preferred boxer briefs. But not just plain black ones. Orange, lime green, electric blue, and yellow options were jumbled up in a messy array. I touched the soft material of the one on top, unable to help myself from imagining him in only those, slowly lowering the fabric over his tight ass, until I could see—

The door behind me opened. I hadn't even realized the water had cut off. I turned to face him.

Steam billowed around him as he stood in the open doorway, water dripping down his chest, the towel around his hips in danger of falling off.

"Change your mind?" He smirked.

"I—" *Holy virgin mother of the sweet baby Jesus.* "I was looking for a clean t-shirt to borrow. For the ride back." Even though the towel covered more than the shorts he'd had on earlier today, the effect of him in a towel with a bed right beside us was almost more than I could take. I wiped my mouth surreptitiously for drool.

Four strides brought him to my side. He glanced down. "Snooping in my underwear drawer?" He plucked out the pair I'd been stroking, dark gray with a red waistband and red stripe right down the crotch. Without hesitation, he dropped the towel, and the glimpse I caught of him before he pulled the boxer briefs on confirmed his earlier statement.

His dick was huge. The story he told me earlier about how he acquired Oscar flitted through my mind. That was definitely a prize-winning specimen.

My whole body felt like it was blushing, and I was damp everywhere.

"Wrong drawer." There was a challenge in his eyes, as if daring me not to react to his outrageous stunt. He reached for a drawer directly behind me, and when he yanked it open, it bumped into the back of my thighs, pushing me forward into him. My hands landed on his abs, splayed across those hard, wet ridges of muscle, and I don't know if the moan I heard came from him or me.

My fingers curled and his abs rippled as I regained my balance, my nails dragging across his tanned skin. It was a study in contrasts, the cool drops of water on his warm flesh, the way I yielded instinctively as he leaned in, my soft sigh mixing with his harsh breaths. Our thighs were pressed together, and I could feel the impressive bulge growing behind that red stripe down the middle of his briefs.

Before I could respond, react, do something, he released me, a blue-and-white shirt with the Rodner University shark logo in hand. "Here." The muscle in his jaw ticked as he pulled it over my head, and by the time I'd wriggled my arms through the sleeves, he was fully dressed.

The shirt swallowed me, despite my height, hiding my

shorts and falling to mid-thigh. I licked my lips and backed up apprehensively, not sure how to gauge his current mood. His gaze raked down the length of me, nostrils flaring, before he turned away.

"Keep it," he said gruffly. "It looks better on you anyway."

The cotton was soft, either by design or from being washed so many times, and it smelled like him, a mix of fabric softener and something muskier, like sweat that came from hot sex instead of cardio. My skin prickled in the spots where his eyes returned and lingered, the neckline, my thighs.

"Thank you." My words landed awkwardly, too loud in the intimacy of his room.

"Don't thank me." His face twisted with a self-mocking smile. "I'll be jacking off later, thinking about you wearing just my shirt, nothing underneath it except those black lace panties of yours."

CHAPTER 10

Laird

REESE DIDN'T TALK TO ME ON THE RIDE BACK TO campus.

Not a word.

A different guy might let that bother him. Feel insecure and try to fill the silence with small talk or flirting or apologies or turn on the radio just to have some goddamn background noise to drown out the nothing.

Not me. Nope.

I let her sit there, two feet away, within a fucking arm's reach and did nothing.

Her mind was whirling. I could tell by the way her gaze would dart around, then fixate on something before going a little vacant when she was no longer paying attention to the college-town scenery Rodner, Alabama had to offer and was inside her own head.

Just thinking.

Because I was an arrogant asshole, I was pretty damn sure those thoughts were all centered on me and the words I told her at my townhouse. That final, dirty promise I made her.

I stole a glance at her when I made a right turn onto her street. Strands of her dark hair were curling from the humidity around the base of her neck where it'd escaped from her ponytail, or maybe it was from when I'd wrapped those long locks around my hand and pulled her head back to expose her throat.

Damn, that'd felt good. When she'd responded by parting her lips and closing her eyes a little, her breathing a little softer and more rapid than it'd been before I'd touched her. When her thighs had rubbed together only to part again at the knees when I moved closer, as if begging me to explore.

And, fuck if I didn't want to learn everything there was to know about her. Which spot made her gasp and tense up, if she preferred to be licked slow and gentle or firm and fast, the perfect angle that made her scream my name. It wasn't just her body either. Seeing her at the hospital had hit me at a visceral level. I wanted to find out what made her laugh, discover the secret to making her smile so big that dimple appeared, and uncover her greatest fear so I could stand by her side when she had to face it. Yeah, this wasn't a girl who'd let me do the dirty work for her, slay her dragons while she cowered in the ivy-covered tower. Reese would be on the front lines, carving her own path and wielding her own sword. And I wanted to be the one to have her back on the journey.

When I pulled to a stop in front of Petersen Hall, her dorm, she didn't react. Her full lower lip was caught between her teeth and she was absently stroking her neck, that soft spot just below her ear where I'd nibbled earlier.

Yeah. She was thinking about me.

It was only after I circled the Jeep, opened her door, reached in, and shook her knee slightly that she responded, jerking back to the present with a little gasp.

I couldn't help the shit-eating grin on my face.

"We're here."

She climbed out of my Wrangler and blinked, as if surprised to find we were steps away from her dorm. I let my hand settle on the small of her back, pleased when she didn't object or pull away, and steered her through the lobby to the elevator that would take us to her room on the fourth floor.

During the ascent, I studied our dull reflections on the chrome walls. I'd never been with a girl as tall as her, but I liked the way we looked together. Height on a girl would have some definite advantages. Longer legs to wrap around my waist. I wouldn't have to contort to try to kiss her lips or suck her nipples while I was buried deep inside her. Shower sex would be a thousand times easier. Even something as simple as reaching down to hold her hand.

Reese might have ruined me on short girls forever before I'd even tasted her.

I walked her to her door, room 407, then followed her in after she unlocked it without waiting for an invitation. While I would never, ever force myself on a girl, I wasn't above playing a little dirty when it came to her.

As she toed off her shoes in the corner, I crossed over to the little basket on the edge of her desk, where I'd found a bottle of ibuprofen the night I'd brought her drunken ass back here and taken care of her. Removing it and shaking it to ensure it wasn't empty, I set it and a bottle of water I snagged from her mini-fridge next to her bed.

"You can have more at midnight," I reminded her. "Don't forget. You're gonna need it to get through tomorrow."

Her glance flickered between the bottle of pills and me, her eyebrows folding down in confusion. "How did you know where…"

I stared at her. Waited for recognition to widen her gaze, for her to bite her lip in embarrassment maybe. Confusion filled her eyes and pursed her lips. I huffed out a laugh of disbelief. "Jesus, you don't remember do you?"

She cocked her head just slightly. "Remember?"

"After the drumline party? The one where you kissed Smith?" My voice dripped with bitterness as I said his name. I couldn't help it.

"I thought Willa…" she trailed off, comprehension dawning. "It was you?"

I nodded curtly. That explained her reaction, or lack thereof, at practice the next day. While I hadn't necessarily expected a thank you, I'd expected… fuck, *something*. An acknowledgement at least?

She rubbed her chin absently before she stiffened, shooting me a panicked look. "I woke up without pants that morning. Without a *bra*."

And I'd beaten myself off more than once to the memory of undressing her, as innocent as it had been. I couldn't help torture her a little right now though. "Yup."

"So you—" she bit off the rest of her words, her face pinking in the best way as her eyes slid closed.

I wouldn't laugh at her though. I'd never do that. Taking the two strides necessary to reach her, I cupped her jaw and tipped her face up to mine. "Nothing happened, Reese. Not like that. Not with you wasted." I paused, let those words sink in before I continued. "When I touch you—and make no mistake, it's a *when*, not an *if*—you're going to remember every fucking second of it. And it'll be because you want it as badly as I do." Her bottom lip was caught between her teeth, and I tugged it free with my thumb. "I took care of you, hung out and watched you like a fucking creeper to make sure you weren't gonna puke all over yourself in the middle of the night, and left before the sun came up."

She cringed.

"Did you know you make this soft little whimper some-times when you're sleeping? Not a snore, it's a different noise." I ran my thumb along her cheekbone, where the pink was the darkest. "It made me wonder what you were dreaming about."

The pink changed under my hand, darkening further.

I dipped down, traced her jaw with my nose. "You bet-ter not have been dreaming about that fucker, Smith. Are you seeing him?"

"And if I was?"

White-hot jealousy pierced my chest and I wanted to roar my displeasure. She. Was. Mine. I tamped down the in-tensity to an acceptable level, forcing a slow breath in and out through my nose. Like fuck would I allow that shit. "I'd hate for you to break his heart when you choose me instead." I nibbled her lobe, followed the delicate shell of her ear with my tongue. My cock jumped when she swayed against me, her hands fisting the sides of my shirt at my hips. I buried my smile in her hair. "Because you will."

With that vow, I released her, pleased as hell when she sank down to sit on the edge of her bed, as if her legs couldn't support her.

"I'm gonna go." I tipped my head toward the door. "You going to be okay? Do you want me to drive you to the health clinic? I think it's just bruised, but if you think one of your ribs…?" I'd probed them lightly at the apartment when she was pressed against me in the bedroom. She hadn't flinched when I'd run my hand down her side until I got to her waist, well past the curve of her ribs.

"No, I'm good." She hesitated. "Laird…" Another long pause as uncertainty flitted over her face, before she seemed to reach some kind of decision. "Your apartment is a thousand degrees. There's no way you can sleep there tonight. I have an extra bed if you wanna crash here." She nodded at the bare twin bed behind us. "You said you stayed the other night…"

I sucked in a breath as my dick leapt for joy. *Stay stay stay*, it pulsed in time to my racing heart. "Reese. If I stay tonight, I'm not sleeping in that bed over there." I held up a hand. "I'm not saying we have to fuck, but I can't take another night of watching you from across the room, and not at least having you in my arms." Sharing a twin bed, there'd be no way to be anything *except* close.

Her sock-covered feet tapped out a nervous rhythm, the first part of the Bon Jovi song we'd been working on earlier today. "What about Oscar?"

"I have a neighbor two doors down with a beagle. Oscar hangs out there sometimes if my classes run late. He could probably stay there tonight."

No more excuses. She had to make the decision herself. I'd laid it out there, but it was her turn to take a step toward me.

She fiddled with the edge of the quilt that covered her bed. It was pale blue and had a crazy intricate pleated type of design. If I was in her bed tonight, she wouldn't need it. I'd keep her plenty warm.

"You should give them a call. See if they can keep Oscar," she spoke to my knees.

"I don't sleep in pants, by the way."

"Jesus, Laird." She tugged that oversized shirt of mine she was wearing away from her body, as if it was hot in her dorm too.

"Or a shirt."

"You have to keep your underwear on!" Her voice was strangled and she wasn't looking any higher than my ankles now.

"Reese." Her hand fisted the edge of the quilt, then smoothed it back down, while her feet segued to the second song. "If I stay, it means something. I'm not saying I have expectations for tonight, but it means something. And I need you to admit it."

Her feet stilled, and she ran her palms down her thighs and back up again, but her fingers were relaxed, not stiff. She raised her melted chocolate gaze to mine and looked me right in the eye. "You should call your friend. About Oscar."

I'd never texted so fast in my life.

And two hours later, after she'd showered and come up with a million inane topics of conversation to delay the inevitable of climbing in bed with me, it was obvious she wasn't going to be able to keep her eyes open much longer. It might've only been ten o'clock, but when you spent as much time being active in the heat as we did, exhaustion was real.

I took pity on her and flipped the light switch, tipping the room into the near dark. The orange glow of the street lights below us filtered through the cheap metal blinds, providing some illumination, but not much.

She fidgeted by the side of the bed. It was adorable.

Without making a big fuss about it, I shucked my shorts and my shirt, making a little pile next to my shoes on the floor at the foot of her bed. Then I pulled back her quilt and sheet and climbed in, laid on my side, and patted the empty space next to me.

"Waiting on you, Reese."

She edged in gingerly, as if she feared that together we were over the weight limit of the standard issue bed frame and it might come crashing down at any second. Positioning herself as the little spoon to my big spoon, she settled in place.

And then wiggled. And squirmed. And shifted. When her last movement produced a soft groan, I'd had enough. "What's wrong?"

Utter stillness. She didn't budge. But then she finally admitted on a whisper, "I'm laying on my bruise like this, and it hurts."

I felt like a grade-A ass and immediately readjusted us. Once I was flat on my back and she was glued to my side with her head pillowed on my shoulder, her leg thrown over mine, and my arm wrapped around her to hold her in place, I was satisfied.

Her free arm lay bent across my chest, her hand resting near the G tattoo on my right pec.

It was almost perfect. Except one thing. "Hey, Reese? What the fuck is poking my ribs? There's no way your nipples can be that hard."

Was it possible to feel a blush? Because I felt her embarrassment like a tangible thing.

"It's... the underwire of my bra."

"Why the fuck are you wearing a bra to bed?" I asked it conversationally, to put her at ease. "Do you normally do that?"

A pause. Then, "No."

There were several ways I could handle this, but considering her smart mouth was MIA, I assumed she was feeling more than a little vulnerable. I bent my neck until I could look down at her, and then brushed her hair away from her face gently.

"Do you trust me?" I pitched my voice low and serious. "Because in case you misunderstood me earlier, I want you. And I'm not really looking to fuck this up. Take off the bra. Get comfortable. I'm not trying to get in your panties tonight." I tapped the tip of her nose gently. "Not until you're ready. I just want to feel you close to me. You're safe, I promise."

Her breath whooshed out in a long exhale, and I could feel the tension melt from her muscles. She leaned up and performed whatever voodoo magic girls do that allow them to take off their bras without ever removing their tops, leaving her in just a soft cotton shirt and some tiny plaid boxer shorts.

She sank down on the mattress again, and I nearly groaned at how good it felt to have her plastered against me. Her leg slid over mine, her thigh perilously close to my dick. Part of me begged her to shift over that last inch, to press against me, and the other part hoped she stayed right where she was, so my burgeoning erection didn't scare her off. I told her the truth when I promised her I was content just to hold her, but that didn't mean I wasn't aroused as fuck.

The curtain of her hair fell over my bicep, and I was careful to keep my hand on her lower back and away from her sore hip. The soft puff of her breath warmed my neck at steady intervals. It was her left arm, her free arm, that was making me crazy.

Her fingertip lightly traced the black ink of the G, once, then twice. My dick swelled, and I flattened her hand against my chest to still her motions.

"What's the G for? Your middle name maybe? Laird G. Bronson? Or an old girlfriend?"

Did her voice get a little brittle there when she said that last word? "No. G stands for Garrett, my brother." My hand pressed hers down harder for a moment, right over the tattoo.

"Aww, that's sweet." She tipped her chin up to me. "Does he have an L for you?"

I blinked hard at the sudden burn in my eyes. "No." Leaning, down, I dropped a single, soft kiss to the top of her forehead. "Enough questions for one night. Get some sleep."

I released her hand and tucked mine behind my head, propping myself up a tiny bit so I could have a better view of her curves against me. Sleep wasn't part of my immediate plan, not when it meant missing out on this.

Her hand drifted lower, away from the tattoo. I couldn't stop my abs from contracting when her palm brushed over them. I growled in a mix of satisfaction and frustration. "You know," my voice was deep, husky, as I whispered to her, "just because I promised to behave, doesn't mean you have to. Feel free to touch me wherever you want, gorgeous."

Reese made a little noise in the back of her throat before those slim fingers of hers slid partially under the waistband of my boxer briefs, brushing back and forth over the sensitive skin just inside my hip. I couldn't help thrusting up a tiny bit, begging her to continue her southward journey. But the little minx retreated, pulled back and snapped the elastic sharply against my skin, and had the gall to laugh at my pained moan.

Then, her pleased grin so big I could see it despite the dimness, that dimple taunting me, she wrapped her arm around my waist, snuggling close and stilling her tormenting movements. "Night, Laird."

As I replayed the last two minutes in my mind with a very different ending, drifting off was the least of my priorities. But I was wrong. Sleep claimed me soon after her breathing evened out, her heart beating the same tempo as mine.

The dream was both the same as normal and different from before, and it broke me like it did every time.

The hospital was cold, like always, but the little boy sitting in the middle of all the beeping machines wasn't wearing Eli's thick glasses. Instead, he stared back at me with the same green eyes I saw in the mirror every morning.

His pale fingers traced the line of tubing that ran from the port in his chest to the pump on the pole next to his bed. "She's pretty, Laird." I followed his gaze to the open doorway, where I saw a flash of dark hair and long legs.

Reese.

"I call dibs on that one," he continued, leaning forward to try to catch another glimpse.

"You can't," I said automatically. "She's mine."

He smirked, those familiar eyes taunting me. "Does she know that?"

I snorted at his trash talking, and flexed my biceps obnoxiously, putting my guns on full display. "Not yet. But who can resist all this?"

He smiled wistfully. "Will I look like you when I grow up? So I can get a pretty girl too?" The blue veins were visible in his thin arms, and there were scars from so many needle sticks and IVs.

No.

No, he wouldn't.

Because he'd never grow up.

"Definitely," I lied. We both knew it was a lie, but I said it anyway, hating the way his eyes dimmed a little.

"Hey, Laird?"

"Yeah, Garrett?"

His face was worried. "She might be out of your league, with legs like that. But don't give up, okay?"

I scoffed, and if he'd had hair, I would've ruffled it. "Are you doubting your big brother? Of course, I'm going to get the girl."

"Never." He smiled up at me, lips dry and cracked. "You never let me down."

But that was the biggest lie of all.

And we both knew it.

CHAPTER 11

Reese

I PARKED MY HONDA CR-V THREE ROWS BACK FROM THE nearest car at the hospital, not for the fear that someone would ding my doors, but because there was a big oak tree at the edge of the lot there, and it was one of the only parking spaces in the shade. If this Alabama heat had taught me anything, it was that shade trumps proximity every time. The black leather interior was great, except it could reach temperatures more suitable for baking a cake when left in the sun. I'd almost burned the backs of my thighs right off on my first day in Rodner. Lesson learned. Now, I parked in the shade or covered my seat with a beach towel when I left.

Since it was new, the interior of my car was still spotless inside. My parents wouldn't dare let me go off to college in anything but the most affordable vehicle on the list of the Safest Small SUVs, according to God knows who. Emphasis on *safest*. If cancer hadn't killed me, they sure as hell weren't going to lose me to a car accident. Their words, not mine. They loved me. And they preferred to show that love via smothering. And hovering. And micromanaging.

In fact, the only way I'd managed to convince them to let me attend Rodner University, the school I settled on both because it had a fantastic drumline and it was geographically the farthest from home, was by threatening to not go to college at all if they refused. And *that*, to my upper middle-class professional parents, was a fate worse than death by helicopter-parenting.

I scooped the handful of grape lollipops on my passenger seat into my small canvas purse. My morning had been unexpectedly busy. After an early thunderstorm washed out today's band camp, I'd started the day by cleaning Marco's dorm room per drumline requirements, then afterward, I'd met Smith for lunch at a small local taco joint. The lollipops were a gift from him.

"Why so many?" I'd questioned, when he dumped five or six in my outstretched palms.

"I was in the bathroom the other day. Ended up at the urinal next to Laird's. Snuck a peek. Decided you probably needed some more practice sucking before things progressed any more between you two. And since I'm such a good sidekick, I brought some extras to help you out." He'd nudged me with his elbow. "You're welcome, Batman."

"Progressed?" I'd stumbled over the word, my mind still lost in the visual of Laird's large shaft stretching my lips wide. "What do you mean?"

He'd leveled an exasperated stare at me. "You mean that wasn't his Wrangler I saw parked in front of your dorm all night long?"

I'd mumbled something about Wranglers being so common, they were fucking everywhere, damn it, like the mosquitoes. I'd hightailed it out of there as quick as I could, my hands full of candy, his laughter following me.

And now I was at the hospital on a whim, desperate to keep myself occupied. The alternative being sitting on my ass in my dorm room with way too much time to think about the fact that I woke up alone this morning, with no note or text from Laird since.

Except for the one he sent to the drumline on behalf of the band director, canceling practice.

And, I told myself for the billionth time, I didn't need to talk to him. There was nothing to discuss, right? We'd... cuddled. Cuddling didn't have to mean something. I mean, okay, I'd seen his junk too. In all its massive glory. But so had Smith apparently, so I wasn't in an exclusive club or anything.

We were cool. No, wait, not *we*. There was no *we*.

I didn't think.

Well, obviously *not*, because if there was a *we*, then surely he would've stuck around until daybreak, when my alarm alerted me to my utter aloneness.

By the time I reached Eli's room, I'd shoved Laird and his big wiener to the far corner of my mind, in a box I'd mentally duct-taped shut.

Knocking lightly in case he was sleeping, I pushed open the door and peeked inside. "Eli?"

"Reese! You came back! Did you bring the tattoos?" Eli shoved his thick glasses up his nose and practically vibrated with excitement.

Sitting on the hard, plastic sofa next to the bed was a thin lady with equally thick glasses who had the same eyes as Eli. There was no doubt from the resemblance this was anyone other than his mom. Plus, she eyed me warily, with the look every mom of every pediatric cancer patient watched someone new approaching their child. "They're temporary, I promise, Mrs. Wagner," I reassured her and introduced myself.

"Mo-o-o-o-om," Eli begged. "It's okay, isn't it?"

She smiled indulgently at him once she realized I wasn't here to poke and prod. "Of course, darling. I bet *Amelia* will love them." Eli blushed and mumbled something under his breath. Rising from the sofa, she squeezed my arm on her way out. "I was wanting some coffee anyway. I'll leave you two to visit. And, Reese, call me Melissa. Mrs. Wagner is my mother-in-law." As she reached the door, she turned around, mouthed *thank you,* and pointed at Eli.

After she left, we got to work on his arms and didn't stop until he had a full sleeve on his right side and a half sleeve on his left. The joy on his face when he saw himself in the bathroom mirror warmed me inside. He wrinkled his brows, narrowed his eyes, and stuck his lips out a little, trying on a tough guy persona. I gave him one of the grape lollipops, and the white stick angled from the corner of his mouth like a fat toothpick, then I took a quick picture on my phone to text his mom later.

"I have a few more suckers," I mentioned casually. "Does Amelia like grape?"

"Only one way to find out!" His confidence was adorable. The sleeves of his gown were rolled up to better show off his badassery, and with candy in hand, we strolled down the hall, IV pole in tow.

Three doors to the right, he rapped on the door twice before sauntering in with so much attitude and swagger, he even gave Marco a run for his money. I bit my lip to hide my smile and hung back in the doorway, happy to let Eli do his thing.

"Amelia, you know what makes chemo like a million

times better?"

A waif-thin girl with huge pale green eyes and a port connected to an IV pump just like Eli's gave him a blinding smile. "What?"

"A view like this." He struck a pose, flexing his biceps like a bodybuilder. She cracked up so hard she got short of breath and had to take a couple of deep pulls from the oxygen in her nasal cannula. "And this." Eli performed an elaborate bow, presenting her with a lollipop like it was a rose.

Amelia accepted it gratefully, hugging it to her chest before tearing off the wrapper and sticking it in her mouth. Chemo wrecked your taste buds, and some had the worst metallic aftertaste. It was one of the weird facts you didn't learn until you went through it—that chemicals pumped through a tube almost straight into your heart had a taste. A little candy could be a life saver sometimes, if the nausea wasn't too bad. The perfect sugary distraction.

"My hero," she said around the stick. "And I like the ink."

"I know. I'm pretty hardcore these days."

I stifled my giggle.

"And that's not all," he continued. "If you're not too tired, I have UNO cards in my room. Want to play a few rounds?"

Her eyes shone. "I love UNO."

"I know." His voice was shy this time. "I asked my mom to bring a deck so we could hang out."

An hour and five rounds later, with Amelia the decided champ with three wins compared to my and Eli's single win each, she was running out of steam and Eli was squirming enough that I suspected he needed to pee but didn't want to miss a moment of time with her.

"Miss Amelia, it was a pleasure to meet you, but I need

Eli to escort me back to his room now." I leaned close and finished in a stage whisper, "Those tattoos of his scare all the bad guys away. He's my bodyguard."

Eli puffed out his chest as he gathered up the cards, and neither kid argued with me putting an end to things.

"Tomorrow," he told her, "I demand a rematch. I was trying to be all gallant and stuff today and let you win because you're a girl, but a man can only take so much. I won't take it easy on you next time."

She nodded solemnly. "I would expect no less."

When we got back to his room, he wrapped his arms around my waist and squeezed surprisingly tight. "Thank you," he whispered. "That was awesome."

"*You* were awesome." I fought back the sting of tears behind my eyes as I tucked him back in bed after he used the restroom. He was beyond ready for a nap.

Nothing compared to the way I felt when I left the hospital after hanging out with the kids there. And yes, I called them kids, not patients. Too many people there saw them as a disease first and a person second. I refused to even think of them in those terms. They were just kids caught in shitty circumstances.

As I walked down the hospital corridor, I pulled my phone out. I'd had it on silent during my visit.

Nothing from Laird. *I guess our little sleepover didn't mean as much as he said it did.* Nothing except three texts from my mom, asking what I'd eaten for lunch, if I'd remembered to take my multi-vitamin, and if I needed her to order more sunscreen via Amazon for me.

I ignored all three.

And when I turned the corner and Laird was only six feet away, heading in the direction I'd just left, I treated him the same way he'd treated me all day. I ignored him too.

CHAPTER 12

Laird

COULDN'T STAY.

That dream. That wonderful, awful fucking dream. Wonderful, because I got to see *him* again, in sharp, bright, high-definition clarity in my mind. And it had been long enough since he passed now that, between dreams, he'd started to blur a bit around the edges. I'd forgotten about that cowlick he had, just above his left ear. And that his smile always tipped at that certain angle. And that he was too motherfucking young to go through any of it.

And it was awful because every time I dreamt of him, I kept getting older. The conversation was always the same, except for what he asked for. Would he get to play the drums too? Would he learn to drive someday? Would he get to graduate at the top of his class?

I lied every damn time. *Yes, Garrett, yes, you'll get to do it all.*

Leaving her bed was the hardest and easiest thing I'd ever done. Easy, because I'd never let a girl see me cry. And Garrett brought the tears.

But there was no place in the world I wanted to be except pressed next to her like a sardine in a twin-sized bed, her thigh over mine, her head over my heart, and her hand over that inked G.

That dream was why I found myself watching the sunrise from a graveyard, sitting in a puddle while the rain fell around me. I traced the numbers that spelled out the length of his life, the dates far too close together. He didn't even get two handfuls of years to be my brother. But I'd be his forever.

My clothes clung to my skin, annoying but not cold. It didn't matter though. It could've been the middle of winter and I wouldn't have budged until I was ready. The discomfort of being wet or hot or cold was nothing compared to what he'd endured. Nothing.

The early morning text from the band director cancelling practice cemented the conviction that I was exactly where I was supposed to be in that moment. With my brother.

The only concession I made to the rain was the baseball hat I'd pulled low over my face. Not that it mattered. My cheeks were as wet as the rest of me.

By the time I finally rose, the thunderstorm had cleared. The violence of it had helped somehow. The angry vibration of the thunder, the sharp, painful crack of the lightning. The endless, endless rain. I understood all of it.

I embraced all of it.

And when it ended, it was time for me to move on too. To go back to living for both of us. Trying to turn my lies into truths. Until I dreamed of him again one day.

When I got back to the Wrangler, the chill from the AC raising goose bumps on my skin, my phone was dead. It didn't matter. I had nowhere to be today with practice cancelled.

Except the hospital.

Maybe there, I could keep Garrett close to me a little bit longer. There were always pieces of him lurking in the depths of their eyes. Parts of him I recognized in their actions. Remnants of when I thought I could save him if I just loved him enough, behaved enough, achieved enough.

But I couldn't. My mom left one year to the day from when we buried him here. I never heard from her again. My dad, he'd stuck around physically, but he'd never been the same. Since love had already failed him twice, he'd come up with new tactics to deal with me. Lists of impossible demands, the strictest of schedules, regimens for both my diet and exercise, and more after-school activities than one person could ever enjoy. He kept me at arm's length, never closer, never farther. And he never, ever said my brother's name again.

I wanted to hate him. So bad. But he was the only connection I had left to Garrett.

And there was nothing I wouldn't do for my brother.

Consequently, I listened to Dad's lectures, did just enough to keep him off my back, and did my best to live my life in what little space remained.

Like drumline, which he'd always considered a colossal waste of time.

I scrubbed my hands over my face, wishing I could wash away the reality of being a disappointment to the only parent I had left just as easily. And then I forcibly pushed him from my mind, refocusing on the present.

On the way to the townhouse, I picked up Oscar, who

spent an inordinate amount of time sniffing me. I played fetch and tug-of-war with him while I ate some cold pizza from the fridge. The AC was working again, thank fuck. By the time I showered, changed, and got to the hospital, it was mid-afternoon. The storm was gone, the August sun having erased any evidence it'd once existed.

When I turned the corner to the oncology floor, she was the last person I expected and the one person I needed to see the most.

And I was finally able to take a deep breath that didn't pinch. My first of the day that came easy. When my lungs filled completely and the pain squeezing my ribs ceased.

But she didn't stop. Didn't even look at me. A sharp, prickly sensation filled my gut.

And when I visited Eli last, after he'd woken up from his nap, she was all he would talk about.

"… and then she covered my arms with all these tattoos, and I could tell Amelia thought I was a total stud, and then we all played UNO, and Amelia kept winning but that's okay because every time she won she *smiled* so big, and her smile is just the best thing, and why weren't you here too? Did you get in trouble with Reese?" He finally paused for a breath while I tried to catch up.

"Trouble?" I repeated. "Why would you think I'm in trouble with her?" *Maybe because she walked right by me as if I didn't exist?* But Eli didn't know that.

He shrugged but looked at me reproachfully from behind those glasses of his. "I asked about you and she smiled, but not like Amelia smiled when she won UNO. She only smiled with her mouth and not her eyes. That's how you know it's not real." Confusion darkened his face. "I thought you liked her? You called dibs on her last time."

"I do like her." Something warm and soft bloomed in

my chest when I said those words.

He laughed. "Well, you're not doing a good job of show-ing her apparently. Maybe you need more tattoos."

"I'll take that under consideration." I nodded seriously.

"Then you can peacock."

"I can what?" *Did he just say something about a cock?*

"Peacocking. I saw it on the Discovery Channel. In na-ture, the male of the species is usually more colorful and bright, to attract the best female. You might need some more colors. Because Reese is the best, after Amelia. Then you can peacock her."

I bit back a laugh. "I'll have to work on my peacocking. Good advice, Eli."

"Just trying to help a brother out." He held out his fist for a bump.

I tapped it, then said my goodbyes. "Sounds like I got some work to do. I'll come back and give you an update in a few days."

"Good luck." His eyes were wrinkled around the edges, like he was truly worried about my lack of game.

Turned out, he was right.

She ignored my texts the rest of the afternoon.

And at practice the next few days, she was glued to Smith. Reese didn't avoid me per se, but she certainly didn't seek me out or hang back to give me a chance to catch her alone either.

And the texts I sent those days? She finally replied. But they were stilted, awkward conversations.

Me: *Hey, how are you?*

Reese: *Good.*

Me: *Busy tonight?*

Reese: *Yes.*

Me: *Want to grab dinner tomorrow? Sammy's maybe?*

Reese: *That's not a great idea. Someone could see us.*

Me: *We could bring it back to my place. Or yours. Or go to the park or something.*

Reese: *Maybe.*

We didn't get dinner. Not together anyway. When I stopped at Sammy's after Thursday's practice, she was there already, turkey and cranberry sub in front of her. But she was sitting with Smith, Cade, Willa, and Amber. Willa saw me first and licked her lips in blatant invitation as I walked to the counter. After my sandwich was ready, I approached their table, aiming for the empty seat next to Reese, but as I sat down, she popped up like a damn whack-a-mole and announced I could have her seat, she was finished anyway. And Willa and Amber were so visibly excited, talking over each other to get my attention, I couldn't change my mind and follow her out without it looking awkward as fuck.

Tomorrow was Friday, the last day of official band camp, and the night of the Countdown, a Rodner drumline tradition.

I was the captain, damn it. And her vet.

She wouldn't be able to avoid me there.

And I planned on peacocking the hell out of her.

CHAPTER 13

Reese

WHILE I'D ADMIT I HAD A DREAM EARLIER THIS WEEK that involved Laird and being tied up at his mercy, I didn't expect to wind up blindfolded in the back of his car on Friday night.

The Countdown had officially begun.

It sounded easy enough. The remaining NADs were paired off, blindfolded, and driven around for however fucking long the vet behind the wheel decided to drive. Then, each twosome was dropped off at a different unknown location, somewhere within a five-mile radius of campus. If you didn't make it back to the party at Bubba's apartment and chug two cups of NAD juice before midnight, you were cut from the line, just like that.

Only six of us were left. Three groups. And, of course, Smith was the only one willing to be my partner.

Fuckers.

Marco and Laird were in the front seat of Laird's Wrangler, arguing about practice times once school started Monday. Marco kept saying we only needed two a week, with the rest of the band, but Laird was pushing for a third, a drumline only one, on Wednesday nights.

The Jeep hit a pothole and I grabbed the door handle for balance.

"We can't get sloppy this year, man," Laird said. "It's our last year."

"Relax. We're better than that. We're not gonna fuck it up. We can always add in Wednesday practices later if we need it."

I bit my lip at the blatant disrespect in Marco's voice.

"We need it now," Laird replied sharply. "We haven't even narrowed down who's earned field spots or started on the snare duel for the drum break."

I couldn't hear Marco's reply over my own swift intake of breath, when the Jeep swerved suddenly to the left and I fell partially against Smith next to me.

He gave my hand a quick squeeze. "You okay?" His murmur was pitched soft enough not to be overheard.

"Yeah." I braced my foot against the bottom of the seat in front of me, trying to stabilize myself a little better. "Pretty sure we just went off road."

Marco snickered. "I take back my earlier comment about girls being dumb."

I mumbled under my breath.

The rock music that had been blaring in the background suddenly went quiet. "Did you just say *scrotum breath*?"

I coughed to cover my laugh, and then lost the battle when I heard Smith choking up next to me.

"Scrotum breath?" Marco asked again. "Are you sucking Smith's balls or something back there? Or is he sucking yours?"

Laird growled and slammed on the brakes before I could reply. The seatbelt cut into me hard, ending my laughter with a hard grunt. "We're here."

The sound of rustling filled the Jeep. I waited, listening as I heard Laird and Marco opening their doors and getting out. A gust of wind ruffled my hair as my door was opened, some of the dark strands landing in my mouth. I felt someone close to me and held my breath.

Gentle fingers traced the curve of my cheek, dislodging the hairs stuck to my lip balm. *Laird.* Marco wouldn't have cared or noticed. He leaned over me, his arm brushing across my breasts as he unsnapped my seatbelt. Warm breath fanned my ear, his lips teasing the sensitive skin around the shell, and he murmured quietly, "I've missed you."

Now was not the time or the place to discuss it, so I nodded for lack of a better response, but my traitorous nipples didn't get the memo and hardened beneath my shirt. I sent up a silent prayer that Marco wasn't watching.

The blindfold around me loosened, then fell in my lap. I blinked at the sudden brightness. Even though it was after dinner, the sun wouldn't set for another hour or so.

Laird blocked my exit from the Jeep, his broad shoulders filling the door frame. I twisted in the seat, nudging his hip with my knee to signal him to get out of my way. Behind me, I could hear Smith exiting, the Jeep shifting with the movement, and then Smith talking shit about where we might be while Marco dodged his questions.

"Move," I whispered.

His eyebrows dipped and his hand dropped to my knee and squeezed. "Look, maybe this isn't a good idea. You don't have to do this."

My eyes flashed to his in surprise. "What do you mean?" *Did he mean us—if there was an us—or the Countdown?*

"You're not from here. I don't want you guys getting lost and …" He lifted his hand to rub the back of his neck as his voice trailed off.

I nudged him again. "Are you worried about me, Laird?"

His hesitation was answer enough.

"No special treatment," I reminded him. "And, seriously, how hard can this be? We do five miles at practice regularly."

"Yeah. It's five miles maximum if you go in the right direction on your first try."

"She wimping out? What's taking so long?" Marco's taunt interrupted our conversation.

Laird stepped back, and I climbed out of the Jeep. "Nah. You'd miss me too much if I wasn't around." I kept my voice light.

Before I could round the corner of the vehicle, Laird's hand snaked out and hooked the back pocket of my denim shorts, stopping me. Using just his fingertips, he turned my hips partially to the left. His touch seared me right through to the skin. "Start that way." His words were barely audible, but I heard him.

Whipping around, I glared at him. "Stop it. I can do this."

He still looked troubled as he nodded at me, then glanced at his phone. "You two have about an hour and twenty minutes of light left. If you haven't found campus by then, you fucking call me." He muttered the words against my temple.

"That's against the rules." We weren't allowed to have electronics for this, because it was too easy to cheat with GPS. Your vet was supposed to hold onto your phone until you made it to the party. Except, when he blindfolded me earlier, Laird had refused to take mine, and had instead tucked it in the back waistband of my shorts when no one was watching, where it was hidden by the hem of my loose tank top.

Internally, I was conflicted. On one hand, his concern was sweet. On the other, I wanted him to have a little more faith in me that I could handle this on my own.

We had a stare-off until Marco and Smith joined us on our side of the Jeep. He looked away first.

Marco eyed the two of us suspiciously, while Smith gave me a shit-eating grin. "Problem here?" Marco asked.

"Just wondering what's taking so long for y'all to leave," I answered flippantly. "We have a party to get to, don't we?"

"Fucking hell," Laird muttered.

"We'll see you suckers later. If you make it." Marco punched Smith on the shoulder and wrinkled his nose at me before shouldering past us and climbing back into the Jeep. He pounded on the roof. "C'mon, Laird. It's time to get our drink on while these two wander around like lost sheep. I'm thirsty."

Smith flicked his eyes at me, and dropped to one knee to re-tie his already perfectly tied shoe, giving me a minute with Laird.

He lifted his hand like he was going to reach for me again, but I stepped back. "I'll see you soon. Have a cold beer ready for me."

With a final searching look, those full lips of his pressed tightly together, he stepped back. "Yes. I will see you soon. Because you're my fucking NAD and you will not disappoint me." And then he winked before he disappeared inside the Jeep.

"That's more like it," I muttered, and Smith snorted.

We watched in silence as they drove off, the Jeep bouncing over the overgrown grass down a barely visible path to a black swath of road about five hundred feet away.

We each had a water bottle, and I had my contraband phone, but other than that, we had nothing to help us on our way.

"Do you know where we are?" I ventured, looking around. I wasn't sure if I should mention my phone or not.

"Yup. I know exactly where we are."

"Really?" My voice was bright with surprise. This area looked vaguely familiar. Did I pass it on the way to the hospital?

The Jeep had turned right onto the road as it disappeared from view. Smith pointed left instead. "Campus is about four miles down that way." The same direction Laird had pointed my hips. I started walking, but Smith grabbed my elbow and stopped me. "Or it's two miles around that lake over there if we keep going down this path."

I looked behind us, where he was pointing. "For real? That's so much shorter."

"Considering they went right and must be taking the long way back to campus, if we hustled, we could probably even beat them. But what's the fun in that?" He started toward the lake at an easy pace, and I fell into step alongside him, matching my stride to his out of habit. "Know what else we pass between this lake and Bubba's house?"

"What?" I watched my feet so I wouldn't trip over any loose rocks.

"Pizza. We have plenty of time. Want to stop for a slice, Batman?"

I pretended to consider it. "Only because I don't want you wasting away, Robin." I patted his perfectly flat stomach. "You're looking skinny these days."

He tugged up his shirt, flexing his abs. "Girl, you don't need to come up with an excuse to touch me. Just ask and I'm happy to let you cop a feel. Especially if I get to return the favor."

"I don't think you watched the same Batman and Robin I did growing up." I rolled my eyes.

He laughed. "A pair of grown-ass men in tights who hung out in a cave together? I think the general public is avoiding making some very obvious conclusions about the two of them."

My eyes got big as I thought about his words. "But what about Catwoman?"

Smith slung his arm around my shoulder. "A hot woman in latex to join in the fun? I'm telling you, Batman is absolutely my kind of hero. He didn't even try to hide his kinky side."

We dissolved into laughter and spent the rest of the hike speculating about the sex lives of various superheroes while sucking on a pair of grape lollipops Smith had brought along.

An hour later, we were settled at Antonio's with a giant cheese pizza propped between us, and the sun was saying its colorful goodbye.

I took a long drink of my Cherry Coke Zero before pulling a hot, melty slice onto my plate, the mozzarella cheese stretching and drooping as it tried to hold itself together. "Oh hey," I started. "I meant to ask you the other day, whose dorm room do you have to clean? Since I got Marco, did you get Laird?"

Smith took a huge bite of his own slice and looked at me quizzically. "What do you mean? I don't even clean my own dorm room."

"You mean one of the vets doesn't have you…" I trailed

off, nibbling on the tip of my slice while I thought it over. Fucking Marco. He made that shit up about NADs cleaning the vets' rooms. I'd bet money on it. I took another bite absently. I could complain. Pitch a fit about how it wasn't fair and refuse to do it. *But that's what he wanted.* Technically, a NAD had to do what a vet asked. The fact that I was the only NAD being asked was beside the point, I was sure.

Smith tipped his head. "You're cleaning Marco's room? How'd he get you to do that?"

"He told me I had to. But you know what, it's fine. If that's the worst thing he can think of to do to me, I can handle some housework."

Smith chewed thoughtfully. "I wonder if it's a gender role thing. If he's trying to put you in your place symbolically. Like, you know, traditional-ass shit where the woman cleans the house and the man goes to work."

I laughed so hard soda dribbled down my chin, and I pressed a handful of napkins to my mouth to mop up the stray drops. "Jesus, Smith. You give him too much credit. You think Marco thinks symbolically? Seriously? Are we talking about the same guy?"

He shook his head. "You're right. My bad. More likely he's just lazy and saw an easy way to con you into doing it. You gonna stop now?"

"I'll handle it. No worries. But for real, what's his deal? Is it just me? Or does he have something against women in general—when he's not trying to fuck them?"

Smith leaned back in his chair and rubbed his chin. "Back in high school, Laird and Marco were a big deal. They ran in the same circle of popular kids. You know, the ones who won Best Looking and Prom King and that kind of shit. But Laird always made it look easy. People just liked him. With Marco, I don't know quite how to explain it, but he always seemed to try a little too hard or fell a little short. He's been in Laird's shadow forever in that sense. Laird was first chair and snare captain back then too, and Marco was second."

I finished my first slice and took a second. "Right, okay. But plenty of kids aren't class president or homecoming queen and don't end up being dickholes. There's got to be more to it than that."

"There were rumors back then. About Marco's mom. That his dad used to hit her and that she tried to leave once, abandon the family. I have no idea if they were true or not, but I never saw her come to any of the football games." Smith fiddled with the edge of his plate.

The pizza in my mouth lost its taste. "His dad beat his mom? Did his dad hit him too?"

Smith shrugged. "I mean, I never saw any marks on him that year. But who knows? His dad was a drunk asshole, so it wouldn't shock me if he had."

I couldn't help thinking back to the day he tripped me and I fell on the curb. I wiped my fingers off on a brown paper napkin and pushed my plate away. "It sucks that he had a shitty childhood. But that doesn't excuse his behavior."

"No. It doesn't. But if that's the only way he'd seen a man and woman interact, it's not surprising that he doesn't know how to treat a woman."

"Are you defending him?" I asked incredulously. Batman was about to fly solo. Who needed a sidekick?

"Not... defending him." Smith drew out. "I'm just saying, especially here in the South, and for a guy who was always second best, I can see how a confident girl like you could bring out the worst in him."

"Wait, so it's *my* fault?" My fingers curled into fists on my thighs.

"*No!* I'm not even remotely saying that. He shouldn't talk to you the way he does. But you have to admit that you go out of your way to push his buttons. You're not exactly helping the situation."

"You *are* defending him." All I could do was stare at him incredulously.

Smith's cheeks turned pink and he looked away.

"Oh my God. Do you *like* him?" My eyebrows nearly reached my hairline, and my voice rose an octave higher than usual.

"I don't like *him*. I don't like the way he treats you or the way he acts sometimes. But do I think he's kinda hot when he gets all worked up and starts strutting around? I know you're blinded by Laird, but have you seen the abs on Marco?"

Now it was my turn to blush at the mention of Laird. "But still… of all people? Marco? Scrotum Breath?"

Smith scrubbed his hands over his face. "I've always had a weakness for the bad boys, okay? I don't want to date him or anything. I'm just saying if he got really drunk one night and wanted to experiment—or offered me a private practice session—I wouldn't say no. He's an asshole, but he's a sexy asshole." He took a long drink. "And Laird isn't the only one I got an eyeful of in the bathroom the other day. Let me just say, Marco has got some *girth*."

I shrieked. "I did not want to know that!"

"But now you do." He smirked without remorse.

I threw a wadded-up napkin at him. "I'm not going to be able to look him in the eye now."

"Perfect. He'll love that. He'll think you're subservient. Less drama for all of us."

We both laughed at the likelihood of that ever happening.

And then we lost track of time as the conversation shifted to classes starting on Monday and roommates moving in tomorrow. Somewhere along the way, we ate the rest of the pizza. When the waitress brought the check, I noticed the timestamp on the top and gasped. "Smith! It's 11:30! We only have half an hour left to find Bubba's and get our drink on."

Smith scooted his chair back in alarm and stood to leave. "Holy shit, Batman. Ready to fly?"

CHAPTER 14

Laird

I PROWLED THE PARTY IMPATIENTLY, NURSING THE SAME warm beer I'd been holding for the last two hours. The sky was dark outside the window over the kitchen sink. And Reese had neither shown up nor called me. I checked my phone for the third time in five minutes.

Still nothing.

Cade and Justin had arrived a while ago and chugged their requisite two cups of NAD juice while everyone else cheered, especially Cade's relieved older brother, Charlie.

I sent Reese another text. The fifth or sixth since I'd dropped her off. All of them unanswered.

Shit. Fuck. Damn it to hell.

What if they were lost? She wasn't from around here. It was doubtful she'd recognized the far edge of the lake on the south side of campus. Or worse, what if one of them had gotten hurt? The sun had set over an hour ago. If they were still on the road, cars might not see them. And it's not like we'd left them with a fucking flashlight or anything.

She has her phone, I reminded myself for the millionth time. Not that she apparently remembered how to use it.

But maybe she was the one who'd been injured? And Smith didn't know she had one and hadn't gone the right way for help?

The cup crumpled in my hand, the last inch of beer at the bottom dripping onto the beige linoleum. I cleaned up the mess with a wad of paper towels and then hunted down Marco.

"I'll be back, man. I'm gonna go pick up some more beer. We're running low."

"We can have someone else do that. There's no need for you to leave." Marco protested. "And Willa was looking for you earlier."

Who gave a fuck about Willa? "Nah, it's cool, I got it. I won't be long." I slapped him on the back between the shoulders and beat a hasty escape to my Wrangler.

I didn't care if it was cheating. I was going to go find her and bring her back. For appearances, I could drop her and Smith at the end of the block or something, let them walk from there. It didn't matter. I just needed to know she was okay.

I just needed *her.*

My foot was heavy on the gas as I returned to the field where we'd left them. It was empty. *Of course, it's fucking empty, man.* I berated myself as I waffled over which way to try next. When we'd driven off, we'd turned right. Guessing they would have followed us, I went that way, driving slow and peering into the tall grass along the side of the road on the way. Several side streets split off and I went down all of them, finding a whole lot of nothing.

The knot in my stomach doubled in size. I sent more texts. Even called twice. It went straight to voicemail both times, indicating to me her fucking phone was either off or had been crushed into worthless pieces when a car ran her over in the dark.

Jesus, what was it about Reese? She'd dug her way under my skin in a way no other girl before her ever had, dominating my thoughts and ruling my dick. I'd started to measure time by the number of hours until I'd see her again. And the answer was always *too fucking long.* I had a feeling when I finally did claim that sexy body of hers, this addiction of mine was only going to get worse.

Using every cuss word I knew and inventing a few new ones, I returned to the empty field and repeated the same meticulous procedure the other direction. My fingers squeezed the leather of the steering wheel harder, my knuckles turning white, as if it would help me see deeper into the darkness beyond the twin beams of the headlights.

By the time I'd traveled every inch of road she could've come across between the field and campus, I was alternating between fear and fury. When I found her again, because, damn it all, I *would* fucking find her, I wasn't sure if I wanted to kiss her senseless or spank her ass until it turned red beneath my palm.

My phone dinged with a text, and I almost swerved off the road in my hurry to check it.

Marco: Where are you, man? You left two hours ago. Everyone's here and wondering where you went.

Me: Everyone? All the NADs made it?

Marco: Yeah, Smith and the girl showed up and drank the juice with a few minutes to spare.

Marco: Unfortunately.

She was there.

She was fucking there.

And despite his words, I couldn't relax. Not until I saw her with my own two eyes.

I floored it the whole way back until the tires squealed into a spot at Bubba's apartment. I practically flew up the stairs, the hinges in serious jeopardy as I ripped the door open. My eyes scanned the party frantically.

With Smith's arm around her shoulders, Reese was tucked into one end of the blue couch, cheeks red and head tipped back as she drank from a plastic cup. I froze in the entryway, chest heaving from my sprint across the parking lot, absorbing every detail. Her shirt wasn't wrinkled, but traces of mud edged her shoes and a few shallow scratches marred those long, bare legs of hers. And was that the start of a bruise on her shin? I had a brief flash of Garrett, those dark bruises that began blooming on his pale skin before we knew it was leukemia. Then I pushed the thought aside roughly. She was fine. I hadn't failed her like I'd failed him. She was right here in front of me, laughing her ass off without a care in the world.

And those conflicting emotions rushed through me again, battling each other for dominance. I wanted to rip her from the couch, crush her to me and devour her lips, feel the heat of her against my body to prove she was real and here and okay. At the same time, I wanted to strangle her for the wild goose chase I'd been on half the night and demand to know what the fuck was wrong with her phone.

She lowered her hand, the movement loose, and when she placed her cup on the beat-up wooden coffee table in front of her, not a drop spilled.

I exhaled. Good, she wasn't tipsy yet, despite the NAD juice. Because, dammit, before the night was over, I planned on claiming her and I wanted her to fucking remember every moment of it.

Time to peacock.

But before I could take a step, a hand clasped my shoulder. "Where's the beer?" Marco raised his eyebrows in confusion.

Fuck. The beer. "They were out."

"Of beer?"

"Yup. Weird, right?" I shrugged. "I guess with school starting back, everyone's having one last party."

"There was no beer," he repeated, disbelief twisting his face. "At all?"

"Sorry, man." I moved farther into the room, shaking off his hand and advancing in her direction.

She hadn't seen me yet. Her head was turned the other way, toward Van, who usually never said a word, but was waving his hands around and making explosion sound effects as he told her some story. Damn, the things that smile of hers could do to a guy. The look on his face was slightly awed, as if he couldn't believe her attention was centered on him.

It won't be for long.

When I was two yards away from her, she sat up straight and whipped those coffee-brown eyes of hers to me so fast, her hair slapped Van in the face. The smug smile that lit her face saved her.

I was going to kiss that smirk right off her lips.

As I passed the couch, I captured her hand and pulled her free of Smith's arm, tugging her along behind me. She stumbled a bit, but I just tightened my grip to keep her from falling.

I didn't stop until we were in the bathroom with the door locked. Didn't glance around to see if people were watching us and whispering, drawing their own conclusions. I was singularly focused on Reese.

On those perfect lips of hers stained red from the cheap alcoholic punch.

"Laird," she whispered.

I allowed myself a handful of seconds to savor the sound of her saying my name, wishing we were anywhere but Bubba's bathroom. Then I hardened my voice. "Give me your phone."

"My phone? Why?"

"It's broken, isn't it? I assume that's the only reason you have for *not* using it like I told you to."

"No. You said I needed to call you if I didn't reach campus before dark," she countered indignantly, her hands behind her back where her phone was likely still tucked in her shorts.

I took a deep breath. "And when it had been dark for over an hour, and you still weren't here, why didn't you fucking use it then?"

She dipped her chin, but I immediately curled a finger under it to raise it back up. Her eyes slid to the side, and her voice was sheepish. "We were back on campus by then. We were at Antonio's, eating pizza."

Closing my eyes, I counted out several four-beat measures in my head. *She was eating pizza.*

"You said to call if we hadn't found our way back by then." The words were mumbled and only faintly apologetic. "And… we were back. We just weren't here."

"So I used half a tank of gas driving all over Rodner, Alabama looking for you while you were busy eating pizza with Smith." I leaned down until our noses were only inches apart. "Is that right?"

Her hand came up to circle my wrist where I still held her chin, and her hot breath fanned my palm. "You were looking for me?"

I backed her up against the locked door and used my other hand to free her phone from the tiny piece of denim she called shorts. "Did you even check it?"

"No." She shivered beneath my glare, but stood tall. "It was against the rules. And I didn't need it. I told you I had this."

"If *you had this*, you would've been here before dark." A quick glance at the screen after I hit the button confirmed that it was powered off. I put the useless piece of technology on the counter next to us.

"The rules just said be here before midnight. And I was."

"Jesus, fuck." I pressed my forehead to hers and closed my eyes. "Yes. I was worried, okay? And I came looking for you because the thought of you out there somewhere, needing me, while I stood around here hoping you weren't lost was unacceptable."

"I wasn't lost."

"But I was, Reese." I opened my eyes and searched her face. "I didn't know where you were, so I was."

She bit her lip, her teeth denting that full lower curve, and I used my thumb to free it, to trace the mouth that had haunted my dreams for the last few days. She whispered my name again, and I crowded my hips against hers, letting her feel every inch of the effect she had on me. God, the sound of her voice saying my name. Made me want to puff out my chest and fall to my knees at the same time.

And nothing, absolutely nothing, made me harder.

Her eyes drifted shut, and when her chin tilted up, offering me her mouth, I'd reached my breaking point. I cupped her face with both hands, my fingers fanning out across her cheekbones before curving around the back of her neck.

With a growl torn from the back of my throat, I lowered my mouth to hers, finally tasting her the way I'd wanted to since that first day.

CHAPTER 15

Reese

HE DEVOURED ME.

Being eaten alive had never felt so good.

His lips. His hands. His heat. My entire being was overwhelmed by him finally, finally touching me.

The kiss started hard, desperate, the inevitable conclusion to the tension that had been building between us for two weeks. With my eyes closed and my breasts flattened against the wall of his chest, I gave into it, surrendered to the moment. My mouth clung to his as he tilted my head to the side, changing the angle to deepen the contact.

His hands moved over me restlessly, hungrily, skimming down my back on the way to my ass, then back up my sides to frame my face, his fingers leaving a trail of heat behind on every inch of skin he claimed for himself. I pulled at his shirt while he pushed me against the solidness of the door. My heart tripped over itself in its race to keep up. Muffled sounds came from both of us, vibrating in our throats but not escaping our lips because we hadn't even parted for a breath yet.

Who needed fucking air when Laird Bronson was kissing them? *Not me.*

His lips were somehow firm and soft at the same time as he slanted them over me again and again. It was like being called up to the major league from the minors. Nothing in my past compared. I shivered from the intensity of it, from the innate authority of his mouth as he consumed me. Like I was made to bend to him, as inevitable as the moon ceding to the sun.

I lifted on my tiptoes to get closer, one of my hands snaking up to tangle in his dark hair. The strands were barely long enough at the top to grip, and when I gave them a tug, he rolled his hips against me, showing me just how much he liked it. I moaned and felt an answering wetness gather at the juncture of my thighs.

Dear sweet rosy-cheeked baby Jesus and all the saints in heaven.

His mouth needed to come with a warning label. *Danger. Highly flammable.*

But it was too late. I'd had a taste and I liked the burn.

We were so close, I could feel his heartbeat thumping against my chest, half a beat off from the *allegro* tempo of my own. The fingers of my other hand slid under the soft cotton of his shirt, impatient to feel more of him. As my thumb mapped the grooves of his abs, the firm squares of muscle flexed beneath me. Laird growled his approval.

His knee nudged my legs apart, his thick thigh filling the opening, and then his hand pulled my leg up, hooking it around his hip. The hard length of his erection throbbed between us, separated only by two layers of denim and some thin cotton. I shifted beneath him and reveled at the heady friction.

His tongue traced the bottom curve of my lip, then the seam, begging for entrance. I parted my mouth, stole a hasty breath, and then welcomed the slick invasion of his tongue. The calloused hand still cupping my jaw shifted, slid down my throat until the pulse at the base of my neck fluttered against the pad of his thumb.

And somewhere along the way, the kiss softened. Conquering melted into exploration. His lips traced a wet path up my jaw to the tender spot beneath my ear, then journeyed south and discovered another, even more sensitive point where the curve of my shoulder met my neck. He lingered there, licking and nipping my skin while I shuddered beneath him, his name both a plea and a homage as I murmured it twice, three times.

Rational thought disappeared.

His hands gripped my ass and lifted until I wrapped both legs around his waist and he propped me against the door. My hands wandered the bulge of his biceps, the breadth of his shoulders, the planes of his chest, and I repeated the path a second time, because I couldn't decide which part was my favorite.

His shoulders. Definitely his shoulders.

Laird's muscles hardened beneath my palms, rising to meet my touch. Our mouths clashed again, my greedy lips seeking his, and the rough stubble on his jaw scratched my cheeks and chin. I'd never kissed a guy with stubble before. The boys I'd known in high school had always been smooth-shaven, and it just highlighted the difference between them and Laird.

I liked the roughness of his jaw, how it tugged at my skin, demanding I pay attention. I wanted to feel it on other, softer places. On the swells of my breasts. The back of my neck. My inner thighs.

"Reese," he groaned, tearing his mouth from mine. But he was back a moment later like he couldn't help returning for another taste, his teeth nipping my lower lip until I yelped. I caught a quick glimpse of the tortured expression twisting his face before he buried it in my neck, exhaling harshly.

I pushed my hips against him restlessly. His mouth was addicting and I wanted more, but his arms tightened around my ribs to keep me still when I tried to recapture it.

"We have to stop," he panted raggedly. His chest rose and fell against me in staccato bursts. "We have to stop or I won't be able to."

My head fell back against the door with a thud, my body protesting every word he just said. I cracked my eyes open to see if he was serious, but his gaze was fixated on the arch of my throat in that position. He licked the length of it and his dick grew impossibly harder.

"Do we?" I barely recognized my own voice.

"Yes." Reluctance was carved on his face as he loosened his grip and I slid back to solid ground. I swayed against him when my knees threatened to give out. "No. We have to pause at least. Relocate. Because we are not doing this in Bubba's fucking bathroom with the rest of the drumline on the other side of that door."

I could see the logic in his argument but my body was screaming at me *more*, *please*, and *now*.

"My place is closer." Who was this person controlling my mouth? "My roommate isn't due for seven more hours."

"Good. Because when you scream my name the first time, I don't want anyone hearing it but me. That moment is mine and I don't share."

He brushed a kiss across my temple, his hands smoothing my shirt back into place. Crouching just a bit, he rattled off instructions against the shell of my ear, his lips skimming my skin with each syllable. *Ten minutes. His truck. Third row over in the parking lot, halfway back. Avoid Marco.*

I twisted my head, until the tip of my nose grazed his. "I only need five."

He caught my wrist, pressed my hand to his zipper. "I need ten."

The door to my dorm room hadn't even fully closed before his mouth was on me again. We didn't bother with the light, and I was already so lost in his kiss, that if I hadn't heard the *thunk* of Laird latching the deadbolt behind me, I wouldn't have even thought to lock the door.

What a difference a change in scenery made.

Gone was the hesitation from before. When I yanked on his shirt, he ripped it over his head and threw it across the room. Mine followed seconds later, and then his hands were covering my breasts, kneading them over the silky fabric of my bra.

I moaned into his mouth, and his tongue delved inside to celebrate with me. Impatient, and feeling bold within the familiar space of my own room, I reached behind my back to unclasp my bra. It sailed through the air, meeting the same fate as our shirts.

And then my bare chest was flush against his for the first time. Laird hissed out a breath of pleasure as I wrapped my arms around his back, sealing us together. Goose bumps prickled the skin of my arms and furled my nipples. Since modesty wasn't going to get me what I wanted, I made shameless and wanton my new best friends. Unable to resist the temptation, I rubbed myself against him like a cat in heat, and Laird threaded his hands through my hair, tugging until I tipped my face up to his.

"You're better than the fantasy I had of this moment," he confessed. His green eyes were dark with lust and something more, something deeper. "And I had a pretty damn good fantasy."

I laughed, leaned up to nibble his lower lip, and then hummed in appreciation when his fingers tightened their grip. "Sounds like it's time for some new ones."

He groaned. "The way you don't hold back in anything you do? It's sexy as fuck, Reese Holland." At his words, the heat inside me splintered. Half of it stampeded to my wet core and the other half settled in my chest, draping me in a soft, fluffy warmth, like a down comforter straight out of the dryer.

"That dirty mouth of yours is pretty hot too," I whispered, dipping my hands into the back of his jeans.

"We've barely started." The husky promise in his voice made me forget any doubts I had about the wisdom of hooking up with the snare line captain. Because right now, that wasn't who was in this room. That guy could've been a million miles away for all I cared. But the person in front of me, the one who couldn't take his eyes off me and whose hands were stroking my breasts like he intended to sculpt them later, was the guy I'd seen whenever I'd closed my eyes at night for the last two weeks.

And I was done fighting it.

Maybe I was just horny. Maybe it was the insane chemistry that sparked to life whenever we were near each other. Whatever it was, I was succumbing to it.

His confidence and innate sex appeal had caught my

attention the first day of auditions, but it was the vulnerability that sometimes slipped through the cracks of his raw masculinity that showed me his real strength. Hell, I think I'd been his since I'd heard him call dibs on me with Eli at the hospital. It was just in my nature to make things difficult, to prove I could do it solo, that had me resisting so much.

But why the hell would I want to be in this room alone, getting myself off with some vibrating plastic, when he could take care of it for me?

"Tell me—" I paused to lick his neck while my fingers undid the button of his jeans, "—tell me what happens next."

My boobs were swollen and achy when his hands dropped lower, his palms rubbing the flare of my hips. "Your shorts come off but not your panties, and you lay across your bed, spread your legs, and wait for me."

I turned around so my back was to him, then bent over at the waist to undo my sandals, purposefully pushing my ass into his groin. And when I worked my hips from side to side to remove my shorts, I rubbed against him some more. By the time they were off, his jaw was clenched tight and the look in his eyes was feral. I was halfway to orgasming already.

"Bed, Reese. Now." He slapped my butt hard enough to make me gasp, but not enough to hurt.

When I was settled against my comforter, head centered on the lone pillow, I bent my knee up and placed my wrist on top of it, crooking my finger at him to come closer.

He laughed. "Do you really think you're running this show?" He took a step closer and stopped again. "Open your legs. Hands on the headboard."

His assertiveness made me shudder with arousal, but

even so I cocked an eyebrow at him, silently asking if he was serious. He stood stone still. Watching and waiting. My panties, only covering half my ass, were the same dusky pink as my sex and if the look he was giving me as he stood at the side of the bed was any indication, probably just as saturated.

I licked my lips in anticipation and rearranged myself.

Laird's eyes were the only part of him in motion as he studied the curves and angles I presented to him. Flared hips. Rounded breasts. Spread thighs.

"If you're waiting for an invitation, consider this it." I writhed on the quilt, never dropping his gaze.

His jeans hung low on his hips, the button popped and the zipper down. The top inch of his royal blue boxer briefs showed above them. What was it about that V of muscle narrowing down from a guy's hips that was so fucking sexy? While I stared, mesmerized, he reached down and stroked himself slowly, the head of his impressive cock coming into view as he fisted his hard length.

I released the headboard with my left hand and slid it down my body, pausing to squeeze my nipple, before continuing south. My fingers made one good pass under my panties and through the slickness between my legs before he caught my wrist, stopping me from repeating the motion. He held my hand captive as he climbed onto the bed, his knees settling between my parted legs. "That's mine," he warned me, his voice thick and low.

And then he licked my fingers clean, looking me in the eyes the entire time, his Irish green gaze making sinful promises. Promises I very much hoped he'd keep. When he finished, he pressed a kiss to my palm, and then to the delicate underside of my wrist, lingering with his lips against my racing pulse. "Headboard." He repeated the husky order as he released my tingling hand. "I told you to hold on to the damn headboard."

My mouth was dry as I followed his direction. While I normally craved control over every aspect of my life, yielding to Laird was instinctive. He waited until my fingers were curled around the nondescript metal bed frame. "That's better."

Planting his hands on the bed near my waist, he dipped his head to place a soft kiss to my flat stomach, the breadth of his shoulders a little overwhelming on my narrow XL twin mattress. But the tenderness of his kiss was nearly my undoing. That single touch of his lips silently vowed that his focus was on my pleasure first, not his.

I trembled beneath him. His eyes filled with dark hunger as he raked them over my body. "Breathe, Reese," he chided. I hadn't even realized I was holding my breath, and the air escaped in a whoosh. He grinned wolfishly. "I won't bite. Unless I think you'll like it."

My head fell back on the pillow. *Unless I think you'll like it.* His words echoed in my head.

Dear Peter, Paul, and all the apostles, even the shitty one, Judas.

I would. I would like it.

His nose stroked a line down the center of my underwear, and then he nuzzled deeper when he reached the part where the damp fabric clung to me like a second skin. He exhaled and the heat of it against my very core had me squirming beneath him.

And then, in the space of a dozen heartbeats, my panties disappeared and his mouth delved into my slick heat, learning my most intimate secrets. That the flat of his tongue, drawn slowly up my crease, made me arch my back to prolong the contact. That short flutters on my clit made me buck helplessly beneath him. That two fingers buried deep inside me made me quake and grip his hair, headboard be damned. That those same two fingers curving upward made me clench my eyes shut until tears leaked out. And that when he closed his lips around my clit and sucked, I came hard and loud, moaning his name as my thighs quivered around his head.

The aftershocks were still making me shudder when he cuddled next to me, hauling me on top of his chest. His fingers combed through my hair while I caught my breath and his jean-clad legs tangled with my naked ones.

"Reese?"

I mumbled incoherently. That orgasm to end all orgasms had completely robbed me of my ability to speak. I raised my head to look at him and forced my heavy eyelids to open a crack. A chunk of hair was blocking half my sight. I mumbled again, some garbled attempt at *so good, can't think, thank you* that sounded like gibberish. My body might have been sprawled across his, but the rest of me was still floating around in weightless bliss, and I was in no hurry to discover gravity again.

He chuckled and smoothed my hair back. "I could eat you all day, every day and never get tired of your taste." His fingers cupped my face and he kissed me, his lips lazy and unhurried. The tang of me on his tongue mixed with his own cinnamon flavor.

When he tucked me back against his shoulder, his hands meandering over my back, my arms, my ass, any piece of me he could reach, I was surprised. Honestly, this was when I'd expected him to rip his pants off and sink balls deep inside me. But he didn't seem like he was in a rush.

I lowered my hand to his jeans in case he was waiting for a signal from me, but he captured it and pulled it back up his chest until my palm rested over the inked G. "Not to-night, hotshot. When you're ready for that, we'll go back to my place." His voice was rough. "We need a larger mattress and a morning after where we don't have to do anything but sleep and eat and fuck some more. You're not something I want to rush."

And just like that, I dropped back to earth, my imagina-tion working overtime on what it would be like to be slowly savored by Laird. I planted an opened mouth kiss on the star tattoo on his other pec. "I could…" I licked his skin, demonstrating what I was offering.

When he shook his head *no* though, insecurity unfurled inside me, sharp and prickly.

"No?" I questioned softly, incredulous.

"If you put those lips around my dick tonight, I won't be able to stop. And I've got bigger plans for you and me than a blowjob and quickie." He sounded like he was in pain.

"Bigger, huh?" I smirked.

He rolled his hips, letting me feel just how big. I whim-pered. As I started to respond in kind, his arms banded around me, stopping my undulation.

"Don't tease me, Reese. I'm completely serious when I say I plan on ruining you for every other guy, fucking you hard and fast, slow and deep, and every combination in be-tween." He paused for a minute to let that sink in before he continued. "And then there's all those other sexy fantasies I've had about you. I've been dreaming of us for two weeks now. Get your rest tonight. You're gonna need it, because my imagination is one horny motherfucker."

CHAPTER 16

Laird

"**G**ET UP!" THE PANICKED WORDS DRAGGED ME FROM the best sleep I'd had in months.

I groaned. "I'm up, I'm up." I nudged my hips into her soft belly, in case she had somehow missed the insistent outline of my morning wood rising to greet her.

"Not that!" She tried to roll away, but I reflexively caught her and resettled her on top of me.

"Stay." I yawned and stretched, keeping one arm anchored over her back. "I like waking up with you. We should do it again. On a better bed. Like mine."

"Laird," she hissed, wiggling around and sending the rest of my blood rushing south.

"Mmm, keep doing that, but scoot a little higher first."

She pinched my hip and I winced.

"What?" I complained.

"It's almost nine!"

I pried open one eye and squinted at her. Mornings weren't my forte. "And? It's Saturday?"

Reese dropped her forehead down to my chin, and I used the opportunity to smell her hair. The scent was soft and girly, but not overpowering. I wouldn't mind it lingering on my pillowcase. "*And* my roommate could be here any minute for all I know."

"You don't know what time she's arriving?"

She shook her head and her hair tickled my nose. "This isn't exactly how I'd like to meet her though."

Damn, I hated it when she had a valid argument. Especially when I wasn't on the winning side of it. I gripped her ass and hauled her up my bare chest before I captured her mouth in a hungry kiss, morning breath be damned.

When I finally let her go, her breathing was ragged and her eyes had that hazy, unfocused look again, the same one she had after she climaxed, moaning my name last night. My hard length throbbed at the memory.

"Fine." I brushed my lips across hers once more. "I'll leave. But only if you promise to come to my place tonight." I tipped her chin up until her espresso eyes found mine. "We're not finished here."

"I'll come."

"Yeah, you will. Multiple times." I winked and shifted her off me, sliding out from under the quilt and yanking on my jeans. My dick protested when I tucked him back down and zipped my pants the rest of the way up. "Seven o'clock? I'll even feed you."

She scrunched her face.

"What?"

"You feeding me. I don't know if that's a good thing or a bad thing. A threat or an enticement." She tilted her head, her swollen lips frowning. "Can you cook?"

I ruffled her hair and then bent over to whisper in her ear. "I guess you'll have to find out."

Her smile spread slowly, like honey melting over a hot biscuit, that dimple I loved so much making an early morning appearance. "I guess I will."

"You eat red meat?" I confirmed.

Her eyes widened and dipped to my crotch before returning to my face, bright splotches of color staining her cheeks. I chuckled. "That's not what I meant, but I'll take it as a yes."

She pulled the covers over her head. "Leave. For the love of all the little fat cherub angels playing harps in the sky, just leave."

My lips quirked at her choice of words as I found my shirt on the other side of the room. One shoe was still by the door, the other had landed in a laundry basket. "Seven, Reese. I'm going to tell Oscar to expect you. Don't be late. He's perfected the sad puppy dog look."

"I'd hate to disappoint your dog." Her voice was muffled from the blanket but the sarcasm came through loud and clear.

"There's nothing worse than an unhappy wiener," I agreed.

I slipped out the door before she could say anything else, so she'd be left thinking about my dick.

As I drove away with a goofy ass smile on my face, I debated whether to go all out and make steaks and a salad or do something more casual like shrimp and grits. My phone dinged and my grin morphed into a full-on smirk, thinking it was her with a parting shot.

Marco: I'm free this morning if you want to work on the snare duel.

Annoyance filtered through me but I tamped it down.

I'd been trying to set up a time for the last week to finalize the duel with him and he'd blown me off three times. For three different girls, I'm pretty sure. But now, *now*, he was free.

Me: One hour. Practice room two.

Punching the gas a little harder than necessary, I headed home to shower. At this rate, I'd barely have time to stop for coffee on the way. And I needed all the available caffeine in south Alabama to make dealing with Marco on a non-game-day Saturday morning tolerable. We'd been friends once, I might have even considered him my best friend in high school, but most of that relationship seemed to have crumbled over the years. What remained was more of a reluctant partnership—like when the teacher paired you up in school and that's not who you wanted to get, but there were worse choices so you kept quiet and made do.

The snare duel was a 64-count chunk of time for me and him to shine.

If we could find a way to successfully collaborate.

The practice itself went about as well as I expected. After wasting thirty minutes arguing back and forth and getting nowhere, we finally decided to split it up into sections. I'd play the first eight counts, then him, followed by a sixteen-count section each, and we'd finish it up with sixteen counts played together with some flashy stick work to show off.

We settled on a Wednesday deadline for our solo sections, which meant all we had to get through today was choreographing sixteen beats. Four measly measures. How hard could that be?

It took two hours for us to agree and another hour for us to perfect it.

Fucking Marco.

Noon had come and gone by the time we'd stowed our snares and gone our separate ways. I had no idea where he was going, which was fine by me. These days, if it wasn't specifically drumline related, we didn't interact. I wasn't entirely sure why, but something about him had shifted subtly over the years. His humor had changed, from laughing at himself to laughing at the expense of others. And the way he treated girls as if they were both disposable and interchangeable left a sour taste in my mouth.

I headed to the grocery store for steaks and fresh veggies. No more of this indecisive nonsense. And I could grill the fuck out of a ribeye. Nothing said peacocking like meat cooked to perfection over a fire. There was a raw caveman element to it that was undeniable.

The Wrangler bounced over the uneven parking lot of Publix as my phone dinged. Dreading a message from Marco and hoping for one from Reese, I checked the screen.

Bastard: We need to talk. I'll expect you here by three today.

My jaw clenched so hard it almost popped. Fucking hell. Could I not catch a damn break? First Marco and now my father? Nothing ruined my day quite as thoroughly as a mandatory trip to Montgomery for a lecture from the man responsible for half of my DNA.

He'd moved about an hour upstate when I started college, claiming he needed a fresh start.

Bullshit.

More like so he could leave without feeling guilty after I started at Rodner as a freshman.

But it worked out. It gave us both an excuse to see each other less. In fact, we didn't see each other at all anymore unless he demanded it. And I only went because he was the last link I had to Garrett, which I couldn't toss aside no matter how much I hated the guy. I rubbed the tattoo on my chest.

Years ago, I'd given up envisioning how different my life would be if Garrett hadn't died. If Mom hadn't left and Dad hadn't lost himself to the bitterness of losing a son and then a wife. If he'd remembered that he still had a son who would've given his left nut to have a parent at least pretend like he loved him.

I laughed bitterly and didn't bother replying.

We both knew I'd be there.

I bought steaks, mushrooms, zucchini, squash, sweet potatoes, and salad fixings. A case of Cherry Coke Zero and a nice bottle of wine covered both my bases beverage-wise. And I picked up a can of whipped cream in case the evening went as well as I hoped. After a pause, I grabbed a second can too. I used to be a Boy Scout and the *Be Prepared* motto still came in handy on occasion. A box of condoms, the shiny gold foil covered ones, rounded out my purchase.

Confident I was fully stocked for my date with Reese later, I dropped everything by the townhouse and spent twenty minutes playing with Oscar. That dog went crazy over tug-of-war. I gave him a good long belly rub and left him with a new rawhide to chew on when I couldn't put off leaving any longer.

The whole way there, I played the *Shrek* soundtracks. Those had been Garrett's favorite movies. We'd watched it so many times and taken turns quoting the different characters. Donkey was my favorite. Donkey was both our favorites. I did anything I could to make Garrett fresh in my mind before I arrived at Dad's house. Anything to remind myself why I put up with him.

Despite the best efforts of Smash Mouth, my muscles were tense with the impending confrontation when I pulled up the brick-paver driveway and parked in front of the three-thousand square-foot house he lived in alone. I used to think the size was excessive, but these days I recognized that he needed all that space to hold the ghosts of the family we used to be and might have been. Or maybe he needed the fifteen-foot cathedral ceilings to have room for all his lingering bitterness.

Six bedrooms in that house and none of them were mine.

I didn't stay here. Ever. Even on holidays. Because extending such an invitation would never occur to him.

After I switched off the ignition, I turned my phone to silent. Not that it really mattered, because meetings with him were never pleasant, but the *ding* of phone notifications made him batshit crazy and I was fucking tired of hearing his lecture on how good manners dictated silencing your cell phone during meetings.

Because this wasn't a son visiting a father to catch up with each other.

It was a *meeting*.

The clock on the dash glowed 2:53. *Hey, Dad, I'm here by three.* But the stubborn streak I'd inherited from him kept my ass firmly planted in the driver's seat of my Wrangler until the numbers changed to eight minutes past. Only then did I reluctantly exit the vehicle and approach the front door.

I rang the doorbell and waited. It wasn't like I had a key to let myself in.

He answered it with a scowl, and I vowed for the millionth time not to turn into him in thirty years. He was just past fifty, but the lines etched around his eyes and the permanent creases carved into his forehead made him seem a decade older.

"'Bout damn time," he muttered, turning away and heading to his study in the rear of the house.

"Good to see you too," I mumbled to the empty foyer as I shut the massive carved oak door behind me. The house was spotless as I moved deeper into it. Even the dust particles were scared of him. He had a cleaning service come daily, and they probably knew him better than anyone at this point. He kept such a chokehold on every aspect of his life, there was no room left for joy, happiness, laughter, love. *Me.* I didn't think he even recognized the concept of fun anymore. It had ceased to exist as a noun in his world. Maybe it was because his job as CFO of the largest chain of car dealerships in south Alabama dealt with numbers, not people. Everything was black and white. Profit and loss.

His back was to me as he sat in his oversized leather office chair behind his equally oversized solid mahogany desk, the view out the window of the perfectly manicured yard obviously preferable to the sight of me standing stiffly in the doorway.

"Come in," he ordered impatiently. "You're late."

I moved a few steps farther into the room and chose the guest chair in front of the desk closest to the door, already planning my escape. The chair was hard and uncomfortable which suited the mood in the room perfectly.

"It's recently come to my attention that you haven't submitted any med school applications yet." He steepled his fingers as he spoke, each word precise, sharply articulated, and dripping with disapproval. "And not only have you not applied, you've changed your major from pre-med to computer science."

My back straightened on the unforgiving chair but I held my tongue. He hadn't actually asked a question yet. The silence lengthened. It was a game he liked to play to make me squirm, one that was losing its power over me the older I got and the less I cared about his opinion.

"What the fuck do you think you're doing? There was a plan. You're going to med school to become a research oncologist because this world needs better doctors than the ones that took care of your brother. You're smart—you got that from me. Your grades are up to par. And you owe it to *him*." The last four words were accented by his fist pounding the desk with each syllable.

Your brother. Him. He couldn't even say his name.

"*Garrett*," I emphasized the name and he flinched, "wanted me to be happy. *That's* what I owe to him."

"And what are you going to do with a computer science degree?" He said it in the same tone you might expect someone to say *finger painting*.

A smile curved my lips. "Design video games."

His head shook in denial before I even spoke. "No. Absolutely not. I forbid it and I won't pay another cent in tuition toward something that asinine."

I held my silence. His decree was both unsurprising and unimportant.

"Well?" he demanded after a time. "Do you hear me? You will change your major at once. School hasn't started yet so you can end this nonsense before it begins."

"I hear you," I acknowledged. "But no, I don't plan on making any changes."

"And then how exactly do you plan on supporting yourself?" His smug tone made it clear he thought he'd won this round.

My shoulders rose and fell in a casual shrug he couldn't see. "I haven't used a dime of your damn money for myself in the last two years."

I knew that would shock him and one side of my mouth

tipped up in a satisfied smirk at the way he whirled around to glare at me with eyes the same color as my own.

"Watch your mouth."

I rolled my eyes. Because that's what we really needed to be worried about here.

The middle finger of his right hand tapped the desk in an angry *allegro* rhythm. A pair of robins flew loops outside the window, and the vapor trail of a jet cut across the clear blue sky. Minutes passed. The tapping sped up.

"Why didn't I know about this?"

Because you only exist on the periphery of my life. Because you quit being a father the day we—not you, we— lost Garrett. Because you're a selfish asshole who never asks about my life. Pick a fucking reason.

I sighed. "Does it matter? Do you really give a fuck?"

"I told you to watch your goddamn mouth!"

My hands fisted on my thighs. "Apologies, *Dad*." My sarcasm was thick as syrup and there was no way he could miss it.

He pinned me with an assessing gaze but his chair remained facing the window. I didn't merit his full attention, even now. Hurt curled into a hard knot in my gut. "What happens to all the money I deposit into your account?"

"Half goes to the children's hospital—yes, *that* one— and the other half funds a scholarship to Rodner for a student who's had cancer." *And beaten it*, I added silently.

Dad's jaw worked back and forth before he twisted back to the window. I wondered what he'd do if I marched over to it and touched it, smeared my handprint right down the center and marred the spotless glass. I was half-tempted to try it.

"And how do you pay your bills? Your tuition? You selling drugs now?"

No, but he wasn't going to like the real answer any better. I rolled my neck, hating how tense I always got in his presence. "Remember all those video games I played as a kid? The ones you hated so much? They paid off. I designed two popular game apps and live off the royalties from the download price and the in-app purchases."

His face twisted like he'd accidentally eaten a piece of gristle.

"In fact," I continued, "I'm almost done developing my third. It should hit the market before I graduate."

He clutched his stomach like he might be physically ill.

"Why?" he boomed. "Why would you waste all your intellect and ambition on something as trite as an app? You could be curing cancer in a few years!" He vibrated in rage as his chair rotated to face me.

I didn't back down from the fury in his pinched eyes. "You're right. I am smart, and I did the research. The problem with pediatric cancer treatment isn't a shortage of doctors willing to put in the time and effort to find a cure. It's a lack of funding. They need money. I'm going to raise it for them."

He shot to his feet. "I donate thousands of dollars each year toward that very goal!"

"They need more."

"And that's your big solution? Throwing money at the problem?" He gesticulated wildly.

"No. That's only part of it. The other part I'm working on is for the kids themselves. Kids like video games." I said it like I was revealing the location of Atlantis after centuries of searching. "Kids fucking love video games."

"*Watch your goddamn mouth!*"

"But nobody," I ignored him and kept talking, "has taken the time to create a game specifically designed for the needs of a pediatric cancer patient. One that keeps their attention, but also, through biofeedback, assists them through the treatment process by helping them manage their own pain. That's the app I'm working on developing now."

He blinked at me and his face wobbled as he fought to hide his surprise. He licked his lips and ran a shaky hand through his hair. Though it was still thick, it was more gray than brown these days.

I didn't care about his reaction though because I wasn't doing it for him. I pushed to my feet and turned to leave.

"Where do you think you're going?"

Pausing on the plush Oriental rug, I asked, "Are we not done here?"

"We're done when I say we're done and not a second before."

I didn't turn back around. He could face *my* back this time. "You finished with me years ago. Fourteen if you're looking for specifics."

The truth was, any remnants of Garrett I'd like to pretend were still buried deep within him had shriveled up and disappeared along with my childhood. The only thing we had in common these days were Irish green eyes, a last name, and half our DNA, and if I could somehow return those in exchange for a clean slate, I would. As I approached the door, I heard the rustle of his clothes behind me.

He somehow reached the door before me and produced a key, locking me in. Who the fuck had a key to lock themselves in their own office? Or maybe he was sealing everyone else out?

"So, you basically stole my money."

His accusation stung.

"I didn't *steal* anything from you. I never *asked* you for it. You put it in my bank account and I used it as I saw fit."

"You let me think it was for your tuition."

True. "If you were so worried about where your money was going, you could've asked. Maybe during one of those family dinners we have. Oh, wait…"

He lurched forward, almost as if he wanted to strike me. I wouldn't have stopped him. I'd have let him get in a free hit just to satisfy my curiosity if he'd physically touch me. I don't think he had in the last decade.

"That money was an investment. In you."

"I'm not a fucking investment, Dad. I'm your son." My chest was so tight I could barely breathe.

"Talk to me like that again and I'll write you out of my will."

Heat burned the back of my eyes. "I never gave a shit about your money. It was never, not once, about the money. You can take every single one of your dollar bills and burn them to ash for all I care."

He scoffed. "You don't mean that."

"I do." The vehemence in my voice had him studying me curiously. As if I was a new species of insect and he wasn't sure if he should protect it for further study or squash it under his hand-tooled Italian loafer.

"Then you're an idiot." *Splat.* Decision made.

"I learned from the best," I muttered under my breath.

"You haven't learned anything yet. You have no sense of family responsibility." His words were cold. Condescending. Dismissive.

"And you do?" I shot back. "You're suddenly the expert on what makes a good parent? A good husband? A decent fucking human being? Because you're right, I haven't learned any of those lessons from you yet."

He got right in my face, but I didn't step back. "You know nothing of what it's like to lose a child. Or a wife."

"No," I conceded. "But I know what it's like to lose a brother. And not one, but *two* parents."

His chest puffed out, almost touching mine. I had two inches on him in height, but right now he seemed taller. "Your brother would be disappointed in you. I know I am. What a fucking waste…" He took a step back as if he couldn't bear to be that close to me any longer, as if my very presence repulsed him.

"It doesn't matter!" I yelled. "It doesn't matter because he died. He died. *He died.*" My chest heaved as I took a ragged breath. "But I didn't."

He shrank back from my words, turning his head side to side as if to ward off the blows they dealt.

The dark satisfaction I expected to feel at my outburst never materialized. Only resignation at the knowledge that our relationship had passed the point of being salvaged.

Striding over to him, I ripped the key from his loose grip, returned to the door, and unlocked it, freeing myself once and for all of the strangling ties I'd let him hold over me for half my life.

I threw the key at his feet. It landed without a sound on the thick Persian wool. "*I* didn't die but you make me feel everyday like you wished it'd been me."

CHAPTER 17

Reese

11:04. My dorm was spotless. All my shit was picked up and neatly stowed in my half of the room. I even went down to the bookstore and purchased a stuffed Sharky, the school mascot, as a welcome gift and had it waiting on the bare mattress for her.

The thought of sharing my living space with someone had me oscillating between nervous and excited. I was an only child. I'd never lived with someone else my age before. Would she like me? Would I like her? How awkward was it going to be getting dressed and undressed in front of a stranger? What if I needed to fart? What if she brought a guy back to the room? Would we have to have a system—the whole sock on the doorknob thing?

Restless, I went to Sammy's to get an early lunch before the crowds got too bad. Getting there was like trying to swim up a waterfall as thousands of students and their parents flooded the campus with suitcases and laptops and posters, their hopes and dreams and fears tucked between folded Rodner University t-shirts and fresh spiral notebooks. When I finally had my turkey-and-cranberry sub and requisite Cherry Coke Zero, I escaped to the center of campus, away from the craziness of the dorms, and found an empty bench shaded by an oak tree.

I checked my phone. No texts from Laird. A twinge of disappointment weighed me down, stealing some of my excitement over our date tonight. I'd just seen him two hours ago, and I'd see him again tonight. Did I really expect to hear from him in between? I shoved the phone aside and nibbled my sandwich. It didn't taste as good as the one I'd eaten with him at his townhouse last week.

4:38. Still no roommate. Concerned, I tracked down Myrna, my resident adviser.

"Oh, Reese, I'd meant to find you earlier today. Yeah, your roommate isn't coming. She switched schools last minute. I'd keep that quiet if I were you—if nobody realizes it, they might not fill the spot with anyone else and you'll get a room to yourself!" She gave me an exaggerated wink and patted my shoulder. "Gotta run. A girl down the hall can't figure out how to log onto the campus wi-fi and her world is crumbling as we speak." With a swish of her long white-blond hair, she was gone and I was alone again, in a sea of girls who'd all been paired off by the housing gods.

I went back to my clean, empty room. I stared at Sharky, alone on the other bed. He looked sad by himself so I moved him to mine, tucked him under my blankets, his head nestled on my pillow.

No roommate. Huh.

And then I did a little dance, in the room I didn't have to share with anyone at all.

I even farted out loud for good measure.

5:41. Even though it was a little early, I started getting ready for my date with Laird. Dinner at his place. And sex, presumably. Lots of sex. So much sex, he expected me to need the whole next morning to recover. I bit my lip. I wasn't a virgin, but my experience level was more intermediate than expert, and I would bet Laird was a high scorer at this game.

Should I stretch? Prepare myself? I glanced at the pink four-blade razor in my shower caddy. Yeah, I needed to prepare. Forty minutes later, I was sleek as a seal, moisturized, blow-dried, and wrapped in a damp towel as I contemplated my closet.

What did one wear to be seduced? Would he expect skimpy lingerie? Would that seem slutty, or was that what he was anticipating? I eyed my bed. Sharky fixed me with his plastic gaze, absolutely no help to me in this situation. "Some roommate you are," I told him. He grinned back at me, his white felt teeth on full display.

7:02. I hesitated outside Laird's door, and smoothed my hands down the soft raspberry pink jersey dress I'd settled on. The sleeveless, scooped-neck design was casual, but the way it clung to my skin was anything but innocent. And the sheer black bra and thong set I wore beneath it revealed more than it concealed. We both knew what was going to happen tonight. Wearing full-coverage cotton seemed pointless.

7:04. Oscar barked on the other side of the door, but Laird hadn't opened up yet. Feeling silly standing on his stoop, I tried to remember our conversation from earlier. *He said seven, right?*

No texts from him with a change of plans, so I sent him one, letting him know I was here. Maybe he'd had to run back out to the store. I peered around the parking lot. His black Wrangler was conspicuously absent.

7:12. I retreated to my car to consider my options. Plus, standing at his door that long probably looked suspicious to his neighbors, especially with Oscar still going crazy. I texted again.

7:31. I left.

7:56. I scrubbed off the last of the eyeliner I'd painstakingly rimmed my eyes with. What a fucking waste. Braless, with comfy cotton boyshorts, pajama pants, and a tank top on, I scooped up Sharky. This whole no roommate thing was going to work out just fine, considering I'd already thrown my discarded clothes onto the other bed.

Me and Sharky were about to get our Netflix binge on. Oh, and ice cream. I'd bought some ice cream on the way back. The good stuff that had a thousand calories in each tiny pint and was hand-churned by magical leprechauns with healing powers for situations just like this.

8:02. My phone buzzed.

Laird: Reese, I'm sorry. I'm just getting home and I didn't realize it was so late.

Laird: I had a huge fight with my dad today and then I drove around to calm down and lost track of time.

Laird: I fucked up. I know I did.

Laird: Can I come see you? I can bring over steaks in 30 minutes?

I wavered. If there was one thing I understood, it was fighting with your parents.

But... he'd left me hanging with no word. I'd put on fucking eyeliner. And sexy underwear. And shaved everything. *Everything.* Yeah, his loss this time.

I took a selfie, framing the ice cream, Sharky, and a decent portion of the curve of my left breast in the shot just to emphasize what he'd missed out on, and sent it to him.

Me: You've been replaced tonight. Maybe we should slow down and try again another time.

And then I turned my phone off, ate the best ice cream of my life, and watched a whole season's worth of *Pitch* while drooling over a bearded Mark-Paul Gosselaar. I didn't think of Laird once.

Except later, I dreamt I had a threesome with both Mark-Paul and Laird and that we rounded *all* the bases and hit some homeruns.

I told you.

That ice cream was magical.

CHAPTER 18

Reese

THE LAST FOUR DAYS HAD BEEN A BLUR AND, DESPITE his best efforts, I'd barely said two words to Laird. Between classes, volunteering at the hospital on different days than each other, and freshman orientation nonsense, the only time our paths had crossed was Tuesday's band practice. The choreography we learned that day was much more technically challenging, not leaving much down time for chatting, and I'd rushed off for a resident advisor meeting as soon as it ended. He'd tried to meet me for lunch yesterday, but our schedules were off by twenty minutes and I couldn't swing it without being late for Calc I.

We'd texted a few times, but the messages were stilted at best. It was my fault. I didn't know how to create distance from Laird without making it weird. How to slow things down without turning them off.

I reread his last words from this morning.

Laird: Can you get to practice thirty minutes early? I miss you.

I hadn't responded, but here I was, waiting like an idiot in the equipment room for him to arrive to maybe get a chance to talk to him alone and in person. Helpless to resist, despite knowing this couldn't end well. I wiped my palms on my gym shorts for the third time. My heart beat an uneven rhythm against my ribs as I checked the time on my phone again.

The door creaked open. I swallowed hard past the ball of nerves in my throat.

"Showing up early doesn't earn you brownie points, hotshot," Marco sneered as he entered the room to collect his drum.

"Hello to you too." I fiddled with my harness while avoiding eye contact, adjusting the padding that didn't need adjusting.

He grabbed his gear and hesitated before exiting. Flustered, I stooped down to re-tie my double-knotted shoelaces.

"Yes?" I asked when it became obvious he wasn't going to leave.

"You missed a spot when you cleaned my room this week. The desk was still a mess. Do better next time." The door didn't quite hit him on the ass on his way out, even though I summoned all my Batman-superpowers and willed it to happen. I flipped him off like a middle-school boy instead, with outrageous exaggeration and both hands, because I knew without a doubt he couldn't see me.

Bubba came in next, followed by Charlie and Cade. A quick glance at my phone confirmed that practice started in twenty-five minutes. Laird was late, and the opportunity was gone—again.

When Smith barged through the door a short time later, I gave up any pretense of fumbling with my gear and fell in step with him to head to the practice field.

Smith moaned about the semester-long project we'd already been assigned in biology, but I barely heard him. My eyes were laser-focused on the dark-haired guy stripping his shirt off in the distance, revealing the abs my fingers ached to trace again. Laird Bronson. Already on the field. I must not have shown up early enough. Or maybe when I hadn't replied to his text, he thought I wasn't coming.

"Right?" Smith nudged me.

I had no idea what he was talking about. "Mmhmm," I agreed, forcibly ripping my attention away from all that tan muscle and sinew.

Must. Not. Drool.

In public, anyway.

"Really?" Smith raised an eyebrow in disbelief. "You've fantasized about drizzling Marco in warm caramel too?"

I screwed my eyes shut and shook my head violently, trying to force that mental atrocity from my mind. "What the fuck, Robin? Why would you even joke about something that bad?"

He tipped his head back and let loose his spectacular laugh at my expense. "Because, Batman, you were ignoring your sidekick. Not cool. I'm not over here talking just because I like the sound of my own voice."

Appropriately chastised, I flattened my lips and dipped my head. "Sorry. I was just preoccupied."

"Picturing a certain someone covered in caramel? Someone li—"

My elbow connected with his ribs before he could complete his sentence, and I narrowed my eyes in a pointed warning to keep him from opening his mouth again. "Watch it. Or I'll partner with someone else for the Bio project and leave you hanging."

The stricken expression on his face had me rolling my eyes. As if Batman could partner with someone other than Robin.

When we reached the edge of the twenty-yard line where the other snares had gathered, Laird and Marco were huddled over a clipboard together, much like they were the first day of auditions. Something about that white plastic rectangle seemed ominous. As though it not only held my fate regarding my position on the field, but possibly a hidden message from Laird.

What did it mean if I earned a spot? Was it preferential treatment? Or what if I didn't? Was it because I wasn't good enough? Because Laird was upset about my request to slow things between us down? Or, on a more basic level, because I was a *girl*?

Marco glanced up at me and scowled.

I couldn't interpret it, but my muscles stiffened in response.

Laird didn't look at me and his body language gave nothing away.

Smith bumped my shoulder. "You okay there, Batman? You're looking a little tense."

"Gotham City has been a little rough this week." I forced my shoulders to relax and unclenched my jaw.

He flung his arm around my shoulder. "Want to grab dinner after this? We could—"

Laird cleared his throat. "Hate to interrupt you guys setting up a date," his green eyes glittered as they pinned me down, "but we have a practice to get through. Our first game is Saturday so today is essentially a dress rehearsal. Before we begin, we need to officially announce who will be marching on the field when the Sharks take on Louisiana State this weekend."

This was it. I couldn't watch.

I studied my shoes instead, the way the rubber on the right one was starting to curl away from the toe and the laces on the left one were uneven. I should fix it. Maybe try to get some of the grass stains out.

"Me. Marco. Bubba. Van. Charlie." His voice carried no particular inflection as he continued down the list. "Morris. Topher. Cade. Smith. And Reese."

Time slowed. Was it just in my mind or did his tone change when he said my name? Almost like a bit of a Scottish burr came through and he rolled the *r* just a little and lingered over the *s*. As if he was caressing my name with his tongue. Or was that just wishful thinking?

I blew out my breath, trying to slow my runaway pulse. I wanted to look at him so bad, but at the same time, I was scared of what I might see in his eyes. That there might be too much there and the others would notice. Or worse… indifference.

Arms wrapped around my shoulder and lips smacked against my temple, knocking me back to reality. "We did it!" Smith's jubilant shout nearly took out my left eardrum.

I grinned at his contagious enthusiasm and returned his hug, pushing thoughts of Laird aside and allowing the news to sink in fully. I'd done it. *I'd fucking done it.* "I told you we would on the first day. Never a doubt." My feet barely touched the ground the rest of practice, I was floating so high. A female snare would march in Rodner Stadium in two days, under the floodlights and with forty-thousand Shark fans watching.

I didn't let Willa's whining at being paired with me instead of Laird for the second song faze me. Not even when she let the cymbal drop too low for the third time in a dozen measures. For the next two hours, my cloud of happiness was impenetrable.

As I put up my drum after practice while solidifying plans for celebratory pizza with Smith, the sudden weight of Laird's presence behind me, heavy and unmistakable, hijacked my train of thought, and I dropped my stick bag twice. My lungs struggled to suck in enough air.

"She'll catch up with you in a few minutes, Smith. I need to talk with her about her timing during the first song before she leaves."

My spine snapped straight and twin spots of fury darkened my cheeks. There was *nothing* wrong with my playing and being called out like that in front of everyone? Oh, hell no.

I whirled around to defend myself but stopped short when I saw his eyes. So many things flickered through his green irises. Confusion, hurt, desire, impatience. His fingers pulled at the hem of the Rodner Sharks shirt he'd put back on, and he stole a look at the time on his phone as if annoyed that it was taking everyone more than eight minutes to pack away their equipment.

My stomach churned with twenty-foot waves of turmoil as Charlie, Cade, and Smith headed toward the door, the last ones to leave.

Silence fell.

Unsure of where we stood on a personal level, I shifted my weight and twirled a drumstick in my right hand, letting the polished hickory tumble through my fingers in a practiced blur.

He took a step forward, halving the distance between us.

"There was nothing wrong with my stick work today." I

couldn't hold that in any longer.

"No, there wasn't."

His easy agreement gave me pause and the drumstick fell to the floor when my fingers lost the rhythm. I bent over to pick it up, and he groaned behind me.

"I've missed you, Reese." His voice was rough and deep, quieter than before. "And I want to apologize again for fucking up last Saturday."

I straightened cautiously, knowing I needed to choose my words with care. He'd moved again, so close I could touch him or he could touch me if one of us reached out the slightest bit. "Look, Laird, maybe it's a good thing we've been busy. That we've been forced to slow down the last few days. Because the way things were headed…"

I trailed off at the blazing heat in his gaze as it slid down my body. It screamed the opposite of *slow*.

"Yeah. About that." And then his lips covered mine in a hungry swoop, one palm cradling my neck while the other supported the small of my back. I responded immediately, no pretense, no trying to push him away. My mouth clung to his as he tasted me urgently, his lips searching for the best angle to claim me.

I sighed into his mouth, and he took swift advantage of the opportunity, his tongue slipping in to tangle hotly with mine. My hands, still holding the drumsticks, fisted the cotton of his shirt for balance as the force of his kiss arched my back over his arm. Because of my height, most guys in my past hadn't been able to manipulate my body this easily, but with Laird, I felt small and delicate in the best way possible. Like there was no safer place than his arms because he'd never let me fall. I melted against him, answering each slide of his lips, each parry of his tongue with one of my own.

He moved us deeper into the room as he devoured my

mouth, until we were tucked away behind the large floor to ceiling cabinets in the far corner, my back against the cool, painted concrete-block wall. His hand slid around the front of my neck, dropping lower until his thumb toyed with my hard nipple. I trembled beneath his teasing touch.

"Tell me you don't want this." Hot breath fanned over my cheek. "Tell me your heart isn't racing as fast as mine."

His hand shifted until the flutter of my pulse against his palm was unmistakable. He tugged one of my arms from around his waist, pried my drumsticks free, and pressed my shaking hand to his chest, where his heart pounded the same rapid tempo as mine.

"Tell me to stop," he dared me.

I couldn't. I was drowning in the incandescence of his hungry eyes, the heat of his embrace, the intensity of his blunt words. He caged me between the wood cabinets and the unforgiving wall, but I didn't feel trapped. I felt alive, bright and shiny and ripe in the way only Laird Bronson could evoke. I drew my hands down his chest and slipped my fingers under the edge of his shirt, needing to ground myself with his solidness.

"Laird," I breathed.

And that was all it took. His name. His eyes blazed and his mouth captured mine in a fiery kiss, while the hand holding the drumsticks lowered until I felt the gentle pressure of solid wood nudging between my thighs. With only a thin pair of shorts and my damp panties blocking him, the soft friction he started as he slid the sticks back and forth had me grinding against him, wanting more of his sweet brand of torture.

"I've got you, Reese." He spoke against my jaw, his mouth nibbling a path to my ear and then down my neck. He nipped the sensitive skin and I shuddered, my nails digging into his muscled back. Laird braced himself with his free hand against the wall, while the other continued the onslaught between my legs. He used the unevenness of the drumstick heads to rub circles around my clit with a teasing lightness that drove me wild. Pleasure began to coil slowly, my breath escaping in jagged puffs as it built.

I pushed my face into his shoulder to muffle my soft cry while my hips rocked in counterpoint to his strokes, seeking more pressure. One of my hands dipped between us, cupping his hardness through his gym shorts. He throbbed as my grip traveled to the base of his dick and squeezed.

Two could play this game.

He growled and sucked the tender flesh on the side of my neck, using the edge of his teeth to scrape my skin. The hand holding the drumsticks moved faster but not harder. I bent my knees, trying to force the issue, and matched his technique, stroking him quickly but softly.

The drumsticks fell to the floor with a dull clatter on the cheap carpet, and his thick fingers replaced the lifeless wood. "I love how greedy you are." His lips tickled my ear as he whispered the words. I slid my hand along his forearm, reveling in the way his muscles flexed as he touched me. I never wanted him to stop touching me. He cupped me with his hand and ground the heel of his palm against my clit, finding a rhythm that drew the coil even tighter, and I squeezed his hip in response as his name fell like a plea from my parted lips.

"Nothing better." His pace increased, and one finger pressed up against the thin fabric. I knew he could feel my wetness right through it. I was soaked. "Nothing better than you saying my name."

The edges of my vision blurred. Everything ceased to exist beyond his hand and the hot, achy anticipation building higher and higher. I was so close. I whimpered, my thighs shaking. He moved impossibly faster, and I bit his shoulder, hard enough that it'd probably leave a mark, but I didn't care. Those perfect fingers stroked and twisted, and then he pinched my nipple, the sudden sting of it snapping the coil, sending me spiraling into my luminous release while I clenched his hand between my thighs. My toes curled inside my shoes, and no air left my lungs as a soundless moan pushed past my swollen lips. I trembled in his arms as I flew to the stars and back, weightless but unbearably heavy at the same time, while he held me close, supporting me when my legs threatened to give out.

Our warm breaths mingled, his exhale becoming my inhale and vice versa. I was dizzy with remnants of my orgasm when his dick pulsed against my hand, reminding me that I still held it in my grasp. I resumed my lazy torment, aftershocks of pleasure making my strokes eager but disjointed. Laird pushed his shorts partway down, and shifted my hand until it wrapped around his impressive length. He was so big my fingers didn't touch. I pumped him slowly, reveling in the contrast of hard steel covered by hot velvet. With a rough growl, he wrapped his fingers around mine until I gripped him harder, and then he showed me how he liked it, tight and slow at the bottom, fast at the top, sometimes pausing for a few shorter passes at the head before dropping back down. The chords of his neck stood out in sharp relief, and his eyes darkened and fell halfway closed as he watched our hands.

Biting my lip, I reached down to cup his balls as we worked together to stroke him off. They were already tight and drawn up, and I knew he was close. I rolled them in my hand, and he cursed when I tugged on them, golden satisfaction swirling through me at his response. He crushed my hand tighter around him, our fists a blur as we jacked him faster.

"Do it again." He pressed haphazard kisses to my neck. "Fuck, Reese, do that again."

I did, twice. He groaned the first time and came the second, his hips jerking with his release as he spilled over our joined fingers. Laird shuddered as he repeated my name in a whisper with each of the half dozen strokes it took for him to finish.

It was the hottest thing I'd ever seen, his face slack with pleasure as he watched me watch him. He made no attempt to hide his reaction, and he held my gaze with a quiet fierceness, as if he wanted to make sure I saw exactly what I did to him, how he came apart because of me. Something inside of me shimmered and sighed when he used his clean hand to stroke my cheek and trace the curve of my lip reverently. "Reese. I—" He broke off and the moment sharpened. The musky scent of our arousal, the hum of the ancient air-conditioner, the stillness of our bodies after the impetuous intimacy. He dipped his head and his lips met mine softly, like he was saying thank you for something he wasn't sure he deserved.

Hot tears I couldn't explain pricked the back of my eyes as he released me, and I blinked rapidly, ducking my head so he wouldn't see. His gentleness in the aftermath was my undoing.

He whipped his shirt off and used it to clean us up, then wrapped me in his damp embrace, peppering my face with aimless kisses, as if he wasn't quite ready to stop touching me yet.

"Forgive me, Reese." His lips skimmed along my jaw. "Forgive me for last Saturday." Across my forehead. "Don't." The tip of my nose. "Please don't push me away." The corner of my mouth.

I shivered. My hands roamed from his waist to his ribs. I couldn't form words.

And then the door banged open, and Marco's sharp voice cut across the room. "What are y'all still doing in here?"

Ice froze my veins and I couldn't move, my wild eyes flashing to Laird's in a panic. He put a foot of distance between us, keeping his back to Marco and partially blocking his view of me.

"She needed to work on her stance some before this weekend. Her shoulders were slumped and her arms were too low at practice earlier." He nudged me fully against the wall and raised my arms parallel to an imaginary drum. "It's nine inches, Reese, not six."

My eyes widened at the double meaning of his words and he winked at me. I choked on my next breath.

Marco snorted in disgust from the doorway. "Told you we shouldn't have picked her."

"It's not a problem." Laird dropped his hands to his sides and moved back a step. I bristled at the insult but held my position. "I'm gonna make her do it over and over and over again until I know she's got it right. Even if it takes her all night."

Images of us doing it over and over again all night long cartwheeled through my mind. *Until we got it right.*

"Need any help?" The offer from Marco was grudging at best, the words sour as they lingered in the air.

"No," Laird responded easily. "I can handle her."

Dear sweet mother Mary and her perfect virgin womb.

Yes. He could.

CHAPTER 19

Laird

"**A**ND THEN AT THE END OF THE SECOND QUARTER, we were down by three to Louisiana State. That fumble on the opener really cost us in the first half." Eli hung on my every word as I recounted Saturday night's game.

"Then you killed it in the halftime show?" His expectant smile took up half his face, the other half mostly hidden beneath a blue knit beanie. Rodner University blue with the shark mascot embroidered on the front.

"You know it." I held up my hand for a fist bump and pretended like my knuckles were sore after he tapped me. "Watch it, man. Don't make it so I can't play this weekend."

"Did someone record it?"

I gave an exaggerated huff and withdrew my phone from my pocket. "Of course. Our biggest fan needed to be able to watch it."

I pressed the screen to make the video play, pointing out which speck was me and which one was Reese. She did well that night, much to Marco's disappointment. She stumbled a bit on the first roll, coming in a beat too late, but it was a minor bobble easily attributed to her first time playing for such a large crowd. No one would've noticed unless they studied her specifically on the video afterward, which I did only because I couldn't take my eyes off her. With her height, she blended right in to the rest of the line, and if it weren't for the fact that I knew she was second from the left, I probably wouldn't have been able to pick her out. Her skill level more than held its own.

A little swell of pride filled my chest as Eli watched our performance, his nose inches from my phone.

As the band marched in perfect sync off the field to a drumline cadence, he glanced at me with a solemn expression. His eyes seemed even bigger without eyebrows or eyelashes, dominating his face now that he was no longer smiling. "She did good, didn't she? I prayed she would do good."

My ribs threatened to crack open from my heart breaking so hard for this kid. "She did great."

"When she comes by tomorrow, I'm gonna tell her she sucked. That she needs to work harder." A sly smile curled the corner of his mouth. "That even I could've done better than her. Don't want her getting a big-ass ego like you."

I reached down for my bookbag and withdrew two pairs of drumsticks. "Big claims, little man. Let's see what you've been working on."

He held the sticks expertly, just the way I'd shown him in the past, but he hesitated. "Can we get Amelia to play with us too? Last time Reese was here, we had a joint lesson. I think Amelia really liked it."

"Yeah, I'm sure wanting Amelia to be a better drummer

is your only motivation," I teased him.

The blush on his face spread down his neck until it disappeared under his green hospital gown. "Suck my dick, Bronson." He used the plastic bedrail to bang out the cadence I'd been teaching him for the last few weeks, not missing a single beat. When he finished, he looked at me expectantly.

I ignored his performance. "You talk to me like that and pray to God with the same mouth?" While I appreciated his spunk, one day he was going to say that to the wrong person.

"Do you talk to God with the same mouth you eat pussy with?"

Little shithead. Now I was the one blushing. "What do you know about," I cleared my throat, unable to say the word *pussy* to him, "...girls?"

"Enough to know that's what makes them crazy." His voice was confident, but his eyes wavered, shifting from side to side.

I held back a laugh. He didn't know what the fuck he was even saying.

My mind drifted back to Saturday. To what happened after the game with Reese that I didn't share with anybody. We'd already put our equipment on the trailer to go back to East Hall and I'd tugged her back inside the stadium to a darkened corner away from security and the cleaning crew that was starting to make their rounds through the bleachers.

I pulled her against me, her back to my front. The boxy polyester uniforms we wore did nothing to hide the sweet curve of her ass. Our military-style jackets with yards of looped braided detailing and a yellow sash had been ditched after halftime, the band allowed to strip down to matching t-shirts in deference to the Alabama heat. The lack of sun did little to lower the temperature this time of year. Her shirt hung loosely around her hips, but clung to the slope of her breasts. The cotton was slightly damp from the pervasive humidity.

"How'd it feel? Your first game, the crowd watching and cheering for you?" My fingers slipped under the hem of her shirt, found the synthetic waistband of her pants. They were unisex, fitting her better at the hips than the waist. I took advantage, letting the pads of my fingers sink under the scratchy black fabric and slide along the smoothness of her stomach.

She gasped at the contact, bowing her back into me and pulling her shirt over my arms to hide my wandering hands. "I doubt it was me they were watching." Her voice caught on one of the words when I plucked at the waistband of her underwear.

"Did your parents watch?" We never talked about her family. But we didn't really talk about mine either. My dad didn't watch, that much I knew for fact.

"They don't have cable. TV is a waste of perfectly good time to them." She didn't tense or stiffen in my arms, nothing to indicate my statement upset her.

"Still," I pushed the issue, not sure why I was chasing it so hard, "to see their only daughter?"

She turned her head and scrunched her nose at me, her eyebrows squeezing together. "I'll send them a link to the YouTube video of it if you're so concerned."

I pulled my hands back, unfastened the button, and lowered the zipper of her pants. The only thing keeping them from falling to her ankles was her ass tight against me.

"Laird! What are you doing?" Her ponytail tickled my chin as she twisted her head both ways, checking on the proximity of the closest cleaning crew.

"Scoring."

Her hands slid to my wrists, not stopping me, just resting there.

I circled her navel with my middle finger. "I couldn't get enough of you the other day before Marco interrupted us." My finger sailed a slow arc down her stomach until I reached the edge of her pubic hair. She only kept a small ribbon of it, closely trimmed. I liked it. My finger trailed through it slowly, and I groaned when she clenched her ass, my growing erection throbbing behind its polyester cage.

"My fingers smelled like you all night." Her breath hitched as I traced down one side of her slick heat and then the other, but avoided the tempting center. "They smelled like you and me mixed together. Better than soap, better than any perfume." I stroked her feather-soft skin and was rewarded when she bloomed for me, swelling to my touch.

She whimpered, her grip on my wrists tightening for a moment.

"I wanted to do so much more. Rip your shorts off. Get on my knees. Lick you until you screamed and keep your wet lace as a souvenir."

I dipped in, found her wet and melting for me. I coated my finger and drew the dampness higher until her hips bucked in response when I reached the right place. My other arm banded across her abdomen, keeping her snug against me, until not even a sixteenth note could've squeezed between us.

"What—" She stopped and licked her lips when her voice cracked. Tried again. "What would you have done with my panties?"

"Later that night, after I'd climbed in bed, I'd have used them while I stroked my dick. Pretended the slight scratch was your nails. Or your teeth. Pumped myself raw into the same scrap of cloth that had been pressed to you all day until

I came." I paused to run the tip of my tongue along her earlobe, and an absurd sense of pride swelled my chest when her breathing stuttered. "Then I'd have done it all over again."

She tipped her pelvis up, her breathy moan floating away on a rare breeze. "Is that a thing you do? Steal underwear from your..." She didn't finish, whether it was because she didn't know how to label herself—label us—or because that was the exact moment I sank two fingers deep inside her with no warning.

Her grip convulsed around my wrists.

"No. I don't have a drawer full of lingerie at the townhouse, if that's what you're asking." But it made me picture a spot for her stuff. Top right of my dresser maybe. A place where she kept some spare clothes for the nights she didn't leave, stayed in my bed—in my arms—all night long.

I'd build her a fucking armoire if that's what it took.

Chop down the trees, cut the boards, and piece the damn thing together by fucking hand.

One day, I'd wake up in the morning and she'd be the first thing I saw. First thing I touched. First thing I tasted.

I twisted my fingers, added a third. She squirmed and my dick jumped, leaking on itself in excitement. "That's it, Reese. There's nothing better than feeling you clench around me. Feeling your heat and knowing it's all for me." She squeezed her thighs, but I used my foot to knock her legs wider apart. Opening her up further to my touch. "I'm not stopping until you're done. Until the guys in the other end zone hear you scream my name."

My thumb found her clit, tapped out a rhythm much like our warm-ups. I started slow, quarter notes with an accent on the third beat, speeding up every measure. I played her faster and faster, listened to her breathing, fine-tuned my touch. We reached the crescendo, little noises coming from her throat.

She was my favorite instrument, one I intended to master.

I strummed her clit, her back arching. She was close. "You're beautiful, so damn beautiful like this." She twisted her face to mine, her eyes wide and desperate, begging for release in those chocolate depths. Her nails dug sharp crescents in my wrists, and I reveled in the small bite of pain. Everything about her was drawn tight. I put my lips to her ear. "And mine. You're all mine, Reese Holland."

My claim sent her over the edge, and she slammed her lips against mine, my mouth catching her scream, my tongue coaching her back down. Each shudder of hers was a victory I savored, until she relaxed fully against me, replete with pleasure I'd given her.

Eli snorted, bringing me back to the present, like he'd already discovered all the secrets girls held over us.

The memory of Reese had me hard and aching and I rose from the bed and walked to the window so I could adjust myself discreetly.

"Easy there, tiger. There will be enough time for practicing the advanced moves when you get older. And if you ever need someone you can talk to and you're too embarrassed to go to your mom, you can always ask me."

He swallowed hard, those big eyes flicking up to meet mine. "Promise?"

"Promise. Bro code and all that, you know?" I came back to his bedside, met his gaze steadily.

"Right. The bro code." He squinted a little, nodding in reassurance to himself.

I rapped out a few measures of my own on his bedrail and did a few tricks with my drumsticks to distract him. "Let's go get Amelia and see your wooing skills in action. But let's keep it above the waist today, yeah?"

"Hey, man, I can't help it if she tries to sneak a peek

at my ass. Have you seen the pickings around here? Pretty slim." He snickered. "And these gowns make it easy to show off the goods."

"Oh, Eli. You have so much to learn." I heaved a big sigh like I was disappointed in him. "You can't just put it all out there like that. You have to bait them, make sure they're still thinking about you after you leave. What's more interesting? A wrapped present or an unwrapped one?" His brow furrowed. I played a little drumroll while he thought about it. "A *wrapped* one. It's the mystery of it that keeps them up at night. Mooning the ladies with your skinny butt isn't your best tool."

He wrung his fingers together and stuck out his lower lip. "Then what is my best tool?"

I immediately thought of Reese, of how I approached every interaction with her. "Figure out what makes her smile, then keep doing it. Remember what worked, and find new ways to earn one. Big smiles, little ones, all the kinds in between. Each one is its own victory. If she's smiling, you're doing something right."

"It's that simple?" He looked skeptical.

I nodded. "It's that simple."

He sucked in a deep breath, exhaling it all in a rush. "I can do that. Amelia always smiles around me."

My chest felt too small for my heart. This kid. He was so much like Garrett, and it hurt and healed some of the rusty, unused parts of me at the same time. I wouldn't fail with Eli though. He'd grow up big and healthy and strong. Do all the things Garrett never got a chance to do.

"Let's go get her. I need to see these moves of yours in action."

We did. And he was right.

Amelia smiled for him the whole time.

CHAPTER 20

Reese

O N Saturday, the Rodner Sharks were playing an away game in Kentucky, a game the band wasn't traveling to for budgetary reasons. Which meant I didn't have plans for Saturday that revolved around school. Which meant... Laird was finally going to cook those steaks for us at his place this weekend. And I'd be packing an overnight bag.

My stomach fluttered at the thought, anticipation and nerves rioting out of control.

But before that, I had to pass tomorrow's calculus exam, a totally different breed of anxiety. Derivatives, bright and early on Friday morning. Every college freshman's dream come true.

The rest of the guys were headed out for pizza and cheap beer after the Thursday night practice we'd just finished, but I trudged the opposite direction, following the cracked sidewalk back to my dorm, where I would be solving differentials into the darkest hours of the morning. At least they'd invited me, which was more than I expected. Smith had asked me to join them and Bubba had seconded the request. Unsurprisingly, Marco had glowered from the middle of the group, a smug smirk splitting his face when I'd declined. I hated that it somehow felt like a victory for him in this battle between us.

And despite my simmering need to knock Marco off his pedestal whenever the opportunity arose, academics had to come first, regardless of how good melted cheese and cold beer sounded.

By the time I emerged from the communal bathroom on the floor of my dorm—eight shower stalls for thirty girls—my stomach growled its demands to be fed. I made my way back to room 407, a cheap towel wrapped like a turban around my head and my pajamas sticking to my damp skin, doing a mental inventory of my food stash.

Some microwave popcorn. Store-brand granola bars. A few apples and half a jar of creamy peanut butter. The requisite ramen noodle packs, chicken flavor. And three cases of Cherry Coke Zero.

It sounded like MSG for dinner with a side of caffeine to balance it out.

I stowed my shower caddy on the floor of my closet and gathered up a bowl to fill with water for my noodles. Except I got no further than opening my door again to head for the fourth-floor kitchen when I found Laird, my white knight with a full bag from Sammy's cradled in his arm, his bookbag hanging off his broad shoulders.

I fumbled to set the bowl down and take the bag from him. It smelled like freshly baked carbs. My favorite.

"What's this?" I inhaled, shoving my entire face into the

bag, opening and sniffing deeply.

"Turkey-and-cranberry subs. Two of them. Plus, chips and brownies." He stepped closer, his shoes inches from my bare toes, and plucked the towel from my head. My hair fell in wet clumps around my shoulders, covering my eyes and clinging to my cheeks. I shook my head, trying to clear my vision, my hands occupied with the more important task of holding dinner. Rough fingers smoothed over my forehead, parting the strands and pushing them back behind my ears. His thumbs lingered on the base of my skull, massaging small circles into the tense muscle. It took all my willpower not to purr like a cat and lean into his touch.

I sighed. "Laird, thank you. But I can't hang out tonight. I have this huge test tomorr—"

"—and you need to study." He reclaimed the bag, moving to the empty bed that would've belonged to my roommate if she'd shown up, and pushed aside the small mountain of dirty clothes I'd piled there. "So do I. I thought we could do it together. Or, not together so much as in the same room. You have Calc tomorrow, right? I have my first Anatomy test too." I paused at the evidence that he knew my schedule so well, wondering if he knew how telling that small fact was.

He pulled out the two oversized sandwiches, kettle chips, and brownies wrapped in parchment paper. He lined up everything and set two jumbo-sized cups on the floor where they wouldn't spill. Laird glanced up to where I hadn't budged from the doorway, and dipped his chin, giving me a stern glare. "You have to eat dinner. And you know you'd rather have this sandwich than those noodles you were getting ready to nuke."

My stomach betrayed me, choosing that moment to rumble an agreement, and I frowned at the pack of ramen still hanging loosely from my fingers.

He grinned and patted the mattress next to him. "Come eat. I promise I'll behave."

My dubious look only made him laugh.

"I'll use this desk all the way over here on the other side of the room to study." The paper crinkled as he unwrapped his sub. "You won't even know I'm here."

I shifted my weight from one foot to the other and finger-combed my hair, highly aware of my makeup-free face and lack of bra. "What's in the cup?" I asked the question as if his fate in this room hedged on his answer.

"Wild Cherry Pepsi."

I gasped, curling my lip in disgust.

He took a bite of his sub, chewing and swallowing before he spoke again, chuckling lightly. "Relax. It's Cherry Coke Zero. Now get your ass over here and eat dinner before it gets cold. And you're welcome, by the way."

Guilt sprouted inside of me, and I blushed, appalled at my lack of manners. "Thank you for bringing me dinner, Laird." I hunched my shoulders as I crossed the room, knowing there was no way I could surreptitiously slip a bra on. "I figured you'd be heading out with the guys for pizza. It sounded like that's where everyone was going."

He took a long sip and waited while I settled myself on the other side of the extra-long twin mattress, standard college issue. "I still have things to figure out about you. Things I couldn't discover if I was there and you were here."

"Like what?" I sank my teeth into the freshly baked bread and wondered briefly if saliva wasn't simply your taste buds ejaculating in the presence of yummy food.

A smile tugged at the corner of his mouth as he watched me eat. "Like if you play music while you study or prefer silence. If you read the facts out loud to yourself, like I sometimes do. If you throw your textbook when you get frustrated.

If you eat to relieve your stress. Or exercise. Or masturbate."
A piece of shredded lettuce fell out of my sub, landing on the
bare skin of my calf I had tucked up next to me. "Personally,
I like the last option the best."

I barely tasted the food after he started talking, the
mouthful I had sliding roughly down my throat before my
teeth finished doing their job. "You want to know a lot of
things." The sentence sounded dumb as soon as I said it, and
I winced as I plucked at the rogue piece of lettuce and set it
back on the wrapper.

Laird put his sandwich down and licked his thumb clean.
I zeroed in on his mouth, on that small glimpse of his tongue
slipping out. His words came out low and careful, but with
authority, the way you'd approach a skittish puppy. "I want
to know it all." I lifted my eyes from the full curve of his
lower lip and his gaze seared me, digging past the superficial
and burrowing into the fragile, hidden depths that I didn't
allow most people to see. The parts of me most people never
thought to look for.

"I feel like you're talking about more than just one study
session." I reached down for my drink and took a nervous
swallow to keep my hands busy.

A faint smile crossed his face. "If that's an invitation, I
accept."

Was it? I turned my focus to the sub as I replayed his
words in my head, needing the distraction of something simple. The tartness of the cranberry played off the creaminess
of the melted cheese, and the hand-carved turkey melted in
my mouth. The bread was soft and yeasty, still warm from
the oven, the perfect contrast to the cool, crunchy lettuce.
Sandwiches were so underrated as a dinner option.

Laird whipped his shirt off and dropped it on the bed behind him, then opened his bag of chips like nothing unusual

had just happened. I lowered the partially eaten half of the sub, my eyes caught on all that skin suddenly on full display. My nipples tightened behind my thin t-shirt, one I'm pretty sure had a hole in the armpit.

"What are you doing?" *Dear fearless gravity-defying Jesus walking on water.*

He crunched a chip. "Eating."

"Without your shirt on?"

"Yup."

"Why?" I asked his abs, unable to drag my attention higher. They looked as tight as my drumhead. Tighter, maybe. My fingers itched to find out.

He glanced behind him at the discarded cotton. "Because I took it off."

I pinched my eyes shut for a minute and tried to find my lost equilibrium. "Yes, but why is it off?"

"Oh." He smiled. "Because I took it off."

I wanted to scream. Or kiss him. One of those.

He held a chip up to my mouth, and I accepted it automatically, my tongue swiping at the salt on the tip of his thumb that lingered on my lower lip. He tasted better than any potato.

His eyes darkened with intent, and I pulled back, using my sandwich to create a barrier between us. "Laird," I warned, my attention hopelessly lost in the flex and stretch of his muscles as he retreated to his side of the bed, "I have to study tonight."

"Right. Equations. Mapping boundaries and finding the edge. Let me know if you need any help. Otherwise, I'll just be over here. Studying anatomy. My test is on the musculoskeletal system. Memorizing the names of what forms all those curves and dips. Looks like our subjects aren't quite so different after all."

I want to map his boundaries.

My eyes must have telegraphed my thoughts because he smirked before raising a pointed eyebrow. "Now who's thinking about things other than studying?"

I blamed my dry mouth on the chips. "Likewise. If you need help, let me know."

"I may take you up on that. In a strictly academic sense, of course."

"Of course," I echoed faintly, my eyes glued to where his obliques dipped beneath the waistband of his gym shorts. My favorite muscles of his. The ones I fantasized about licking.

But, true to his word, after dinner was over, he settled in at the other desk and studied on his laptop, completely ignoring me. I was torn between being annoyed at him for being able to tune me out, and grateful that he was taking me seriously when I said I needed to study.

By quarter to midnight, I'd waded through as many practice problems as I thought I could handle without my brain turning into absolute mush.

I stopped, stretched my arms above my head, then padded to the spare bed to retrieve my brownie. I'd been saving it as a reward for finishing.

Laird glanced over, a banked hunger in his gaze as it raked down my body. "That offer earlier to help me. It still on the table?"

Surprised, I nodded around a mouthful of chocolate. "Of course," I answered, holding my hand in front of my face to hide the fact that I was talking with my mouth full.

"Stay there," he ordered. Scooping up his computer, he settled on the mattress behind me and brushed my damp hair over my shoulder until the side of my neck was bared to him. I was nestled between his legs, framed by his strong thighs, the heat of his naked chest warming my back through my shirt. With one finger, he traced a slow path down the curve from my ear to my shoulder. "The muscles here have terrible names for such a sexy place." The stubble on his chin caught me off guard as he pressed his mouth to my skin, and I giggled before the sound morphed into a low moan in response to his tongue.

I forgot about the brownie. I forgot about everything except what he was doing to me in that instant.

"The sternocleomastoid and the platysmus."

Laird tugged on the loose neckline of my shirt until it slipped over one of my shoulders. His lips swept along the newly exposed flesh, and a spark zinged down my spine while my arms erupted in goose bumps.

"The deltoid."

His strong hands massaged my back, thumbs digging into the stubborn knots along my shoulder blades, tight from the weight of the snare.

"Then there are the muscles of the rotator joint. Supraspinatus, infraspinatus, subscapularis, and teres minor."

I whimpered and tipped my head back to rest on his chest. His hands swept down my torso, brushing the sides of my breasts and causing my nipples to bud.

"Latissimus dorsi."

He traveled back up my spine, rubbing out all the tension from the week. Tingles spread to my scalp, that same addicting feeling I'd gotten after someone played with my hair when I was younger.

"A trio of muscles here, remembered with the mnemonic *I love spines*. Iliocostalis, the longissimus, and the spinalis, from superficial to deep."

Laird was thorough when he studied. After he finished with my back, he barely paused before reaching around to my pec major and pec minor, his hands cupping and kneading my bare breasts under my shirt. I melted beneath his expert touch, heat simmering between my thighs. When he rolled my aching nipples between his fingers as my breasts swelled to fill his palms, a moan escaped my parted lips, but he didn't linger nearly as long as I would've liked.

He continued his journey southward, his palms skimming down my stomach, and he rattled off more names as his fingers followed the flare of my hips.

"The sartorius starts here," his thumb pressed just below my hip, "and wraps around the front to the inner thigh before finishing just below the knee." He mapped the distance, his fingers so close to my damp panties I held my breath. "It's the longest muscle in the body, and damn if it doesn't cover some of the best ground too."

Laird retraced his path, his fingers pushing aside my tiny sleeping shorts and flirting with the lace edging the thin cotton between my legs.

"Except for the gracilis. That one might be my favorite. It connects down here," he drew a soft circle on the inside of my knee, his voice deeper, rougher than before, "just behind the sartorius, but it's a little more direct. It runs right up the inner thigh until it runs out of leg. A straight pathway to heaven."

He demonstrated, and this time, he didn't stop until his palm cupped me fully. I dug my nails into his hard thighs and arched my back, wordlessly asking for more. One long finger traced my seam, and I bucked against him.

"I think it's my favorite too," I whispered raggedly.

"I'm thinking I need to study that one a little closer." His lips closed around my earlobe and I shuddered.

"Wouldn't want you missing"—and my breath hitched as his thumbs hooked the waistband of my shorts and pushed them over my hips—"that one on the test."

After he memorized the path with his hands, he slid to

his knees on the floor and retraced his steps with his tongue.

And I lost the ability to think altogether.

The heat from his mouth ripped a harsh exhale from my throat, and I rolled my hips in response. The mere sight of his dark hair between my thighs was enough to have me panting. I don't know why, perhaps just from my past experiences, but I didn't expect a guy like *him*, who could have his choice of girls servicing him at a moment's notice, to put my pleasure first. But, fuck, that dark glow in his green eyes when he peeked up at me erased any doubt I had that he was just going through the motions. It was the look of a man who was finally getting something he'd been denied for far too long. Bold and greedy, but tinged with a certain softness I'd never seen before.

His hands closed around my waist, dragged me to the side of the bed, and settled my thighs over his shoulders, before slipping lower to cup my ass. There was no time to feel shy or embarrassed or self-conscious, because his tongue swept away everything except for an achy restlessness.

He licked me, traced my opening, learned all my most intimate secrets. And all I could do was fist his hair in my hands and pull him closer, his name the chorus to the incoherent chant I mumbled, curses and pleas forming the verses.

When he sucked on my clit and hummed a primal sound deep in his throat, it sent me over the edge, and my thighs closed around him like a vise, my toes curled and tense. He continued, the suction and the flutters of his tongue relentless as I hovered in that place of blinding ecstasy, suspended between heaven and earth.

When my fingers loosened their grip on his dark strands, he lessened the intensity, but didn't stop. It wasn't until I'd said his name for the third time that he lifted his head, his face smeared with my release.

"Laird," I repeated, scooting his direction, until he had no choice but to sit back on the floor. I followed him, straddling his lap, my wet core throbbing anew as his hard cock rose against me beneath the thin barrier of his shorts.

The satisfied smirk barely had time to settle on his face before I took his mouth in a hungry kiss, thanking him without words. One of his arms circled low on my hips, while the other aligned with my spine, his hand gripping my neck to angle me the way he liked.

His hot length pulsed under me and I rocked on top of him, relishing in the deep groan that vibrated his broad chest. I tucked my knees on either side of his hips, then leaned forward into the kiss, until he fell back onto the Moroccan-style area rug I'd brought from home.

And once I was astride his hips, I pulled back and grinned down at him before biting my lip. His lips were full and dark, his cheeks flushed, the green of his eyes barely visible beneath his hooded gaze. A sense of wonder slid into the silence between my heartbeats. I'd put that look on Laird's face. *Me.* Those gorgeous arms of his were relaxed as his palms rubbed my legs softly, in contrast to the steely tension in his thighs as he pressed himself to the damp heat between my legs.

I leaned down and licked his neck, closing my eyes when he sucked in a sharp breath. My lips pressed an open kiss to the angle of his jaw as my fingers gripped the waistband of his shorts.

"My turn," I whispered.

And when his shorts were gone and my tongue was sliding over the swollen head of his dick, I got it. With past guys, blowjobs had always felt more like a chore, performed more out of expectation than desire on my part. But with Laird, I understood the sweet power that came from taking a man in your mouth, knowing at that moment, he was completely at your mercy.

I savored the way Laird lost himself to my touch, and the unselfish way he shared his surrender. As I hollowed my cheeks and took him deep, my hand rolling his balls at the same time, his fingers traced my jaw and tugged my hair into a messy ponytail. Rough sounds of pleasure came from his throat, and he flexed his hips. The pressure from his hands never increased though. He let me control the tempo and depth.

I remembered the lesson from the storage room, how he liked it, and when I switched from soft and fast to slow and deep, I was rewarded with Laird hissing out a curse before whispering my name.

And when I lightly squeezed his sac and brushed my thumb over that thin skin just behind it, he spilled in hot spurts into my mouth, his strangled warning coming too late for me to do anything but swallow him down. Those green irises were nearly molten as he watched the motion of my throat, his fingers tightening in my damp hair.

With an impatient growl, he hauled me up to his chest, seizing my mouth in a fierce kiss that had me thinking things I had no business thinking when it came to him.

"Fuck, Reese," he murmured against my lips, his hands slipping up to frame my face. "What am I going to do with you?"

I lost myself in the nocturne of his kiss, the endless way his mouth slanted over mine, our bodies tangled together like a chord. I kissed him until I was breathless, the answer to his question settling quietly between my ribs.

Everything.

CHAPTER 21

Reese

A s I left Martin Hall after my calculus exam, headed for some desperately needed caffeine, my phone vibrated.

Laird: Hope your test went well. I'm sure you nailed it. Drumline party tonight. 9pm. Mandatory.

I hesitated, not entirely sure how to respond. The first half had been personal, but the second half sounded all business. It also didn't escape my attention that he didn't ask me to go with him to the party.

Well, you're the one who wanted to keep it quiet around the drumline. It probably wasn't fair of me to get mad at the guy for respecting my wishes. But still...

I weighed my options, finally deciding to answer in kind.

Me: I think I did pretty good, thnx. Good luck on yours later! See you tonight.

My thumb pressed send before I could overthink it further.

It's just a text. Just a text. Just a text. I chanted to myself as I crossed the quad. *With the guy I'm probably sleeping with tomorrow.* My feet quickened their pace, as if I could out walk my nervousness over our first official—albeit secret—date.

Laird: Looking forward to it.

Laird: But not as much as Saturday.

I smiled, one of those goofy, dorky smiles dumb girls get when hot guys flirted with them. This was bad. Like, butterflies and rainbows and big puffy hearts bad. I refused to turn into a goopy, brainless mess around him. He could hang with the cymbal girls if he wanted that.

My phone buzzed again a few minutes later as I skirted around the fountain of the shark, thought to bring good luck if you rubbed his dorsal fin. I gave it a quick pat as I walked by, because, hey, it couldn't hurt.

Smith: Drumline party tonight. Have you heard? Want me to pick you up?

Me: I just got a text. And, yes, that'd be great.

Smith: What are sidekicks for?

Me: For insider information, duh. Hint hint. Have you heard anything about this party? Anything I should be prepared for?

There was a long pause and I entered the student center, joining the line in the food court for a soda. By the time I reached the front, the smell of the oversized cinnamon rolls had completely seduced me and I added one to my order on a whim.

It shouldn't take him this long to answer. Something was definitely up.

Me: Robin?

Smith: Yeah, I've heard rumor of something. I just don't think it'll affect you.

Me: Spill.

Another pause. *Dear holy avenging archangels with lightning bolts and personal agendas.* How bad could it be?

Smith: I heard there's going to be a literal dick measuring contest. So, I think you're safe for this one.

I almost choked on a bite of pastry, the white icing on my finger suddenly reminding me of something much, much dirtier.

The story of how Laird acquired Oscar had my brain spinning. I had to be prepared. I needed a way to top his prank, to hold my own with the guys.

I did a couple of quick Google searches on my phone, crossing my fingers we weren't too deep into the Bible Belt for what I had in mind.

Bingo! Only twelve minutes from campus. And I only had one more class today.

Me: You're right. I should be fine. Thanks for the heads up though.

Smith: I see what you did there.

Me: I expected no less, Robin. There's a reason you're my sidekick.

Smith: You know it. I'll see you at 8:45.

Me: Wait! You're not expecting me to be your fluffer, are you?

Smith: Nah, I think I can manage. But as your sidekick, you totally should've offered.

Me: …

Smith: I bet you would've said yes if it was Laird asking.

Smith: Just saying.

Me: Shut up.

208 | STACY KESTWICK

I finished my cinnamon roll, trying really hard not to think about Smith or Laird or their dicks as I licked the cream cheese frosting off my fingers. They weren't going to ruin my breakfast treat. Nope. Not happening.

Okay. I lied. I thought about Laird. And his cock. *Especially* when I was licking my fingers.

Smith: I'm down here. You ready?
Me: I need two minutes.

I adjusted the long skirt of the sapphire blue maxi dress, double checking my reflection in the mirror. My hair was in a casual updo, a sort of fauxhawk from where I'd pinned it back in a column of purposefully messy knots. My back was mostly bare, except for a few skinny straps holding the dress in place, and I was trying out those bra cups that adhered right to your skin. Putting them on wasn't bad, but I wasn't looking forward to the removal later. Pale gladiator sandals that showed off my bright coral nail polish completed the look.

For a moment, I second guessed everything, wondering if I should change into jeans and a tank top like last time.

But, no, I could do this.

Me: Okay, I'm coming now.
Smith: That's what she said.
Me: Are you going to be like this all night?
Smith: Absolutely.

I rolled my eyes as I waited for the elevator. *Greaaaaat.*

When I walked out of the dorm, Smith was waiting by the open passenger door of his truck, ever the gentleman. Except then he wolf-whistled as he caught my hand and spun me around so he could view me from all directions, effectively ruining the illusion.

"Do I look okay?" I winced a little at how anxious I sounded. "Is this too much? Does it look ridiculous?"

I held my breath as he ran a critical eye over me again.

He reached out and rubbed a spot by the corner of my mouth. "A little smear with your makeup, but it's fixed now. You're gorgeous. Are you looking to make Laird crazy or piss off Marco by making Laird crazy?"

My lips parted in a mischievous smile I couldn't smother fast enough. "Oh, I'm definitely hoping for a reaction tonight. I'm just not sure what it'll be yet."

He squinted at me and tipped his head slightly. "You're plotting something." His tone made it clear it was a statement, not a question.

I plastered an innocent expression on my face, and he pointed at me, waving his finger around.

"Nope. Not buying that. Not even for a second. You gonna let your sidekick in on it, or am I supposed to be surprised too?"

"Well, it wouldn't exactly be a surprise if you knew it was coming, now would it?" I winked, then sobered. "Just be ready to help me escape if it all goes to hell."

"I got your back, Batman. Let's go start some trouble. You know Willa and Amber aren't gonna appreciate the level of hotness you're bringing to this party tonight."

"Yeah, they'll live." I rolled my eyes. "And they're welcome to Marco. In fact, I would love nothing more than for one—or *both*—of them to distract him all night long."

Smith had a weird look on his face as we got in the car and he cranked the engine.

"What? Is there something else about tonight you're not telling me?" I demanded.

"Nope. I'm just as curious as you are as to how it's all

going to go down. I feel like we need one of those—what are they called? Safe words? And if one of us says it to the other, we're gone."

I thought for a moment. "Scrotum Breath."

He choked as he turned left. "Seriously, Reese?"

"It's not like it's a phrase that would just come up in conversation. Plus, if I needed to leave early, I'm sure it'd be because of him." I shrugged.

We were almost there. It was just off campus.

"Fine. Whatever. If one of us says Scrotum Breath, we jet, no questions asked."

Two minutes later we walked inside, the volume on the wireless speakers cranked almost uncomfortably loud. Everyone was already in various stages of getting their drink on, and it looked like a cymbal player was already hooking up with a bass drummer in the corner, wasting no time at all.

The first hour was fine. I nursed a cup of NAD juice that was pushed into my hand and made a point to stay on the other side of the room from Marco. Charlie, Cade, and I got into a heated debate about the best brand of drumsticks to buy. I was a fan of Vic Firth, Cade liked ProMark and Zildjian, and Charlie was adamant that AHEAD's synthetic drumsticks were going to eventually gain a majority market share over the traditional wood style.

When I found my way to the kitchen for a cup of Goldfish crackers to help absorb some of the alcohol, Laird cornered me, reaching around for some snacks of his own while effectively caging me against the counter in the process.

"I've never seen you in a dress," he murmured against my ear, his stubble brushing the sensitive skin on my neck and sending a shudder through me.

"You would have," I returned smoothly, "if you'd been at your townhouse the other weekend when I showed up."

He pulled his head back, but not his arms. "Fair enough." His gaze dropped down my body before starting a slow journey back up, his attention lingering on my boobs. "I saw you earlier from the back and almost didn't recognize you. You're not wearing a bra, are you? In that dress? I'm not gonna lie, it's making me crazy. On one hand, I love the idea that your tits are right there, just under this one little layer of fabric. On the other, I don't want anyone else but me enjoying the view."

"You think I wore this for you?" I pinched his forearm, sending him a subtle signal he needed to back up to keep this from looking too suspicious in front of everyone else. He begrudgingly put twelve inches of linoleum between us, disappointment clear in his eyes. "Maybe I just got tired of wearing pants?"

"You don't ever have to wear pants around me if you don't want to." His voice was just loud enough for me to hear him, but there was no way to miss the heat in his green eyes.

"Does that mean you want me to wear a dress tomorrow too?"

"I don't care what you wear as long as it includes those lace panties from the other night. I have plans for them."

I turned as pink as the punch in my cup.

"I'll see what I can do."

He swore under his breath. "I can't fucking wait to see what you do tomorrow, Reese. Can't fucking wait." With one last searing look, he grabbed a beer from the cooler on the floor and headed over to Bubba and some of the bass drummers.

I retraced my steps past a group of cymbal players

grinding on each other to find Smith again when Marco let out one of those piercing whistles that I thought only PE coaches in tiny shorts knew how to make. I was still cringing when I walked the last dozen steps to stand with Smith and Justin. Justin ended up being an alternate for a field spot—meaning, if someone couldn't perform for any reason, he'd step in. I think he was secretly hoping someone would get drunk and break an ankle or something. He'd been fetching drinks like he was majoring in bartending instead of chemistry.

"All snares, listen up!" Marco motioned for the music to be cut. "It's time for—hey! I'm talking!"

Despite the eardrum piercing whistle, the suddenly quiet sound system, and his repeated demands, people ignored him, continuing their conversations.

Laird stepped in and slapped his hand on a wooden console table and paused. Heads swiveled and talk dissipated when they realized who it was.

In his normal voice, he said, "Good evening! We had a great first game last week." He smiled as hoots and cheers filled the room. I wondered briefly who lived in the apartment under this one—if they'd left for the night or been paid off to ignore the noise we were making.

"Now, I know y'all have all been waiting for this moment. Time to stand tall and be measured against your fellow drummers. Who should we have do the honors tonight?" Laird glanced around the room. Willa and Amber had their arms in the air, both waving frantically to get his attention.

"Marco?" Laird threw him a bone. "You want to pick?"

Amber, who had been flirting shamelessly with Topher earlier, fluttered her fake eyelashes at Marco. He shot her a scathing look and turned to Willa, the sweetest smile I'd ever seen from him curving his lips. "Well, traditionally, the most beautiful woman on the whole drumline is picked. So, I'm thinking the obvious choice here is Willa, right, Laird?"

Clever. He was snubbing Amber and baiting Laird, all in one fell swoop, and the smirk he wore said he was well aware of it.

Laird didn't even pause. "I gotta let Marco win at something tonight, so Willa it is!"

Snickers came from one corner of the room where beer pong was set up, and Marco glared at them until they fell silent.

"All right, snares, front and center!" Laird set his drink down and rubbed his palms together, like he was looking forward to the contest. He probably thought he had it in the bag. Which, to be fair, he might. Laird by far had the biggest dick I'd seen with my own two eyes.

Smith handed me his cup. "Mind holding that?"

I took his drink as he navigated to the middle of the room, following behind him so I had a good view.

All the snare players were arranged in a haphazard line except for me. No one seemed to notice or care that I wasn't included in the group, but I let it slide.

Willa, a shit-eating grin stretched across her face, tossed her platinum blond hair over her shoulder and sidled up to Bubba, making a production about feeling his junk. She puckered her face like she was concentrating hard as she ran her hand up and down the zipper of his jeans before moving over to Van and repeating the motion. As she groped each one, she arranged them in order, sometimes pausing to check her placement with a repeat performance.

She was almost done.

Topher, despite being one of the tallest guys on the snare line, apparently had the smallest drumstick in his briefs. Poor guy.

Maybe he's a grower, not a show-er, because he doesn't seem all that concerned.

At the other end of the totem pole was Marco.

Laird, who'd been laughing and joking the whole time, was next. As Willa approached, his eyes flew to mine, wide with panic, as if he just now realized I was going to have to watch her stroke him as part of this whole event. As Willa slid into position beside him, he shuffled back half a step, one eyebrow cocked as he kept his gaze on me.

He's asking permission. It took me a second to interpret his actions, but as soon as I did, I gave him a wink to let him know it was okay.

It wasn't okay. Not in the least. Jealousy boiled, hot and angry, in my gut as I curled my hands into fists, my nails digging into my palms as I forced myself to hold still, to not launch myself at her like a psycho and rip her arm away from his pants where she was lingering way too fucking long. The only thing keeping me still was the fact that Laird's focus never wavered from me. He held my gaze the entire time as if trying to reassure me the only way he could that I was the only one he was thinking about in that moment.

But when she shifted her grip lower, to cup his balls, I was a fraction of a second away from detonating.

No, she fucking didn't…

Laird coughed, taking a step back and twisting away as he covered his mouth.

I stopped breathing, waiting to see she if went for him again.

Go on, bitch, I dare you.

But instead of grabbing his crotch, she caught his elbow and slid him into place—in front of Marco at the head of the line.

I exhaled in a relieved *whoosh*, forcing my jaw to unclench. Laird's eyes were soft with apology, and I gave him a wobbly smile to let him know I understood.

The only person left to be measured was Smith.

Willa ran her hand down his groin, pausing as her eyes widened and her mouth dropped partway open, then squeezed again. She glanced from his crotch to the blush high on his caramel cheeks back to his crotch, then she mimed fanning herself before putting him squarely ahead of Laird.

Smith met my surprised gaze with a bashful grin, slouching next to Laird. I wasn't sure if he was trying to sink into the floor or go for nonchalance.

Willa turned to the rest of us. "And the cockiest snare *this* year—"

Clearing my throat, I stepped forward, interrupting her little speech.

"I think you forgot about me."

Willa scrunched her nose. "You?"

"I'm a snare player too, right? No special treatment? Shouldn't you check the size of my balls? Just to be fair?"

She glanced back at Marco and Laird. Marco was nodding like a rabid bobblehead, leaning closer in his eagerness. Laird had a suspicious gleam in his green eyes when he met my gaze for a quick second before I focused on Willa again.

Practically salivating, Marco stepped out of line to stand next to Willa, clearly not wanting to miss a second of some live girl-on-girl action. "Reese is right for once. You need to rub her down too, Willa. Do it slow." He licked his lips. "Real slow."

Spreading my legs slightly, I held my breath as Willa approached me. She reached forward gingerly, almost as if she was worried I had cooties and was contagious.

"For fuck's sake, Willa, it's not like you've never touched a vag before." I caught her wrist in my hand, pulling her forward and placing her palm boldly at the apex of my thighs. "You've got one of your own, and if you haven't gone exploring down there by now, let me tell you, you're seriously missing out."

Marco groaned and several of the other guys made similar noises.

This was almost too easy.

I rubbed her hand down my inner left thigh, watching her expression closely. There was no way she could miss it.

Her fingers closed around me through the soft jersey of my maxi dress, stroking the length of the gigantic dildo I'd tucked into a pair of Spanx before I left my dorm room.

Willa's mouth fell open, her eyes first widening in shock, then narrowing in confusion as her fingers retraced their path. "What the..." she whispered.

"How do I compare?" I used my most innocent voice.

She gaped at me, and I dragged her palm along the silicone length one last time, pressing firmly.

"You... you win." She snatched her hand back as if she'd been burned. "Reese has the biggest dick out of any of you."

The people closest to me stepped back like I was on fire and they had no intention of helping to put out the flames, confusion twisting their faces.

Marco snarled and half-pushed her out of the way, shoving his hand between my thighs and cupping me crudely.

And then the blood left his face as his fingers met the firm length he didn't expect to find there.

"What the fuck?" After yanking his arm back, Marco stooped down, caught the hem of my dress, and bunched it in his meaty fist until I was exposed from the waist down.

The head of my newly acquired gigantic black cock stuck

out beneath the bottom hem of my mid-thigh shapewear.

In the back of my mind, I registered that a crowd had pushed close to us when he'd raised my dress, everyone eager for a free show. Hoots of laughter filled the room, some of them pointing. Their expressions ran the gamut from mirth, awe, and respect from the guys to disgust and confusion from the girls.

Except for Willa, who just looked relieved that it was a sex toy and not a real dick.

"Still want to give me that private lesson, Marco?" I blinked at him.

And then he was stumbling backward, bulldozed out of the way by Laird as he tore the dress from Marco's hand, covering me up, then tucking me behind him and shielding me from Marco's view with his broad back.

"You don't touch her. Ever." Laird seethed as he barked out each word, the fierceness of his glower enough to melt the polar ice caps. "You don't touch *any* woman like that." He turned to extend the warning to the rest of the snare line, glaring at each in turn. "Like you have the right to just reach between her legs without permission. I don't care if she has the sweetest pussy known to man or the biggest, blackest dick to grace this planet—you *ask*. You get *consent. Always*."

If my dick were real, I'd have just gotten the most epic erection of my life. Raised a fucking obelisk. Laird Bronson had never been sexier than in this moment, a gladiator among mere mortals, laying down the law.

Laird turned a full circle, staring down every male in the room. "Do I make myself crystal fucking clear about how this drumline works?" He didn't raise his voice as he said it.

He whispered.

And his warning was all the more chilling because of it.

But afterward, when Marco caught my eye and I saw

the rigidness of his stance and the dark hatred pinching his mouth, I regretted my decision. Despite my momentary victory, I had a feeling I'd be paying for this little prank of mine tenfold. A shiver of foreboding skated down my spine.

I found Smith in the crowd—Amber damn near accosting him after discovering the size of his dick—looked him in the eye, and said the two words I'd been hoping would be unnecessary tonight. "Scrotum Breath."

CHAPTER 22

Laird

WHERE IS SHE?

A minute ago, she'd been right behind me, so close I could feel her ragged breathing against my back. But by the time I finished staring down Marco and two other assholes—damn bass drum players—who seemed to think my outburst was just for show and I wasn't one hundred percent dead fucking serious, she was gone.

I pushed through the crowd that was still amped up from Reese's outrageous stunt. Not in the kitchen, not on the tiny balcony, and not in the bedroom or the connected bathroom.

I ran my hands through my hair before gripping the back of my neck in frustration.

Where the fuck did she go?

I made one more pass, double-checking where Marco was—shoving his tongue down some girl's throat—and confirmed that Reese was nowhere near him.

My blood ran hot, then cold.

The image of Marco's fingers curled around Reese's waist as he held her dress up, baring her whole bottom half to the entire drumline played in technicolor inside my skull.

On repeat.

I wanted to roar, to wrap my fingers around his skinny neck and squeeze until he turned purple, to punch my fist right through the flimsy drywall of this shithole apartment.

But mostly, I wanted to make sure Reese was okay and I couldn't do that if I *couldn't fucking find her*.

My phone buzzed in the back pocket of my jeans. The plastic case was in serious danger of cracking as I crushed it in my hand, punching the passcode in viciously.

Reese: I left. I'm sorry I didn't say goodbye, but I couldn't stay any longer.

She's safe. Thank fuck, she's safe.

But my relief was short lived as the messages continued to arrive in quick succession.

Reese: I shouldn't have done that.

Reese: Maybe tomorrow night is a bad idea.

I stilled, a thousand denials wanting to rip from my throat.

My fingers shook as I typed a reply.

Me: Because of me? Or because of some asswipes on drumline?

There was a long pause and my heart faltered, beating in triplets instead of quarter notes.

Those three gray dots appeared, telling me she was replying. Then they stopped.

I walked out of the apartment, not speaking to a soul, uncaring as I shouldered past a cluster of guys near the front door.

My lungs breathed easier just getting out of that room, but my legs failed me, and I sunk onto the steps, laser focused on those gray dots that were blinking again.

Reese: You're the captain. I'm the girl trying to fit in where I'm not wanted.

Reese: How can you not see how bad of an idea this is?

Not me. It isn't because of me.

The tightness around my chest loosened. This was a fumble, an interception. But I wasn't out of the game yet.

Me: You're the best damn idea I've had all year. And if you show up tomorrow, I'll prove it.

I hesitated. I couldn't force her to come—I didn't want to force her to do anything. I wanted her of her own volition, this whirlwind of a woman who'd been driving me crazy from the moment I laid eyes on her.

My fingers twitched on the phone, a melody unfurling in my marrow. The song I only heard when I thought of Reese.

Me: Are you really going to let Marco and some shitheads you don't even care about stop you? Are you going to let them win?

I sat there for another hour, until my ass went numb from the edge of the step and the first drunk guests started to stumble home, tripping past me as they left.

And the longer I sat there, my phone quiet in my hand, the calmer I became.

She hadn't answered with another excuse. Hadn't listed a litany of flimsy reasons to beg off. Hadn't invented a friend with a family emergency she had to rescue at the last minute.

No, if I knew my girl, she was fuming on the other end, because *nobody* held her back from doing what she wanted.

Not cancer. Not a hundred and eighteen years of drumline tradition. Definitely not some insecure motherfucker who couldn't stand not being the center of attention.

And—if I was right—Reese Holland wanted me almost as badly as I wanted her.

She'll be here.

I returned the vacuum to its home in the corner of the front closet, having done one last pass in the never-ending battle against Oscar's shedding.

She'll be here.

The salad was prepped and in the fridge, classic Caesar with fucking homemade croutons that I'd made following the instructions on a YouTube video, because she was worth the extra effort.

She'll be here.

Steaks from a local butcher shop, not just the refrigerated section of the Publix around the corner, were marinating, ready to be thrown on the grill.

She'll be here.

The asparagus, bundled with thick slices of peppery bacon, was ready to go, wrapped in heavy duty foil that could withstand the flames.

She'll be here.

The whole apartment smelled like the sweet potatoes that had been baking in the oven for the last hour.

She'll be here.

I took the fastest shower known to man, making sure my pits and prick were clean and rushing through the rest. I didn't shave. She liked the stubble.

She'll be here.

I opened a beer, needing to do something with my hands, needing to do *anything* to distract myself from the fact that she was fifteen minutes late.

She'll be here.

Maybe I should change? I glanced down at my shirt, a soft gray tee that had an outline of Alabama on the chest and said *Homegrown* in thick, blocky letters below it. It wasn't fancy, but if she showed up tonight, it wasn't because of what I would or wouldn't be wearing.

It would be because she couldn't deny the chemistry between us any longer.

She'll be here.

Oscar brought me his favorite tennis ball, raising his eyebrows expectantly. I threw it twenty-seven times before the doorbell rang.

She was here.

CHAPTER 23

Reese

THE DOOR OPENED. LAIRD'S SCENT REACHED ME FIRST, soap and bad ideas and fairy tales all mixed up in a pheromone cloud I was powerless to resist.

"I shouldn't be here." My voice sounded weak and a bit defensive as I looked at his neck, his chin, his nose—anywhere but his kryptonite green eyes.

"Wrong. This is exactly where you should be."

His hand closed around my wrist and he pulled me out of the endless Alabama heat into the coolness of his townhouse, then crowded me against the wall. Before I could protest, before I could even take a breath, his mouth was on mine, desperate, hungry, and so damn hot. Rational thought fled my mind. My knees buckled and I clutched his shirt, letting his arm around my back support my weight.

"Right here. With me. In my arms." The husky words hit me like bullets.

His tongue licked the seam of my lips, then plunged inside. A greedy noise spilled from my throat. I'd never get enough of the way he tasted, of the way my skin seemed to hum whenever he touched me. His other arm fell to my thigh, tugging my leg up to wrap around his waist as he arched my back. That dirty mouth of his wasn't the only thing pressing against me.

I raised my arms to his wide shoulders, feeling his muscles bunch under my palms. My nails scratched along his scalp, and his answering groan had me shivering in wanton desire.

There was no spark, no slow build-up. This was an instant inferno of need.

"Laird." I rubbed my cheek against his stubble, then tipped my head to the side as he trailed kisses down my neck. "We shouldn't."

It was my last attempt at logic, at sane reasoning, although it was half-assed at best considering my words came out more as a moan.

"Says who?" His eyes bored into mine, snaring me in their frustrated heat. "You? You want this. I can feel how much you want it. Your nipples are already hard and begging, your mouth is swollen and pouting, and there's no doubt in my mind, if I reached between those sweet thighs of yours right now, that you'd be wet and ready."

He rocked his hips, his hard length obvious behind his zipper. "That's just the start of what you do to me, Reese."

Laird traced his fingers along my face, rubbing at the crease between my eyebrows with his thumb. "Tell me you don't want to be here."

Before I could open my mouth, he stopped me with a grunt and a sharp shake of his head. "No. Not whether you *think* you should be here, tell me you don't *want* to be here. That you don't want me to cook you dinner, and tell you how damn beautiful you look, and kiss you until you've been kissed every single way there is to kiss."

I bit my lip, unable to lie to him when he held my gaze like this, wringing the truth from me whether I wanted to give it to him or not.

"You didn't even take the time to see what I was wearing," I pointed out with a soft laugh.

"Doesn't matter." His eyes never wavered from mine. "You're gorgeous in everything."

He released my thigh, letting it drop until I was standing on my own two feet again, albeit a bit wobbly.

"Besides," he pressed his forehead to mine, "Oscar's missed you. And there's nothing worse than a sad wiener."

I finally registered the ecstatic dachshund weaving around our feet and head-butting our calves, a well-loved tennis ball wedged in his mouth. I crouched to rub his soft ears, and he flopped on his side in blatant surrender.

"Fuck, Oscar. You don't have to be *that* whipped. You could make her work for it a little." Laird watched his dog snuffle in happiness, tail thumping out a blur of eighth notes. "I'm gonna leave you two to your little reunion while I throw the steaks on the grill. How do you like yours cooked, Reese?"

"Make mine like yours. I don't eat steak that often, so I'll trust your judgment."

He paused at the corner to the kitchen, eyebrows scrunched. "Why not?"

"Why not what?"

"Why don't you eat steak that often? Steak is awesome."

Fuck. Me and my big mouth. I tossed him a shrug I hoped passed for nonchalant. "My parents didn't let me have too much red meat. You know, the free radicals and stuff..." My voice trailed off in embarrassment. Fucking cancer. Fucking overprotective parents. A steak wasn't going to kill me, no matter what psycho article they'd read.

Laird looked stricken.

"No!" I hastened to reassure him, to not be *that* girl. The one he'd look at differently—treat differently—because of some stupid fucking rogue cells that had once wreaked havoc on my body. They were gone. Had been for years. I was safe. *Healthy.* Strong.

Normal.

And if he brought out the kid gloves my parents used around me, this was going to be over before it ever really started.

"Laird, it's fine." I rose from my position on the floor, crossing to his side and squeezing his arm. The muscle beneath my hand was rock hard with tension. "My parents... Look, my parents were crazy overprotective. But I've been in remission for a decade. A *decade.* I can have steak. I can march on drumline." I offered him a wicked smile. "I can even have naughty, wall-banging sex with a hot guy if I want. I'm *fine.*"

He swallowed hard, his eyes searching every inch of my face. Slowly, by tiny degrees, his forearm relaxed, and he reached out to tug on a wayward lock of hair.

"How 'bout this? No cancer talk tonight. At all. Not your history with it or mine. We won't even talk about the hospital. Eli, Amelia, none of that." He looped his arms around my waist and drew my hips to his. "Tonight, we'll eat some fantastic fucking steak—medium rare because that's the only way to eat it—and talk about happy stuff. Then maybe afterward we can revisit your statement about banging on walls."

I beamed at him. "Sounds perfect."

And it was.

Over a salad with the best croutons I'd ever had, I told him about my early childhood, when I explored the Appalachian foothills, climbing every tree I could, and swam in the Monongahela River, chasing minnows and Canadian geese as they migrated south, and how I made the biggest damn mud pies in three counties.

While we ate steak so tender we barely needed knives, and sweet potatoes drowning in butter, brown sugar, and cinnamon, he told me about Mario Kart tournaments with Garrett, building Lego empires, and the tire swing in their backyard, the one Garrett fell off when he was four because Laird had pushed him too high and he'd gotten scared. Garrett had broken his arm, and Laird had felt so bad, he found the steepest hill in the neighborhood, the one three streets over from where they lived, and raced his bike down it as fast as he could—then purposefully crashed into the Morrisons' fence at the bottom, fracturing his elbow and breaking two fingers. They'd had matching bright blue casts the whole summer.

"See right here?" Laird held up his hand and pointed at his little finger, which was just a bit crooked at the joint. "A little memento from that day."

I snagged his hand and pressed a kiss to the old injury. "There. All better."

His eyes turned darker, laced with lust and something deeper I wasn't ready to examine.

I ducked his gaze, took a sip of water, and traced a pattern into the condensation on the side of the glass.

He picked up the last bite of steak from his plate and held it up to my mouth.

I parted my lips obediently, letting him feed me, letting him perform one of my most basic needs. It didn't feel demeaning or belittling, the way it did when my parents micromanaged my life. Instead, I felt cherished, protected, taken care of as if he was honored to do so, not because I was fragile and delicate.

I swallowed, then wiped my mouth with my napkin.

"I'm wearing them," I blurted out, no finesse, no segue. "Like you asked."

"Wearing what?" His eyes drew together a bit in confusion.

I rubbed my damp palms on my thighs. "The black lace panties."

CHAPTER 24

Laird

BLACK.
  Lace.
  Panties.

Just like that—with three little words—all the blood in my body rushed to my groin. I ran my eyes over her, letting her outfit finally register in my sluggish mind. Bright pink shorts highlighted her tanned, endless legs and practically screamed for me to notice her ass. A soft white shirt with an oversized neckline in danger of slipping off one perfect shoulder, a hint of a matching black bra visible beneath.

And then, with the kind of speed Usain Bolt would be proud of, I swept up our plates and deposited them in the sink—safely out of the reach of Oscar—before rounding back by the table and scooping Reese into my arms on the way to the bedroom.

I didn't just toss her on the bed though.

I wasn't a fucking caveman.

Instead, I sat her on the dresser in front of the mirror. Watching my actions in the reflection, I gathered her hair in one hand, drawing it to one side, exposing the long curve of her neck to my view. I buried my nose in that tempting spot where her collarbone flared out.

She smelled so fucking good. Like cherries and flowers that thrived in the South. Magnolia, maybe?

I nibbled her skin as her thighs separated to make room for me. While my mouth started the journey north to her ear, my free hand drifted down her arm, dragging her shirt a bit until her shoulder was bare. Her pulse thrummed in her wrist beneath the pads of my fingers, warm and alive and deliberate as a Sousa fanfare.

"Do you like it when I tell you what to do, Reese?"

Her breath hitched, but I didn't stop the lazy trail of kisses I dropped along her jaw.

"Like with the underwear?"

She shivered in my arms, and her heartbeat picked up pace, more of a circus march now than a military one.

"I think you do." I rubbed my nose down the length of hers. "I think, deep down, there's times you don't want to be the one in control, when you get tired of trying to prove yourself."

Reese whimpered and lifted her chin, trying to capture my lips, but I pulled back just enough to get her attention.

"You've never found the right person, have you? Someone you trusted enough to let your guard down, and let him take charge for a while."

She bit her lower lip and peered up at me from beneath her lashes, but there was nothing innocent about her expression.

"I can give that to you tonight. I can be that for you." I

freed her lip, running my thumb along its curve. "Just say my name. Say my name and tell me *yes*."

I pulled on the hair wrapped around my fist, tipping her chin back until she was forced to meet my eyes fully. Her chocolate irises shimmered with a passion I couldn't wait to explore. I leaned down and whispered in her ear. "You're beautiful tonight, Reese. More beautiful than I deserve. But I'm greedy, so fucking greedy when it comes to you. I want to see your face when I make you come, taste it on my lips, feel it around my cock. I want you on top, underneath, on your knees, against the wall. I want you spread out on the kitchen table, bent over in the shower, tangled up in my sheets, and in my arms. Always in my arms. Do you want me to give that to you? Find all the ways to make you scream my name?"

I pulled back just enough to see her face. She let out a ragged breath, her eyes impossibly dark.

Without breaking my stare, she cupped my aching hardness in her palm, drew her hand along its length, and squeezed.

This girl. She was so fucking perfect.

"Yes, Laird."

That's all I wanted to hear her say the rest of the night. Loud, soft, desperate, begging. Over and over again.

I stole her mouth in a searing kiss, plunging inside the second she opened for me. Her hungry moan filled the air when I sucked on her tongue, my cock pulsing reflexively at the sound. I released her hair. I needed both hands to frame her face, to tilt her head to that angle that let me kiss her the way she liked best, the one that made her wrap her legs around my waist and twist my shirt.

I could kiss Reese for hours and never get tired of it. Get lost in her lips, dueling with her tongue, taking control, then backing off to let her lead. It wasn't just an appetizer to the main course. It was everything, all by itself.

When I had to pause to take a breath, I pulled back. "Take my shirt off."

She didn't hesitate, her nails scratching deliciously along my skin as she fought to tear the cotton from my torso. I squatted down to help her get it over my head, paying no attention to where she threw it.

"Now yours."

It was gone before I could blink, leaving behind those perfect breasts of hers just peeking over the edge of her sexy bra.

"Lean back."

Her eyes flew to mine as she reclined against the mirror, her hands reaching for me in quiet protest.

I caught her wrists and directed them to her chest.

"Play with them. I want to see you touching yourself up here while I'm touching you," I paused to run my hands from her knees to the tops of her thighs, not stopping until my thumbs rested right over the zipper of her shorts, "down here."

She bit her lip, her disheveled hair falling over her shoulder.

I worked on unfastening her shorts blindly, unable to tear my eyes away from the sight of her hands cupping and plumping her sweet tits. There was an awkward moment when I struggled to get her pink shorts down while she was sitting on the dresser—she had to drop her hands to help raise her hips—but then she was naked except for scraps of black lace.

"Squeeze your nipples." My voice was deeper than before, and my cock was hard as granite.

Reese pulled the cups of her bra down, letting those

creamy mounds spill over the sheer fabric. Her nipples were darker than I anticipated, a deep rose where I'd been expecting dusky pink. It'd been dark the first time in her dorm room, and she'd kept her shirt on the other times. The sight of those tightened peaks in the light were nearly my undoing, almost breaking my resolve to go slow this first time.

"More," I rasped.

I slipped my hands under the leg holes of her panties. With aching slowness, I softly traced the margin of her hot core, giving her the barest taste of the friction she craved.

She twisted and tugged those rosy buds, and it took all my self-control not to bend forward and pull one into my mouth. I shifted my thumbs closer together, able to feel the slickness of her now. I stroked around her clit but never quite touched it, watching the frustration grow on her face as she parted her lips and furrowed her brow.

Yes, Reese. Just like that.

"Laird," she panted, rocking her hips up to meet my roving hands.

"Not yet." I couldn't resist any longer. I captured one sexy nipple with my lips, sucking hard. Her hand slid around the back of my head, the scrape of her nails like thunder in my ears, and pulled me tighter to her chest.

I shifted. One hand slid behind her to work the clasp of her bra, the other stayed behind, my thumb finally, finally settling on her clit, making light circles meant to torment, not satisfy.

When her bra unsnapped, Reese removed it without needing prompting.

Good girl.

The hand on my head nudged me toward her other nipple.

"This one feeling neglected?"

She shivered and arched her back, propping her perfect mounds up higher like an offering. "Just a little."

I switched sides, using my tongue and the hard edge of my teeth to work her until she was undulating her hips in an increasingly desperate rhythm.

"I need you," she cried.

"You have me," I countered, kissing a wet path down her stomach until I reached the waistband of her underwear. I paused, then stood back to take a second to just look at her.

God, the sight of her in only those black lace panties. It did things to me that defied explanation.

My pulse skipped and settled into a new pattern, one with her name embedded in it, a rhythm that was more than just her and more than just me. It flowed through every blood vessel, strong and sure, a harmony more resonant than any symphony ever composed.

I never wanted it to end.

A strong bass note echoed off my ribs, bounced off my vertebrae.

I think I'm in love and I've never even been inside her.

I swallowed, oddly comfortable with the idea.

"Take them off," I ordered in a voice like gravel. "Slowly. Watch my face the whole time. Watch what you do to me."

I moved at the same time she did, undoing my shorts and dropping them to the floor in a well-practiced move. Without preamble, I reached inside my orange boxer briefs and gripped my aching dick, squeezing tight at the base to slow things down on my end.

"Now, Reese."

Her dark eyes were dilated as they flicked down to my groin, where the head of my hard length peeked over the top of the elastic.

"I promise, you can play with him all you want in a bit.

But right now, watch my face."

Slowly, her eyes trailed up my body, bouncing over the squares of my abs and pausing on my pecs before reaching my burning gaze.

"You're so incredibly sexy. I need to know that *you* know that." My focus dropped to her slender fingers, sliding the lace off one flared hip.

I shoved my boxers off, desperate to free myself.

To her credit, a quick glance showed her eyes were still glued to my face as directed.

"Keep going." My voice cracked as she lowered them off the other hip, until just the most intimate part of her was still hidden from view.

My nostrils flared and I clenched my jaw so hard, the muscle in my cheek jumped. I was mesmerized by the sight of her being slowly unveiled in front of me, but I was also so damn proud at the way she was responding to my orders. She wasn't shrinking back in shyness, or coyly refusing to play the game with me. Oh, no. Reese was right here in the moment with me, the perfect treble counterpoint to my bass.

I ran my hand over the head of my cock, where a bead of precum had already formed.

Lifting my eyes to hers, I caught and kept her gaze as she squirmed in front of me. One more wiggle and she was bare.

"You're beautiful."

She huffed out a small breath of disbelief. "You didn't even look yet."

I stepped forward, the underside of my dick pressing against her slick core, and ghosted a kiss over her swollen lips. "I don't need to see your pussy to know you're beautiful, Reese."

Her breath hitched, and her eyes got shiny. I tipped her

chin up, capturing her mouth in a kiss that was a blatant imitation to what I wanted to do to her somewhere lower. I rocked my hips, torturing us both by sliding along her seam, but not giving either one of us what we really wanted.

She felt exquisite. Petal soft, beckoning me closer with her wet heat. I wanted to bury myself in her and never reemerge.

When the urge to slip inside her grew too strong, I eased back and reached over to my nightstand to grab a condom, sheathing myself in milliseconds before returning to my spot between her legs.

With a grunt of anticipation, I positioned myself at her opening, rubbing the head through her wetness.

"Eyes down there now, Reese. Watch your body take every inch of me. You're so damn soaked, it's only going to take one push to be deep inside you, to have you squeezing me tight. Fucking hell, I'm ready to explode right now, just thinking about it." I pulled her forehead to mine, cupping the back of her neck as we both looked down. "Once I'm there, once I'm pumping in and out of you, I expect to see your hand on your clit. Understand?"

I felt her nod against me.

And then I couldn't wait any longer.

I flexed my hips and when her warmth enveloped me, hugging me tight within her snug channel, I ground out a primal sound that every man since the beginning of time would recognize. *Mine.*

"Now, Reese. Let me see you touch yourself." I shifted my hands until I gripped her legs beneath her knees, giving me the leverage I needed.

I didn't start slow. I didn't need to. She was ready, I was beyond ready, and waiting was no longer an option. My hips pounded a steady rhythm, and I tilted back a little so my thrusts focused on her front wall. That same position also gave me room to appreciate the way her middle finger rolled fast, hard circles around her pink nub. I moved faster, hammered my hips harder, knowing it was the right move when the muscles on her forearm tightened and her thighs squeezed and her breath came in ragged little pants.

"Laird," she gasped. "Yes. Like that."

"Keep rubbing, Reese. I won't stop if you don't."

She shook her head. "It's too much."

"It's not." I groaned as I bottomed out, pulling her forward on the dresser so my balls could slap against her ass with each plunge.

"I don't want it to end yet."

"We're not even close to done, beautiful," I promised. The night was young and my balls were full. I'd take her again and again, as long as she'd let me.

She whimpered, her knuckles on her free hand turning white as she squeezed the edge of the dresser.

"I'm close, Laird."

"I know. I got you."

Gently, I brushed her fingers from her mound, replacing them with my own. I found her most secret spot, tapping it lightly with my thumb.

"You ready?" I asked.

She nodded, the movement jerky.

I increased my pace, and pressed harder with my thumb, fast, tight, unrelenting circles.

She exploded seconds later, clamping down like a vise around my dick. As she cried out my name, I heard Oscar scratching at the door and howling in panic.

I thrust half a dozen more times, then followed her over the edge into the bright oblivion, slowly rocking my way through my orgasm.

"Reese." My voice was reverent. I wrapped her legs around my waist, gathering her in my arms and burying my face in the crook of her neck.

I couldn't help but steal little tastes of her damp skin as I nuzzled into her, not ready to let go yet.

Not ready to let go ever.

"It's never felt like that before," she whispered.

I paused, then leaned back and pushed her tangled hair behind her ears so I could see her face. Using my finger, I nudged her chin up.

"Like what? Did I hurt you?"

She chuckled and the knot of fear in my gut loosened a fraction. "Oh, I imagine I'm going to be feeling this tomorrow." Her dimple popped out, and unable to help myself, I bent down and kissed it. "But it'll be the best soreness I've ever felt."

My dick pulsed where it still lay nestled inside her.

"Then what?" My question was soft, cautious, as if she'd suddenly gotten skittish and I didn't want to scare her away with quick movements or loud sounds.

She blinked at me, long black lashes framing the most expressive brown eyes I'd ever seen.

"Right."

Fuck, I love you. The words burst inside me, but I clamped down hard on them, keeping them caged within me.

She wasn't ready for that. Hell, I wasn't sure I was ready for that.

And yet there they sat, the words thick and viscous, clogging my veins and drugging my mind.

"Oh, Reese," I murmured, banding my arms around her back and squeezing her to me. Even hugging her felt sublime. "There's nothing more right than you and me in this moment." I dipped my head until I could speak right into her ear. "Except finding it again and again and again."

Reluctantly, I pulled out of her, quickly taking care of the condom.

Then I hoisted her off the dresser, and took a step back until I felt the bed at the back of my knees. Holding her close, I lay back on the bed until we landed on the mattress with a soft thud, her on top of me. I groaned in contentment, loving the weight of her on my hips, her hair draping around my face, her little gasp of delight when her breasts rubbed against my chest.

"I've got a few more things I want you to do tonight. For starters, I need you to scoot up a little higher on my body."

"Higher?" She sounded sleepy, but I knew how to fix that.

My fingers flexed around her hips, urging her up. "Higher. Until you're riding my face. I'm ready for dessert."

CHAPTER 25

Reese

"**S**O, ON THE WAY BACK FROM THE GAME ON THE BUS, you just… slept?" Eli's eyebrows pinched together in disappointment, referring to the return trip from the football game against Mississippi last week. "Even though you won in overtime with the most fantastic play of the season? And then after the game ended, all the Sharks rushed the field and tore down their goal posts? You just… took a damn nap?" He screwed up his face like he'd just sucked on a lemon. "What's wrong with you, Reese? You're a college girl! You're supposed to be wild and crazy and stay up all night celebrating after a game like that. Even sick cancer kids know that much."

He shook his head in disgust, the striped beanie slipping down over one of his eyes until he shoved it back up. His small, pale fingers plucked at the plain white blanket covering his legs. "Did you ride back next to Laird at least?"

I narrowed my eyes at him. I hadn't seen Eli in almost two weeks, not since before I pulled the whole dildo stunt. When I'd volunteered the last few times, he'd been out of his room, in either physical therapy or radiology. But his last comment made me wonder what Laird might have said to Eli during *his* visits.

"No. Laird's a senior. I'm just a freshman. I sat next to my friend, Smith, since he's a freshman too. We got the crappy seats near the front of the bus."

"Bummer."

"Yeah, bummer," I echoed.

"I think Laird likes you. He told me you were pretty." Eli peered up at me, a sly expression crossing his face. "Are you dating him? I bet he'd like to date you."

I paused, snagging his hospital-issued pitcher and crossing to the sink under the pretense of getting him more water.

I don't know if I'd call what we were doing *dating* exactly. He'd made me dinner that one night last month, and I hadn't gotten dressed again until minutes before I walked out the door Monday morning, just in time to make my calculus class. And he'd stayed over at my place twice, fucking me as quietly as he could on the squeaky bed. But, unless I counted a group meal after band practice two days ago, we hadn't done anything else *date-like* since that first time because of our busy schedules.

Well.

Maybe.

He'd met me half a dozen times before my horrendously boring Humanities class to give me a giant Styrofoam cup of Cherry Coke Zero from the student center, making sure I had some caffeine to take in with me. It wasn't a date necessarily, but it was *something*, wasn't it?

And there was last Thursday when he'd skipped his second class, just so he could eat a turkey-and-cranberry sub with me next to the shark fountain. *Had that been a date?*

"You think so?" I stalled a bit longer as I wiped off stray water drops that had splashed around the sink.

"You *are* really pretty. And he has tattoos and muscles and stuff, so I bet you like him too. He's a really cool guy."

I found myself smiling softly in agreement. "He is a really cool guy." I rearranged the cups and pitcher next to the emesis basin on the wheeled table next to his bed. "So… you think I should date him?"

"Totally. And then maybe you guys can go on a double date with me and Amelia sometime. Y'all can take us down to the Starbucks next to the cafeteria or something."

"Oooooh, wait." I picked up his cold hand and squeezed. "Did you ask her out?"

He dipped his chin, hiding his gaze from me. "Sorta," he mumbled. "I tried."

"What happened?"

"That asshole Jaxon interrupted us before she could answer. He totally did that shit on purpose too."

I was no longer fazed by Eli's cussing. At this point, I would've been more concerned if he didn't drop an f-bomb during one of my visits.

"Did you try again?" I tucked his hand under the edge of the blanket, trying not to make it obvious I was fussing over him as I adjusted the covers.

"Not yet." He slumped against his mountain of pillows. "I want to make it special for her, you know? But I think I might be running out of time before I go home."

My heart broke over the longing in his words and I hurried to reassure him. "No, Eli. I promise. It's *never* too late for love. Haven't you learned anything watching TV around here?" I winked, because we both knew how tedious TV got after a while when you were stuck in the hospital. The morning shows, then *The Price is Right* and the court shows, then Lifetime movies until the primetime dramas started around dinnertime. Nothing decent worth watching until late night.

"Yeah. You're right." But his voice was dejected and quiet. "I heard her talking about the cake pops the other day. She likes the birthday cake ones the best because they're pink. I wanted to take her there to get one and a smoothie or something. But that's probably stupid."

"No. I think it sounds perfect!" I dug a pen and pad of paper out of my purse. "Let's work on what you can say when you ask her again. And before I leave, I'll run downstairs to buy a cake pop you can take to her now, so you have an excuse to go talk to her."

He raised his head, hope shining hesitantly in his eyes. "Yeah?"

"Yeah. Now, let's see how good your pick-up lines are."

Not that there was ever any doubt, but an hour later, Amelia said yes without even hesitating.

CHAPTER 26

Reese

EMPTY CEREAL BOX. CHECK.

Crumbs from stale candy bars. Check.

Dirty clothes strewn about in half a dozen places. Check.

I sprayed the room with Febreze to cover the stale scent of sweat and sour milk that seemed to linger in the air, then started working my way methodically around the room, from the far corner to the door. Something crunched under my foot—a mostly Styrofoam cup from the student center, the last dribble of soda now leaking out the side. I hurried to scoop it up before it made an even bigger mess.

Marco is fucking disgusting.

The same kind of yellow rubber gloves my grandma used to wash dishes were on my hands as I picked up a crusty wad of tissue near his trashcan. He'd apparently missed and couldn't be bothered to pick it up himself.

Empty condom wrappers hid underneath.

But—*interesting*. Two different sizes, hell, two different *brands*, one larger than the other. And just a few inches away from those was—

I stopped cold.

No. No, no, no, no, no, no.

Lollipop cellophane and a partially eaten grape lollipop.

I squeezed my eyes shut as I tossed it all in the trash, as if that would prevent the mental image of Marco *and Smith* from materializing in my head.

He wouldn't. He couldn't. With *Marco*?

He obviously did.

Twice, if I was judging by the condom wrappers I'd found.

At least I didn't find the actual used condoms. I gagged, dry heaving over the trashcan I'd just filled, the thought *that* repulsive. It wasn't the gay sex part that was weirding me out, it was picturing Marco naked in any way that was making me nauseated. I shuddered.

But actually, that explained a few things. Those times he ran right next to Smith on the track, picking Smith as his NAD, the way he seemed to overcompensate with the PDA at parties. Marco was either deep in the closet, or secretly bi. Or maybe he was just experimenting with Smith? Testing the waters?

I cleaned the rest of his room as best I could in ten minutes. I couldn't stand to be in there any longer than that. Everywhere I looked, I saw them.

Did they do it bent over his executive desk chair? Or on the rumpled bed? On the rug?

Oh, fuck. Did they have something going on regularly—like me and Laird? Was I somehow now part of their deception? I wanted absolutely no part of being in a threesome privy to that knowledge.

Trash bag in hand, I shuddered as I left Marco's room, careful to lock the door behind me.

Ugh, what was Smith thinking? Marco? Of all people?

I groaned as I walked into the already crowded building at 8:00. In the morning. On a Saturday. The Rodner Sharks were playing a non-conference away game against Maryland of all places, so it should've been a day off, a day to sleep in, a day to do *nothing*.

Instead, I'd be doing the 24-hour challenge known as Shark Day, where the entire band stayed within the confines of Boldt Auditorium from eight on Saturday morning to eight on Sunday morning. They called it a challenge to get around referring to what it really was—hazing. Anyone who slipped out or went unaccounted for at any point during the event was benched from the next halftime show. Supposedly, your final grade in the class would be knocked down ten points too, but I wasn't sure if that rumor was fact or fiction.

The first twelve hours were relatively uneventful. We practiced the new song we'd be adding to the halftime show, did stupid group bonding activities, and ate way too much pizza. But people were starting to get prickly, breaking off into groups, forming clumps in the dozen or so rooms that made up the music building, half of them just small practice rooms.

Even the bathrooms had turned into a sanctuary, people hiding out in the stalls trying to get a few minutes of privacy to text or scroll through Facebook without someone else looking over their shoulder.

And there were so many people around, I hadn't had a chance to corner Smith and ask him about the whole Marco situation I'd discovered yesterday. It was making me act weird around him, answering his questions tersely and staring at him in puzzlement when he wasn't looking, until he'd twist his head around and snap, "What?" in exasperation.

I made a lap around the building, weaving through the high-pitched giggles of the flutists and the third-grade humor of the trombone players. There was nowhere to escape, just noise and body odor and the gradually rising tension of people who knew they were trapped together for another twelve hours when they'd give their left big toe to be any-where, *anywhere* else because as much as marching band is a family, twenty-four hours is a fucking long time.

Free pizza only does so much for morale and goodwill toward your fellow man.

I was avoiding Laird too. Not because I didn't want to spend time with him, but because I was scared if I got close to him, it'd be obvious just how *much* I wanted him. It was getting harder and harder to pretend to only be platonic around him in public.

I wanted to hold his hand, or lean against him, or feel his arms wrap around me. I wanted to kiss him senseless, until his hand tangled in my hair and the world around us went hazy. I wanted to bask in that warm glow that filled my chest when his gorgeous green eyes followed the motion of my hips as I walked.

And this wasn't the place to do any of those things.

My phone dinged.

Laird: Where are you? Practice room 4C. It's empty right now. Except for me. Knock twice, pause, then twice again.

A quiet space. With Laird.

It was almost too good to be true.

Maybe I could give into my urges, if only for a few minutes.

I sidled around a trio of trumpeters who were arguing about whether bull sharks or great whites were the deadliest.

"Bull sharks," I muttered under my breath, and the ginger one raised his fist in solidarity.

"See? *Everyone* knows it. Even the little drummer girl."

I paused. My spine stiffened and I swiveled back around. "What did you call me?"

The blond one snickered to the tall one. "Didn't you hear? Apparently, there's nothing little about her. Especially not the size of her sex toys. She must have the loosest vag on the line, probably from overuse. All those private parties they have? You know they're getting a taste of that."

My ears were so hot, they threatened to spontaneously combust.

What.

The.

Fuck.

I struggled to pull air into my lungs, not sure whether I wanted to punch him in the throat or cry. Humiliation burned like acid as I tried to swallow. I hadn't realized news of my little stunt was being twisted in such a vulgar way, that I'd been given a fucking *nickname* on top of it all. And even though they never said his name, my thoughts shot straight to Laird.

This.

This is what I'd been worried about when it came to getting involved with another drummer.

And not just any snare player.

The fucking captain.

I opened my mouth, not even sure what I was going to

say, but ready to explode nonetheless.

But just then, Marco materialized at my side, looping his arm around my shoulders and pulling me into an awkward half hug, half headlock. "Just the hotshot I've been looking for. I need to talk to you about the stuff you left behind in my room."

The trumpeters snorted and elbowed each other knowingly.

My eyes burned and my hand shook as I balled it into a fist.

"I didn't leave anything in your room, Marco," I said with venom, reluctantly following him as he led me down the hallway. Room 4C was this direction anyway.

Fucking trumpet players. Fucking Marco. Fucking stupid guys with their stupid fucking opinions.

He stopped at room 3A, shoved open the door, and ordered the pair of clarinet players making out in the corner to leave.

Then he locked the soundproof door.

"I found some fuzzy black shirt on my desk chair. I assumed it was yours. I threw it away. Hope you didn't want it back."

Shit. My favorite North Face fleece from home. It had been a little chilly that morning, but I'd warmed up cleaning the room and forgotten I had taken it off.

I clenched my jaw. "Nope. Wasn't mine."

"You sure?" He watched me closely.

I shrugged. "Maybe it was Smith's?" I was so mad, the words fell from me without thinking, but when I saw the look of panic flash across his face, I followed my instinct, sensing a rare weakness in his armor.

A ball of guilt sat heavy and leaden in my gut, but my anger at those dumb pricks and Marco burned hotter, erasing my normal tendency for caution.

I'd beg Smith for forgiveness later, but right now, the line of questioning had been cast, and I couldn't take it back.

Would he take the bait?

My heart tried to burrow right out of my chest it was beating so hard.

Marco narrowed his eyes, and the fingers of his left hand tapped restlessly against his thigh. "What makes you think he was in my room?"

The condom wrapper that was way, way too big for anything you have tucked in your too tight pants.

"I picked up some grape lollipops near your desk. I thought maybe you'd had him over or something. You know, since you're his vet and all." I scratched at a spot near my elbow where a mosquito had gorged on me the day before, trying to look casual.

"Oh. Yeah. That."

Hook. Line. *Sinker.*

"Or maybe it was Amber's?" I added sweetly, tossing out the safety net only after he was thoroughly caught in the trap.

"You know what? The fleece was probably hers. She's been coming over. And coming. A lot." He snickered and my stomach churned.

Riiiiiiight. because you're such a stud. I rolled my eyes. I started to turn away but he moved into my path, shoving his face too close to mine. I jerked my neck back, but kept my feet planted.

"You didn't see anything, Reese. You hear me? Nothing." His voice turned ugly and vaguely menacing.

Whoa. The aggression in his stance and tone took me off guard. "Nope. Sure didn't," I agreed, hurrying to placate his prickly temper. He'd already confirmed what I wanted to know. No reason to dig deeper. And, honestly, I felt bad for Smith. I couldn't imagine Marco as anything but a selfish lover. I motioned toward the door he was blocking. "Can I leave now?"

He grinned, sitting on the floor, his back against the locked opening, and tugged his hat low over his face, an action that brought his eyes level with my crotch. "Not for a few hours. I need a nap. I also need someone who can verify I didn't leave the premises. I pick you."

I took a few hasty steps back, not liking the way I filled his line of sight. A sliver of fear snaked around my ribs, squeezing the breath out of me. *Did he think I was going to sleep with him?* The locked door, the soundproof room, the rumors the trumpet players were spreading...

My rising panic must have shown on my face because he sneered at me, wrinkling his nose in distaste.

"Relax, hotshot. I'm not gonna touch you. Hell, you can take a nap too as far as I'm concerned. I don't care what the fuck you do over there, as long as you stay quiet and don't leave." He pinned me with his stare. "Is that really such a hard request from the snare line lieutenant to a NAD?"

I swallowed down my angry retort, knowing fighting him on this would result in something much worse than listening to him snore for a while.

"Nope. Sounds just *peachy*. I'll take this corner over here, if you don't mind."

"Don't care what the fuck you do. Just shut your mouth and wake me up around midnight or so. That's usually when they bring more pizza."

Hot resentment flooded through me. He was holding me hostage to be his damn alarm clock.

I pulled out my phone.

Me: Can't. I'm stuck with Marco in 3A until midnight.

Any chance you can rescue me?

I hit send, but nothing happened.

I tried again.

My phone powered off, the battery dead. My charger was in my bag in the other room.

I banged my head uselessly against the soundproof padding on the wall.

A dozen cutting remarks shuffled through my mind, but I kept my mouth shut. And anyway, his chin was tucked to his chest, his breaths coming slow and easy. Like this, Marco looked softer, as if he would be the type to hold the door for gray-haired ladies at the grocery store. Except—his arms wrapped around his lean torso, almost protectively, and his hands were curled up tight. It wasn't quite the loose-limbed sprawl of someone at home in their own skin.

I didn't like him, plain and simple. At the core of his being was something mean and little, someone who thrived on getting ahead at the expense of others.

But I only had to get through a few more months of his bullshit until football season ended. After that, there wasn't any reason to interact with him again—assuming he graduated on time.

With a resigned sigh, I surveyed the room. Beyond the piano along the far wall and a group of chairs and music stands, there wasn't much in the room besides a whiteboard with a few bars of music scrawled across it. The door was windowless, and there was no way to open it and leave without waking Marco. His legs stretched out across the opening.

I could do this. I could let him win this stupid little round in the battle between us. This was nothing. And maybe the boost to his ego would buy me some peace for a week or two. Let him think I was firmly under his control.

Minutes passed.

I counted the ceiling tiles. Four hundred and sixteen. Or was it eighteen?

I started counting again. Before I could finish the second time, Marco was snoring, phlegmy little snorts as he inhaled.

It was annoying as hell.

Yet I must've dozed myself at some point, because a particularly loud thud outside the door startled me awake. The clock on the pale blue wall read 11:49.

Thank God.

Eleven minutes later, I kicked his ankle. "Wake up. Pizza's here," I said flatly.

Then I reached over him, and pulled the door open just enough to slide out, forcibly pushing his body a few inches along the floor. He tipped over, grunting out a surprised protest, but I didn't pause, squeezing through the small crack to the overly bright hallway.

Laird rounded the corner and spotted me instantly, concern furrowing his brow. He quickened his step, tipping his head toward the water fountain two doors down. I met him there, my frayed nerves soothed just by being near him.

"Where have you been?" His voice was rough and his eyes ran over me quickly, as if assessing for damage.

A door shut behind us, and he twisted around to see Marco exit the same room I'd just come out of. A scowl marred his handsome face when he turned back to me.

"You okay? Did he try to do something?" Laird's muscles bunched under his shirt, threatening the integrity of the seams around his biceps.

"Nothing I couldn't handle. Just some stupid mind game." I shook my head, and stooped to drink some tepid water from the fountain. "My phone died—I tried to message you."

He started to reach for me, but caught himself, letting his arm drop back to his side. "I waited for an hour, then I came out to look for you. I was starting to get worried, but then I thought maybe you were mad at me or something." He shuffled his feet and ran a hand over the back of his head, gripping his neck. "I sent you a bunch of texts, but I guess you didn't get them."

My shoulders drooped. "I'm sorry."

His smile didn't quite reach his eyes. "I polished up all the snare harnesses in the equipment room. Made myself useful for a few hours."

I winced. That was a task NADs usually did, not a senior. *Definitely* not the captain.

"Laird," I whispered, not sure what to say.

He leaned his weight against the wall, blocking anyone in that direction from seeing his hand as he tangled his fingers with mine. "Spend the rest of Sunday with me—when we get out of here. I can make it through the next eight hours if I know I get you all to myself afterward."

"And do what?" A small grin lifted the corner of my mouth.

"Fuck, that dimple of yours," he breathed. "You have no idea how crazy it makes me."

My lips spread into a wicked smile, and I peered up at him from under my lashes. "How crazy?"

He took a step closer and pulled my hand to the front of his shorts, where I could feel him hardening. I ran my palm down him once, twice, before I remembered where we were and stopped.

His eyes were closed, lips parted as he inhaled deeply. "I can smell you from here. Cherries and flowers. I want my pillow to smell like that before I fall asleep tonight." He opened his eyes halfway, Irish green lust simmering back at me. "How do you feel about that?"

"I think that can be arranged," I murmured, feeling an answering tingle between my thighs. I smoothed my hair behind my ears, trying to keep from launching myself at him.

"Well. This looks cozy." Marco's dark gaze flashed back and forth as he stepped in between us to get a drink of water. "I'm not interrupting anything, am I?"

Laird shifted, standing to his full height. "Nothing I need your help with."

Marco wiped his mouth on his shirt sleeve. "Reese. Funny, I haven't seen you around for the last few hours." His voice rose, attracting the attention of the assistant band director and a few drum majors coming down the hall. "Did you sneak out? You know that's against the rules."

I gaped at him. *Was he fucking kidding me right now?*

The band director paused, trying to get a read on the situation. "Is there a problem here?"

Marco shrugged, a triumphant smirk on his face. "Just asking Reese here if she can tell me where she's been for the last three hours or so. I know I haven't seen her around anywhere."

The lying son of a bitch. If I told the truth now, he'd deny it. I knew it in my marrow.

Laird cleared his throat. "She's been with me."

Marco's eyebrows winged up. "She has?" His voice had a hard edge to it, blatantly challenging Laird's claim.

Laird turned and stared him right in the eyes. "I've had her polishing all the snare harnesses. With a toothbrush. Since *I'm* her vet and all." He took half a step back and gestured toward the equipment room. "Feel free to double check her work. She did a good job, even on yours."

Marco's mouth pinched closed, and he glanced between Laird and me. "So, it was just the two of you? How convenient."

The assistant band director opened his mouth to speak but Laird cut him off. "Nope. Smith was there for a while too, but since he worked faster, I cut him loose after the first hour. Made Reese finish up solo." Laird cocked his head in fake concern, his voice soft but steely with an underlying challenge. "Do you have a problem with my methods? Are you questioning how I'm handling things?"

Oh shit. I tried to blend into the wall, because—all the sudden—this wasn't about me anymore. I mean, it was, but it wasn't.

Marco knew Laird was lying. It was in the way his face was screwed up in confusion, as if he couldn't figure out why the captain would go out on a limb for *the little drummer girl*. But he also couldn't call Laird out on it without revealing his own deception.

They had one of those weird staring contests guys have sometimes, each trying to out intimidate the other.

The assistant band director turned to me, flustered. "So…"

I widened my eyes and painted the most angelic smile on my face. "I was scrubbing hardware. Like Laird said."

Marco snarled at me, tearing his gaze away from Laird in the process, before turning and stomping away down the hall.

Dear holy angels in heaven who kept track of all these white lies on a never-ending tally sheet.

Sides had just been taken.

Laird and me against him.

And he'd just lost.

CHAPTER 27

Laird

THE LITTLE YELLOW OCTOPUS ON MY SCREEN REFUSED to swim higher, regardless of how many times I woodpeckered the button. He'd stop, go, turn right or left, and sink lower, but *not* swim up and follow the bubbles. For the fourteenth time, he got stuck in the coral and the timer ran out on the level.

Fucking hell. I almost threw my phone across the room. The code for the app I was developing as part of my Video Game Design class had been fighting me since last weekend. All the earlier design steps—the graphics, the sounds, the scoring algorithms—had gone smoothly, but *somewhere* there was an error in the programming that I just couldn't find. Oh, and this next stage of the project was due Monday night, four days from now.

I should've spent more time on it earlier in the week when I first integrated the graphics, but I assumed it'd be an easy fix—like all the other stumbling blocks I'd hit with the project so far. A little tweak and it'd be handled. And despite staying up until after three this morning trying to rework the directional commands, the little fucker still refused to cooperate.

Swallowing back my frustration, I switched out of the app and checked my texts to see if Reese was going to make it to practice today. If she didn't show up after already missing Tuesday's practice, I'd have no choice but to give her spot in Friday's game to an alternate. I hated to do it, but those were the rules.

Me: Feeling better?

Reese: No. Still puking. I already emailed the director and he told me I was benched from the Georgia game. This fucking sucks. My guts hate me.

She'd had a wicked stomach virus for the last three days. I'd spent the last two nights in her dorm room with her—because she refused to come to my townhouse—microwaving cups of broth and forcing her to drink plenty of water and Gatorade in between her trips to the bathroom.

Reese hadn't wanted me to be there, hadn't wanted me to see her like that. Pale, sweaty, damp hair clinging to her face—none of that mattered to me. She was still beautiful and there was no place I would've rather been than by her side. Her nausea didn't make me squeamish, maybe because I'd seen Garrett like that so much when I was younger.

Eventually, she'd given in and let me fuss over her a bit. She'd laid in my lap on that little bed, cool washcloth over her hot forehead, making a sound that was halfway between a groan and a hum as I ran my fingers through her tangled hair. I'd murmured nonsense words to her until she fell into a restless sleep, shivering under the blankets and then kicking them off her sweaty body as the fever rose and broke.

Ignoring her protests, I'd skipped two classes, only going to the ones with mandatory attendance, because I'd needed to feel like I was *doing* something to help her, even if it was just to sit by her side while she napped in between bouts of vomiting.

But I couldn't help worrying it was something more.

I held her thin wrist and counted her pulse while she slept, watched the rise and fall of her chest for her respirations. Her long, tan limbs showed no unusual signs of bruising, and my fingers didn't trip over any enlarged lymph nodes when I massaged the back of her tense neck. *But was she paler than normal?* I told myself it was dehydration, not anemia. I googled all the signs of leukemia reoccurrence and alternately reassured myself and fretted over the multitude of subtle symptoms.

Fatigue.

Loss of appetite.

Dizziness.

Fever.

Night sweats.

Weight loss.

All things that could've resulted from a normal, garden-variety stomach virus.

Not cancer.

Not like Garrett.

And so I pushed my worst fears to the darkest recesses of my mind and shoved them behind a steel door. I focused on making her laugh until her dimple appeared. Showed her stupid YouTube videos and rubbed her feet. Changed her sheets and washed her clothes. Helped her memorize the Krebs cycle for biology and reassured her that missing a football game if she wasn't better wouldn't be the end of the world.

Friday's game pitted the Rodner Sharks against the Georgia Bulldogs, who we were expected to crush on the scoreboard. Those games were never as exciting as when the teams were more closely matched and the predicted winner was not only highly debated, but conference rankings hinged on the outcome. She'd still get to play in the stands and be part of the whole game day, she'd just miss marching in the actual show.

I hadn't seen her yet today. Thursdays were my busiest days, with an anatomy lab and a computer lab session back to back.

Me: Do you want me to come over again tonight?

I winced as I typed it. I *wanted* to be there. I wanted it almost more than I wanted to breathe. But I also needed to focus on my damn video game project, and it wouldn't be easy to do that from her dorm.

Reese: I keep telling you, you don't have to take care of me. You're a computer science major, not a nursing one.

Me: I'll bring you dinner at least. Think you could nibble on one of your favorite subs?

That way I could check on her, I rationalized. I wouldn't stay, I'd just drop off some food and make sure she was set for the night. Reassure myself that she was on the mend and didn't need to be hauled down to the Student Health Center.

Reese: That actually sounds really good. First time food has sounded tempting in days. But you don't have to, Laird. It's out of your way. I can call and have it delivered.

She could, but I'd rather bring it to her.

Reese had tried to get me to leave every time I'd shown up, protesting she was perfectly capable of taking care of herself—but that wasn't the point. Reese didn't *have* to take care of herself.

She had *me*.

And if there was one thing I'd promised myself after watching my mom disappear and my dad fade into an emotionless shell of a human after Garrett's death, it was that you didn't just abandon the ones you loved when it wasn't pretty. When it wasn't fucking *convenient*.

That's when you loved more. You loved *harder*.

And since I hadn't said the words to her yet, all I had were my actions.

All I had was myself.

And I wanted it to be enough.

I wanted to be enough for her.

And, project be damned, the least I could do was pick her up a fucking sub.

Me: I'll be there. As soon as practice is over.

Content that I'd gotten in the final word, I tucked my phone away and slogged through what felt like the longest two hours of the day.

I gave Reese's spot on the field to Heath, and the choreography only seemed to confuse him. Instead of rising to the occasion, he wandered aimlessly from point to point, always a little too fast or a little too slow, sticking out instead of blending in.

Keeping my frustration in check exhausted the last of my patience, so when practice ended, and Marco called my name as I headed toward the exit after stowing my gear, my tone was clipped and to the point. "What?"

"I was thinking we should make a new snare duel for Saturday. It's been the same for the last few shows; it's about time to switch it up, don't you think?"

Why? Why, why, why? What we had worked great and, most importantly, we already had it mastered.

I leveled a barely concealed glare his direction. "And

you want to change it *now*? For the show we play in two fucking days?"

"Hey, man. You're *the best player on the line*, right?" His sarcasm came through loud and clear. "I didn't think it'd be that hard for you. I know I can handle it."

He threw the challenge down like a grenade.

The muscle in my jaw ticked as I searched for any last shred of self-control lurking in my sleep-deprived body. Anything to help me deal with his habit of talking out his ass.

"Next week. You want to rework it, we do it next week. You know the drill. We have to pass off any changes with the director before it makes the show. And he's out of town until the game Saturday."

The assistant director had run practice today.

I shifted my bookbag on my shoulders and fished my car keys out of my pocket.

Marco scowled. "What? You don't think we can get it ready in a few hours and get it checked off before game day starts? Where do you have to run off to so fast?"

I retreated a step from the thread of aggression in his tone. Not because I was scared. But because I wasn't entirely sure how we'd gotten to this point. We'd played side by side for years, and while our close friendship had faded over time, we'd always still maintained a certain camaraderie. But these days, if felt more like we weren't even on the same team.

"I've got a project due. It's called homework, Marco. And I don't have some cymbal girl under my spell doing all my assignments for me."

His face turned a blotchy, ruddy color. "What are you implying? Go on and say it outright."

I tipped my head back and focused on the thin white

contrail from a jet passing overhead. I sighed. We only had five games left in the regular season. Five games left before my career as a snare drummer was *over*.

And I was starting to look forward to it, just to escape this asshole.

"I'm *saying*, your whim to redo the snare duel all of the sudden is *not* my main priority. It's just not. Maybe next week, man. I'm out of here."

I didn't wait for him to respond.

I didn't have to.

I was the fucking captain of the best damn snare line in the whole Southeast.

And I had a turkey and cranberry sub to deliver.

CHAPTER 28

Reese

DESPITE SUMMER MELTING INTO FALL, TEMPERATURES still hovered in the eighties as we slogged through the choreography for a new song at Tuesday's practice. This would be the final song we added to the show—Bon Jovi's "Who Says You Can't Go Home".

It was a pointed reminder I'd only answered my mom's endless calls with short texts for the last two weeks. Guilt added to the weight of the snare drum hanging heavy on my shoulders.

And maybe it was some lingering dehydration from the stomach virus, or the fact that I'd barely seen or heard from Laird since last Thursday while he wrestled with his video game project, but I was off today. I couldn't concentrate on the footwork, I struggled with my entrances on the chorus, and I'd quit sweating twenty minutes ago—never a good sign.

By the time practice ended, I wasn't even sure I'd get to reclaim my spot on the field that I'd been forced to yield to Heath last week. He'd been on point today, and I wouldn't blame them for picking him over me. I needed to step it up on Thursday.

As we put away our equipment, the room reeking of male sweat and trampled grass from the practice field, I tucked an extra pair of drumsticks in my bag, planning to practice on the drum pad in my dorm later. I didn't want to lose that damn spot. I'd worked too hard for it.

Glad to be rid of the cumbersome snare harness, I rolled my stiff shoulders and in the process, glanced over and spotted Laird slumped against the wall a few feet away, scrubbing his face with his hands.

"Did you get the bug in the game worked out by midnight?" I knew that's when he'd needed to turn the next stage of his project in.

Around us, guys packed their bags and traded insults, typical after-practice behavior.

"No." His voice was curt as he looked at his phone impatiently, checking something on the screen. "But I got the professor to give me an extension until tomorrow night since my game was more ambitious than most."

"That's good!" I winced as my words came out weaker than I'd intended, sounding almost sarcastic instead of encouraging. I'd been hoping to grab some dinner with him tomorrow, and I tried to wipe the disappointment from my expression.

"Yeah." He waited as I drained the last of my water bottle. "You feeling okay? You had a rough practice."

My ears burned. He was right, but I was hoping it hadn't been noticeable. I peeked around the room to see if anyone was listening to us, but everyone seemed engrossed in their own conversations.

"I'm good. Just a bad day. I'll review the music some more before Thursday so there won't be any problems for this weekend," I assured him.

"Good."

My brows pinched. I didn't like this distracted, short-tempered version of Laird. He was still gorgeous, those tanned forearms crossed over his broad chest and his full lower lip sticking out in a slight pout, but stress radiated from him like steam from the sidewalk after the rain.

I slid a little closer, leaned against the blessedly cool concrete wall next to him, and bumped him softly with my hip. He shot me a questioning glance. Laird was shirtless like half the other guys on the snare line, and while I tried hard not to openly ogle the carved lines of his abs, seeing that inked G on his chest gave me an idea that might cheer him up.

"I can tell by the way you've talked about him that you're close with your brother—have you thought about giving him a call? Seeing if he can make it to the game this weekend?"

"My brother?" His words sounded strangled and unnaturally loud.

The whole room froze as if someone had paused a video while they ran to the kitchen to grab a soda. No one moved or spoke, but a dozen pairs of eyes volleyed between Laird and me.

He'd gone rigid, the blood draining from his face.

Alarm rippled from my spine outward, until my fingers tingled with it, until I could barely breathe from the weight of the stares on me, heavier than a thousand snare drums.

"What?" I whispered.

Marco's voice lashed out. "Wow, hotshot, I can't believe

you went there. Bringing up his dead brother like that. Good one." He started a slow clap, staring at me pointedly. No one joined in.

"Wh-what?" My eyes whipped to Laird, but all I caught was his back as he charged out the door, pushing it open so hard it slammed against the wall in his wake. I looked back at Marco, the words not making any sense. "He's dead?"

My mind spun, trying to put together the broken puzzle pieces of our prior conversations, trying to see the whole picture instead of just the edges.

The inked G on his chest. Does he have an L on his? I'd asked. But Laird hadn't answered.

The stories from when they were kids. But none from when they were older.

The way Laird seemed so taken with Eli at the hospital.

Dizziness swamped me.

"What happened?" My voice was thick and garbled as I forced the words out. "When? How?"

Marco snorted. "You really don't know?"

I could only shake my head mutely, silently pleading with him to tell me, to tell me so I could figure out how badly I'd just fucked things up.

"Cancer. Leukemia or something when he was a kid. It messed Laird up real bad for a long time." Marco's face softened infinitesimally.

Leukemia.

The word hit me like a sledgehammer, and I slid to the floor, covering my face with shaky hands.

Marco huffed derisively. "Fucking girls. *This* is why we never had them on the line." Grunts of agreement came from the corner.

He walked out before I could reply, not that I could find any words.

Leukemia. Like me.

But I'd survived. And his brother, his brother that he'd clearly loved, had died.

What did that mean? How did that affect him? And did that—did that affect *us*? Was that part of why he was with *me*? Pity? Or some weird hero complex? Did he want to try to save me where he'd failed his brother?

But I don't need saving—or pity, dammit. I'm not a fucking victim.

My stomach churned, and acid rose until its bitter taste filled the back of my throat. Had I misread everything? Was this thing between us, this murky, undefined thing that had started to feel so damn real—the most raw, real thing I'd ever felt in my life—was it all built on the memory of a ghost?

I vaguely registered the other guys filing out, until Smith was the only one left. He crouched in front of me, waved his hand in front of my unseeing eyes until I blinked and he came into focus in front of me.

"What have I done?" I stared at him, stared *through* him, asking my best friend, asking the universe.

My world sublimated with one innocent question, leaving me lost in a cloud of gray vapor with no sense of direction.

Smith just shook his head and moved next to me, wrapping his arm around my shoulder as I sat there, stunned and blinking.

Minutes passed—or maybe hours, time seemed irrelevant—and my confusion morphed to anger.

Why hadn't Laird told me? The other guys on the line all seemed to know—even Smith. I was the only one who was surprised.

Was it purposeful? Had he been hiding it? It's not like

he never mentioned Garrett. He told me all those stories from when they were kids—about the tire swing and the broken arm.

Did he not think I could handle the truth? That I was too fragile to hear it? *Of course,* I knew some kids died of leukemia. That had been the biggest danger of making friends during treatment—the day when your friend never showed up again and you were left behind, fighting the invisible enemy alone.

Or had I not been important enough to mention it to, even in passing? Especially after all the times I'd seen him at the hospital volunteering? Or had he thought we wouldn't be together long enough that I'd need to know some of the most basic facts about his family history?

And if he'd lied about something that major in his life—by omission or otherwise—what else had he lied about?

My heart cracked, a searing heat filling the hollow cavity in my chest, until even breathing hurt.

Everything hurt.

A tear snaked down my cheek and Smith pulled me to his side, not saying a word, just letting me lean against him as I cried silently.

For Garrett, who I'd never get to meet.

For Laird.

For me.

The truth hit as hard as cancer. Out of the blue. When I wasn't expecting it. When I'd made myself comfortable and my defenses were down.

I wasn't sure what to think or believe.

Except…

I wasn't sure I could trust Laird. Not anymore.

Not when it came to my heart.

CHAPTER 29

Reese

I CALLED HIM FROM THE HAVEN OF MY DORM ROOM about an hour after the bombshell dropped, hating to text about something so deeply personal.

"Hey," he answered, his voice low and raw.

I hesitated, not sure how to broach a subject he'd purposefully avoided around me. "Laird…"

"I know," he paused, a rasp filling the silence as if he'd blown out a hard breath, "I know I should've told you about him. And I will. But not right now, not while I have this damn project hanging over my head. I need to focus on getting it done. No distractions."

I blinked, not saying anything, because suddenly I fell under the *distraction* category.

"Look, this project is my whole fucking grade for this class, and—"

He kept talking, some justification about needing the

elective to graduate on time, but it was just noise in my ear at that point.

That word—distraction—echoed in my head.

"Okay? We'll talk later."

I didn't get a chance to reply before he hung up.

I hadn't heard from him since.

Not later that night. Not this morning, and not once during classes today.

The rejection stung and jagged insecurities swamped me.

I was in the middle of wiping the sticky crumbs from my peanut-butter-and-honey sandwich off my hands when the phone buzzed after dinner on Wednesday. My anxiety bubbled up and I grabbed it, ignoring the honey I smeared across the screen in the process, both hoping and dreading it was Laird telling me he'd finished up early.

While part of me couldn't see past the hurt and humiliation, the other, bigger part argued that he deserved a chance to explain his side of the story. To tell me why he kept such a huge part of his life a secret from me for months.

But the text on the screen wasn't from Laird.

Marco: Extra practice tonight because somebody didn't have their shit together yesterday. 7 @ Shark Tank. No drums. We're just going over choreo.

Marco: Laird won't be there, he's got that project due, so I'm handling this one.

I pinched my lips with a flash of irritation. It was already after five. And a quick glance out the window confirmed heavy, gray clouds were rolling in from the west side of campus, covering the sky and making it seem later than it really was. Frowning, I typed out a response.

Me: There's a storm coming.

His answer came swiftly, almost as if he'd been anticipating it.

Marco: Scared of a little water, hotshot? Gonna melt?

I bristled, but refrained from texting back a snarky reply. Instead, I sighed and spent the next hour flying through my calc and biology homework before changing into running tights and tank top. I dug out my oldest tennis shoes, since sandals weren't allowed for practices and whatever I wore was going to get soaked.

By the time I reached the stadium on the far side of campus, the clouds had moved firmly into the offensive position, angry and squatting over the field, which was fine by me because it matched my mood perfectly.

This was going to suck.

As I emerged from the North archway, entering the field near the end zone, it became clear this was either a private practice or everyone else was late.

Instantly wary, I slowed, pausing to stow my bag with my phone where it'd stay dry under an overhang. Wiping my sweaty palms on my thighs, I reminded myself that I could handle Marco. I'd dealt with him since the season started and there were only a few weeks left. But my eyes flickered everywhere, searching for anything out of the ordinary.

I've got this.

Marco leaned against the opposite goal post, looking tiny and inconsequential in comparison, and watched me from under straight dark brows as I walked closer. The rain started with a hiss, small, prickling drops that lowered the temperature a handful of degrees.

I shivered as I approached, wondering what fresh hell he intended to dish out tonight.

"You sucked yesterday at practice. I noticed. Laird

noticed. Everyone fucking noticed."

"I'm sorry." It made something twist and pinch inside me to apologize to him for anything—but he was right. And damn if that didn't sting to admit.

"I think you're weak, Holland. I don't think you can keep up. I don't think you belong on the line, yet here I am, taking time out of my busy-ass schedule to come down here just to *help* you." The drizzle dotted his gray shirt.

I sucked in a breath, purposefully keeping several feet between us. There was venom in his voice. Not just simple dislike, but something that went deeper than that. I threatened his fragile masculinity, had made him look like a fool in front of his peers—his friends—at the party. And I'd known he couldn't just let that go.

"I had a bad day." I internally grimaced at the defensiveness of my tone. "I practiced the snare part for an hour earlier, I've got it down now. I'll be ready for the game."

He curled his lip. "We'll see." Straightening, he indicated the damp field in front of him with a tilt of his head. "I've got the music on my phone. Get out there and show me you know the movements."

My brow furrowed. This—this wasn't standard, not that Marco had ever followed the rules unless it suited him. To some extent, I memorized the drill by my relative position to the drummers next to me, to the rest of the band flowing around us. The whole idea of marching the song solo seemed awkward and wrong and doomed to fail from the start.

I took my mark on the midway point of the thirty-yard line and looked over to where he'd positioned himself on the fifty.

"Ready." I pitched my voice to be heard over the rain

that was falling steadily now, making my clothes cling to my torso.

He pressed his screen and I could barely hear the end of the previous song over the wind.

5, 6, 7, 8, and *move.*

I kept my shoulders back and rolled my feet as I crossed to the forty and then shifted back along the painted line. I normally stopped when I was even with the trumpets, who of course weren't there to use as a landmark. I fumbled through the rest of the song, marching with confidence at times, and haphazardly at others. How did I mime weaving in and out of the other snare players when they weren't here?

When the last note of the song faded out, I was two steps off the thirty-five, closer to the sidelines than the middle of the field. Right where I was supposed to be.

He stalked over to where I stood, my ponytail dripping down my back and water squishing in my socks.

"What the fuck was that?"

"A new Bon Jovi classic stunningly reimagined by the Rodner University marching band?"

He didn't appreciate my smartass answer, if the glower darkening his face was any indication.

"You seem out of breath, NAD. Is stamina the problem?" He reached out to wipe the precipitation off my cheek, a useless attempt considering the full-on storm we were standing in.

I recoiled, not missing the way his eyes dipped down, assessing the way the cold had made my nipples bead behind my sports bra. Hunching my shoulders, I tugged at my sodden shirt.

Thunder echoed in the distance like a timpani, and bursts of lightning lit up scattered fragments of the sky.

I licked my lips, tasting the sweetness of the raindrops, knowing it was pointless to deny his accusation.

He smiled, an earnest, magnanimous smile. "Maybe running some stadiums would help? A little extra cardio for missing practice last week?"

My eyes skipped up the endless rows of seats. While the Shark Tank wasn't as steep as Death Valley at Clemson, it was still a long way to the top.

A bone-jarring boom of thunder crashed nearby, making the hair on my arms stand up. I ducked reflexively. Marco stood stoic, as if he didn't feel the wind or the storm pelting us, as if the clouds were an audience he was performing for.

Then he shrugged indifferently, turning toward the end zone. "I'm just trying to help you, hotshot. I'd hate for you to lose your spot on the field this week too."

The threat hung between us despite his nonchalant posture, the implicit dare that I couldn't hack it.

Fuck that.

And fuck him.

Yeah, I could leave, but then what? Lose my spot because of a bully who was threatened by a girl? I'd never been one to back down from a challenge, if for no other reason than for years people gave me a pass, an exception.

Oh, Reese. The cancer girl. Well-intentioned teachers offering breaks on homework, more time to take the test or run the mile, giving me a different—easier—version of the exam everyone else was taking.

Everyone treated me differently and I was fucking sick of it.

If nothing else, Marco's scorn was refreshing in a sense. Not only was he not cutting me any slack, he pushed me harder than everyone else. And I refused to back down, the same way I'd refused to be held to different standards in school.

Watch me prove you wrong might as well have been my motto since I'd been declared cancer-free all those years ago.

I wrung out my ponytail uselessly. "Stadiums, huh?" I indicated the closest staircase with my chin. "How many?"

He shrugged, like he suddenly didn't care anymore, but his eyes glittered with challenge. "I normally do the whole West and South sections myself. Since you're a girl though… maybe just the West?"

Oh, *hell* no, he did not just go there. The smirk twisting his face had my hands clenching into fists and my elbows stiffening at my sides.

"The West *and* South. Got it."

Without looking back, I took off at an easy lope, knowing I needed to warm up my muscles before I ratcheted it up to a faster pace. The seats rattled as lightning hit closer. I faltered, but kept climbing. All the way up, and all the way down. Over and over and over.

As I splashed up and down the steps, my mind drifted to Laird and what he'd think of this whole evening. No doubt he'd be furious and would've put a stop to things long before now. But I couldn't bring myself to tattle to him, to ask for help in dealing with Marco.

No special privileges.

If I was going to make it on the drumline, I was going to make it on my own.

I clenched my jaw and kept climbing.

By the time I'd finished the West and halfway through the South, the storm raged as if it had a personal vendetta against empty college football stadiums. My sweat mixed with the downpour, the combination burning my eyes, and

I concentrated on where my feet were landing, the sky dark and the steps slick.

Marco lounged near the bottom of the section I was on, watching me from beneath the soaked brim of a Rodner Sharks baseball hat. He seemed bored with the whole thing, but I refused to stop, to allow him the satisfaction of me giving up.

I was about two dozen stairs from the bottom when it happened.

My right foot slid right out from under me, and I threw my arms out instinctively to catch myself as my momentum sent me hurtling down the unsympathetic concrete steps. I cried out once, sharply, before my jaw smacked the ground, silencing me.

I rolled and tumbled to a soggy stop at the bottom, pain radiating from everywhere at once. The horizon wavered through a curtain of water. I blinked, and shoes stopped in front of me. I followed the legs up, pausing when I reached Marco's face, split with a smile and shining brighter than a Christmas tree.

"I warned you. Drumline isn't a place for girls."

He reached down and patted my head, the same way you would a dog. And not just any dog—a motherfucking *poodle*, like I was a harmless ball of fluff. As I lay there, stunned and gasping, he sauntered away as if he was just going to grab a beer and he'd be right back, leaving me a crumpled mess at the base of the stands.

My pride wouldn't let me call out to him.

When the reality set in that he'd left—really and truly just left me here, I took stock of my injuries.

My jaw ached but I could open my mouth. My hip, the same one I'd bruised before, was tender, as were a few other spots that had taken direct impact. But my left wrist was the worst—already turning purple and swelling. While I could wiggle my fingers okay, bending it forward brought tears to my eyes, and a gasp of agony escaped only to be swallowed by the storm, unheard by anyone.

I pushed carefully to my feet, relieved to see that I could walk okay. Blood dripped in places, running in watery pink tendrils down my limbs, superficial scrapes that looked worse than they felt.

But my wrist, I couldn't ignore the throbbing pulse of pain there. I cradled it to my chest as I made my way to the exit.

Dear sweet gilt-winged guardian angels on call on this shittiest of nights, please don't let it be broken.

Marco had ignored my bag as he left. My phone was there, salvation delivered in the form of an Apple. Who said God didn't have a sense of humor?

But my smile of relief wobbled as I dug the phone out.

I needed a damn ER.

And a ride. Driving myself wasn't an option. Plus, I knew the drill. The lawsuit-cautious doctors would only dispense the good pain meds if I had a driver. And, tonight, I needed the good stuff.

I dug my phone out. Despite everything, my first inclination was to call Laird for help. The thumb of my good hand hovered over his contact info in my phone, hesitating. Last week, I wouldn't have thought twice about it, but now I second-guessed my instinct. Things between us still felt serrated and brittle.

And his project. Shit, his project. He couldn't work on it in a noisy ER. And again, I knew from experience, nothing about an ER visit was fast. It'd be at least three or four hours from now, minimum, before I'd be discharged.

Fuck.

I tapped on the screen, waited while it rang twice, three times.

"Hello?"

"Robin?" My voice cracked, and a sob broke through. "Batman needs help."

CHAPTER 30

Reese

WHEN THE NURSE WITH THE BOUNCY PONYTAIL walked out after taking down an initial medical history from me, Smith was scowling.

No, it was more of a glower, the way his whole forehead and nose were puckered too.

Because, yeah, I hadn't thought the whole ER visit through. I didn't lie to doctors. Ever. They couldn't effectively help me if they didn't know the real story. And I had too much respect for them after my childhood to fib and make their jobs more difficult. I just kinda sorta maybe forgot that Smith would overhear that I had leukemia as a kid, or that I'd fallen down two dozen concrete stairs in the middle of a thunderstorm.

"Tell. Me. What. Happened." His expression hadn't wavered, his jaw clenched.

I shifted my wrist to a more comfortable position on the

pillow I'd propped it on while we waited for the doctor. As luck would have it, the ER was pretty empty because of the rain and I'd been taken back to a room immediately. The exam room was more modern than I expected, with a glass wall facing the hallway that could be curtained off and a flatscreen TV perched on one wall above a whiteboard.

"Just a little bit of hazing gone wrong. You know how Marco is around me." I tried to shrug off the rest of the story, but Smith wasn't having it.

"Tell. Me. What. Happened," he repeated, leaning forward and gripping the bedrail.

I shivered, still soaked to the bone. What was it about hospitals and overactive air conditioning systems?

Smith softened long enough to fetch me a pair of warmed blankets from the nursing station before he resumed his position, scowl and all.

But the doctor came in before I could speak and I recapped the night's events a third time. And she wanted more details.

Did I hit my head?

My jaw, but not my skull.

Did I ever lose consciousness at any point?

No.

Did anyone witness the fall?

I hesitated before nodding.

And did he call for help?

I studied the growing bruise on my wrist, the way it extended over the heel of my palm now. My silence was answer enough, and Smith growled beside me, his hands in tight fists on his thighs.

We followed the rest of the timeline until I arrived at the hospital, including the fact that Smith was a friend I called for a ride and that he hadn't been present when I'd been injured, and then the doctor led me through a series of range of motion exercises, both passive and active, before ordering x-rays for my hand and wrist.

"After the tech gets the images, the nurse will start cleaning up some of your other scrapes while we wait for the films to be read. There are a lot of bones in the hand and we want to make sure you didn't fracture anything. Some of them, like the scaphoid, you have to be careful with. Are you allergic to anything? We'll go ahead and get you some pain meds ordered too."

I shook my head. "No, nothing. And thank you."

She smiled, but glanced at Smith suspiciously. No doubt I looked like a possible domestic abuse victim. "Is there anything else you'd like to tell me?"

"No, ma'am."

The nurse with the bouncy ponytail brought me a pair of pain pills along with a nitrile glove full of ice to hold on my jaw while we waited for x-ray, and I couldn't help but notice the way she surreptitiously checked out Smith's hands while she fussed over me.

I felt bad for the things they were probably accusing him of in their heads, but his knuckles were smooth and clean, the skin unblemished and unbroken, so they'd realize soon enough they were barking up the wrong tree.

While the tech wheeled me to radiology, he continued the line of questioning they'd started earlier, probably to see if I'd answer differently now that I was alone—if I felt safe, if I needed help, if I needed to speak to a social worker or the doctor privately. He finally point-blank asked me if the guy who brought me here had hurt me, which I adamantly denied.

I admired their thoroughness even as embarrassment flooded me.

But after the imaging was done and my body adorned with bandages in half a dozen places where I'd been bleeding, Smith wouldn't be put off any longer.

"The doctor just went in the room with some old guy who was wheezing. She'll probably be a while. Talk to me, Batman. Let me in. Leukemia? You had it too? Like Laird's brother?"

I closed my eyes. "Yeah. I guess. I mean, I didn't know until yesterday that Garrett had had cancer, let alone that he died from it. And since I'm still here, it's not quite the same, is it?" My brow wrinkled as I thought about it more. "I don't even know if he had the same kind of leukemia. Laird isn't really talking to me right now."

"Why? Because of your question after practice the other day?"

I shrugged, a flush creeping up my neck. "I guess? Maybe? He said he had to finish his video game project too. I know he's been busy with that all week."

"Oh, yeah." Smith's shoulders relaxed. "His project. I'm sure it doesn't have anything to do with you. There's no doubt, that guy is crazy about you." He pointed toward my phone on the other visitor chair in the room. "Do you want to call him?"

That's the million-dollar question, isn't it?

I licked my dry lips, my emotions a jumble. "What time is it?" Hospitals didn't put clocks on the wall in patient rooms.

Smith checked his watch. "A little after ten."

"His project deadline is midnight. He's probably still working." I clung to that excuse so I wouldn't have to examine why my gut felt leaden, my chest a little too tight as I thought of Laird hunched over a computer, his fingers flying as he debugged his program in one of those weird computer languages that just looked like gibberish to me. "I'll text him when we get out of here."

It was a lie.

I wouldn't.

But Smith nodded, looking relieved.

"And the stuff with Marco? It's been worse than you've told me, hasn't it?"

I scrolled through my memory, trying to sort through the events that he'd witnessed versus the ones he hadn't.

"He tripped me a few months back during band camp. I'm sure he'd claim it was an accident or I was clumsy or something, but I bruised my hip pretty bad when I landed on a curb."

Smith swore loudly, and scooted his chair a little closer to me, reaching out to squeeze my ankle at the bottom of the bed. "What else?" he pressed. "There's more, isn't there?"

I started to scrunch up my face but it made my jaw hurt so I settled for shrugging instead. "You know I clean his room—wait, speaking of that." I fixed Smith with a penetrating stare, as if to make better sense of what I'd seen that day before I'd scrubbed it from my mind. "The other week I found grape lollipops and two condom wrappers near the trashcan. Different brands. Different sizes. Anything you'd care to share with *me*, Robin?" I tried to shift the focus back to him.

But Smith just furrowed his brow as a telltale flush tinted his cheeks. "Nothing worth sharing. After too many beers one night, Marco hit on me. And…and…" Smith faltered, tightening his fingers around his knees and not making eye contact with me. "Look, when the guy focuses all his attention on you, it can be downright flattering. He's a hot senior, and yeah, it's obvious now he's a fucking prick, but he'd noticed *me*. And it felt good, you know?"

His words came faster, as if he just wanted to get them out and say it once and put the whole thing behind him. "But he's the most self-centered guy I've ever gone to bed with, and let's just say we didn't both have a happy ending that night. Then of course, the next day when I alluded to it, he looked at me like I was crazy and he didn't remember any of it and *I sure had an overactive imagination* and *he didn't swing that way.*"

"Smith…" My voice fell to a sympathetic whisper. "You can do so much better than him."

"No shit. Have you seen me?" He rubbed his eyes with the heels of his palms and laughed humorlessly. "But I thought about it later. With him, I don't think sex is about pleasure. I mean, it is, but I don't think that's what really gets him off. I think it's a dominance thing. He's turned on when he controls someone, whether in the bedroom or the practice field… or even this whole creepy situation with you. I honestly think deep down he's a scared, insecure little kid, and he tries to grab any resemblance of power he can to make himself feel like a man."

I stared at Smith as I turned his words over in my head, nodding slowly when I realized his insight was spot on. "That's fucked up, you know? Building himself up by tearing others down? A real man—"

"—doesn't need to do that shit. Period," Smith finished harshly. His knee bounced in agitation.

The door creaked open and worn tennis shoes squeaked on the floor as the doctor returned, putting a momentary halt to our conversation.

She smiled at me halfway, like she was too tired to fully commit to the motion. "Ms. Holland, how are you feeling? Pain meds kicking in some? I see your minor scrapes are taken care of now."

"I'm fine," I replied automatically, trying to read her body language for some clue of what the x-rays showed.

"Well, the radiologist didn't see any fractures, so it looks like you've just gotten yourself a nasty sprain there." Her intonation changed slightly as she delivered a spiel she'd obviously given countless times. "We'll give you a brace and an ortho follow-up next week, some anti-inflammatories and pain meds, and get you out of here shortly. The nurse will go over basic RICE therapy when she brings the discharge paperwork, but you're going to want to take it easy for the next few days. If it gets worse, your fingers turn cold or pale, or the pain increases out of proportion to what you expect, you need to come back immediately for further workup. You can take the brace off to shower, but you're going to want to wear it for support for the next couple days until you can get in with ortho. Any questions?"

"No, ma'am. Thank you."

Thank you, thank you, thank you, thank you.

The doctor left as quickly as she arrived, moving on to the next patient.

Smith looked at me somberly. "What are you going to do about Marco? And all this? If nothing else, he should have to cover your medical bills."

"Me?" I snorted. "You think *I* can get Marco to do anything? And anyway, he'll say I tripped, which is technically true. He didn't push me, he didn't hit me. He just happened to be there when I *had an accident*." The thick sarcasm wasn't lost on Smith.

"We both know he's responsible for this."

"And he'll say I'm a weak girl who couldn't hack it and you're a jealous one-night stand."

"Fuck *that*." Smith was quiet for a moment. "What about Laird? He's going to be livid."

I took a deep breath. "Not if I don't tell him."

"You *have* to tell him, Reese. Besides, he'll see the brace."

"And I will tell him. That I *tripped*. Which is the *truth*."

The nurse chose that moment to enter, sheaf of papers in hand, and she blinked at the vehemence of my outburst, eyeing me in concern once again. "Everything okay in here?"

"We're good," I hastened to reassure her, and listened attentively as she went over the aftercare instructions, the prescriptions, and gave me the card with the orthopedic appointment neatly printed on it. As she talked, she wrapped my wrist in a reinforced black brace and secured the Velcro strips.

"Want a sling? It's more for comfort than anything else, but I'm happy to send one home with you."

"I'll pass, thanks." There was no way I was wearing a sling for the next week. And either those meds were really starting to work their magic, or my wrist wasn't nearly as bad as I first thought.

I turned to see if Smith was ready to go and the room spun for a moment.

Yeah, the meds were working.

Surely that was the reason I wished, despite everything, it was Laird here next to me, Laird who was taking me home, and Laird who, in my imagination, stayed with me all night, holding me close and helping me forget about secret dead brothers and asshole snare lieutenants.

I blinked back hot tears, refusing to let them fall.

"Take me home, Robin. I don't want to talk about Marco anymore. Or Laird. I'm tired. It's been a long night."

He collected my phone and bag without arguing, and helped me to my feet.

"Let's get you to the Batcave so you can sleep. We'll fight the bad guy tomorrow."

CHAPTER 31

Laird

AFTER A FORTY-HOUR MARATHON WHERE I reprogrammed my video game from scratch, stopping only to attend the few lectures I couldn't get away with missing, I slept.

I slept like a rock.

I slept right through all my classes on Thursday, mandatory or not, and woke up an hour before band practice, with just enough time to brush my teeth, shower, and rush to campus.

But, damn, it felt good to finally have my app working properly—knowing not only would I ace my class, but I could finish developing the back-end business aspects and release it commercially over Christmas break.

My classmates might have felt like it was stupid of me to fixate over it so much, that I should've taken a C in the course and moved on, but I couldn't ignore the pressure of my looming graduation and my pending entrance into the real world.

The bitter reality where my dad had disowned me, my mom was long gone, and I was essentially alone.

So, yeah, maybe it made me a nerd, but I wanted to be taken seriously as a responsible adult in a few short months—be my own boss, pay my own bills, and tick off the boxes of my five-year plan.

But mostly, I wanted a certain brown-eyed, dark-haired freshman to know I could provide for her.

For us.

Reese was my motivation, my end goal, and not fucking it up was pretty damn high on my priority list, especially after that mess at the last practice.

I needed to apologize for the way I rushed out, when her innocent question about Garrett had caught me off guard, and explain why I didn't talk about his death very often, even though I had no qualms reminiscing over his good years.

It was one thing to talk about Garrett with *her*—and I owed her that much—but it was *not* a topic I wanted to go into detail about in front of all the guys. While his death was relatively common knowledge for those who lived in the area due to the news coverage and fundraising we did for him back then, it still hurt like a motherfucker to discuss.

That said, I was wrong for running out the way I did, for not staying long enough for her to realize I wasn't upset with *her*. And I should've put Marco in his place immediately for his dumbass comment mocking her for her innocent question. I was just in too much of a hurry to escape to think things through at the time.

It wasn't Reese's fault I hadn't told her about all the baggage in my past.

An eager smile lifted the corners of my mouth as I approached the auditorium to grab my snare, just knowing I'd get to see her in a few minutes, because, damn, I'd missed talking to her the last two days.

I wonder if she wants to grab dinner tonight?

My pace increased.

I wonder if she'd let me have her *for dinner tonight?*

You know, after we'd had our talk and kissed and made up.

A flash of tan skin and whipping ponytail caught my eye through the glass door to the building, and I ran up the steps to catch her, but by the time I yanked open the door, she had already disappeared into the equipment room.

Damn. I'd really been hoping to snag her in the hall, to have a private minute with her before practice started without attracting a lot of attention.

When I pushed through the door of the room, Smith was already huddled next to Reese, talking in hushed tones. She had some kind of black brace strapped on her left wrist, and it looked like she was trying to tug it off while Smith adamantly refastened the Velcro she'd just loosened.

As I approached, he jabbed a finger at her arm, pointing, and whispered words I couldn't make out. His face was scrunched in anger or frustration or some weird combination of the two and my hackles rose in automatic response.

"What's going on? Reese? Did you hurt your wrist?" I reached for her arm, but she finished removing the apparatus, flung it into her bag, and hid her arm behind her back, out of my sight.

"Nothing." She shot a loaded glance at Smith. "It's *nothing*. Just a little tendonitis flaring up. I'm fine for practice."

Smith swore under his breath and stalked away after throwing her one last dark look.

"Reese?" My tone had her reluctantly shifting until I could see her hand.

She held it up and wiggled her fingers, but she pulled back when I tried to touch her.

That stung, but I kept my expression neutral.

"Are you okay for practice or not?" My brows furrowed as I studied her arm. It looked a little swollen, but otherwise okay.

"Of course!" she answered quickly, her tone a little too bright.

I hesitated. Reese knew her own limits better than me, and if she said she was okay, who was I to argue?

"Would wearing the brace help?" I prodded.

She licked her lips, and her eyes flicked down to her bag for a second. "I'm good."

From behind me, Smith snorted and shook his head. I watched him a second and raised my eyebrows. "Anything I need to know?"

Smith opened his mouth, taking a step forward, but when Reese elbowed him not so subtly, he clamped it shut again, frowning. "No," he muttered sourly.

"All right then, grab your gear and hit the field. Reese, can I have a word with you after practice? And if your wrist starts acting up out there, sit out for a few minutes or let Heath take your place." I pinned her with a stare that would've made my dad proud. "Got it?"

She nodded, stooping down and avoiding eye contact.

I wavered for a minute. Something about this whole situation just seemed *off*, but I couldn't pinpoint what.

The feeling didn't go away during practice. She was slow, stiff, and off the beat more than on.

And Marco noticed, riding her harder than normal until I shut him down after he called out her mistake for the third time.

"Shut the hell up already, man." I got in his personal space, blocking his view of Reese, who was wincing after a particularly upbeat section. "She heard you, she told me her wrist hurt, and you screaming at her isn't going to change things. Why don't you go help Heath in case he needs to take her place this week, huh? His performance wasn't so hot the other day, if you need to micromanage someone."

Marco held his position, our drums flush between us. "You don't even know what you're talking about, Laird. Me and Reese, we have an understanding. I've wondered about the two of you—what y'all do off the field, but I promise you, you're not the only one she's spending time with. She likes it when I'm rough. If you don't believe me, maybe you should ask her why she has a key to my room? Or ask her where she was last night. I bet you anything she lies, doesn't mention me at all. But check her phone. I met her for a little one-on-one practice session, if you know what I mean." He waggled his eyebrows and licked his lips before blowing me a lewd kiss.

My eyes flew past him to Reese, who was trying to pretend she hadn't been watching the confrontation between me and Marco.

Would she...?

No. She hates him.

But that niggling feeling of unease came back from before practice. That something wasn't right.

Doubt curdled in my gut, sharper than a sucker-punch.

The rest of practice was a blur. I don't remember whether our lines were on point or our stick work tight—it was just two hours of noise and movement until the drum major blew the final whistle, signaling the end.

Not even waiting for the relief of the air-conditioned

auditorium, I beelined straight for Reese.

"Follow me," I snapped, harsher than I intended.

I forced myself to walk normally over to the edge of the field, and when I reached the deserted sideline, I spun back around so fast, my snare slammed into my hip. Impatient, I yanked it over my head, and set it on the ground near my feet. I removed Reese's rig too, setting her drum next to mine, and when I saw a third snare hitting the grass, I realized Smith had joined us.

Sweat from the harness had my shirt sticking to my chest, and the breeze felt cool as it drifted over us, but I barely appreciated the sensation.

My head was all over the place, thoughts zinging from one extreme to the next. I took a deep breath, trying to figure out where to even start.

"Do you have a key to Marco's apartment?" I asked without preamble, praying she'd say no, that Marco was just talking his fool head off like normal.

"I—" Her startled gaze flew to mine, and it was obvious that wasn't the question she was expecting. "Y-yes."

"Why?" I snapped before she even had a chance to continue her earlier answer.

"To clean his room."

"Why the fuck are you cleaning his room?" What kind of bullshit was that?

"He-he said it was a drumline thing. That all NADs were assigned to a vet. You know," she lowered her voice a bit, even though no one else was around us except Smith, "a hazing thing."

I whipped my head back, trying to make sense of her answer. That had never been a drumline *thing* since I'd been on the line. "Why didn't you tell me? That's bullshit."

She gave me a tiny shrug, cradling her wrist against her

stomach. "It wasn't anything I couldn't handle. I had it under control."

"That shit ends now," I ordered, knowing I sounded ridiculous and possessive, but unable to stop myself.

A dark spot on Reese's arm caught my eye, and without giving her a chance to pull back, I captured her hand and gently ran my thumb over the purple mark.

"Okay," she agreed hastily, attempting to free her hand.

I held it tighter.

The discoloration spread, the purple growing with each pass of my thumb. "What the fuck?" I looked at my thumb. It was covered in a beige cream. "Makeup?"

I whipped my shirt off, and Smith watched grimly beside me as I wiped the remaining concealer or whatever the hell it was from her skin.

An enormous bruise covered the medial aspect—thank you, Anatomy class—of her wrist from mid-forearm to mid-palm. It had to hurt like a bitch.

And now that I'd seen that one, I noticed other smaller, more superficial scrapes. On her knee, her shin, her elbow. *What the fuck happened?*

I wanted to strip her down, right then and there, and check the rest of her, run my hands over every inch of her body just to assure myself that she wasn't still hiding a bigger, more serious wound.

"You *played* like this today? *Why*? What happened?" I growled as I traced the margin of her injury, where the purple bled into green. "And why didn't you *tell* me?"

The last question was the one that mattered the most to my rattled brain.

"It was rainy last night, and things were slippery. I lost my balance on some steps and fell. No big deal."

I pointed to her wrist. "This is *not* something minor.

This needs medical attention."

"She had it," Smith interjected quietly. "I took her last night."

My gaze swung to him wildly, even as I refused to release Reese's hand. "*You* were there?"

"Yes. No. Kinda." The snarl on my face must've had the desired effect, because he rushed to explain. "I wasn't there when she got hurt, but she called me, and I took her to the ER downtown. She sprained it."

"Jesus, Smith, just tattle on me, why don't you?" Reese muttered, frowning at him.

"But. What. Happened?" My pulse throbbed in my neck as I stared between the two of them.

Reese yelped, and I realized I'd inadvertently tightened my grip on her. I let go immediately, and she hugged her arm to her lower abdomen.

"Are you okay?" I softened my voice. "Did I hurt you?"

She lowered her chin, but not before I saw the sheen of tears in her eyes.

"*Fuck.*" I ran my hands through my hair, pulling at the short strands in frustration. "Smith. Give me the short version before I go crazy here."

"She was doing cardio at the stadium last night and slipped down a bunch of steps. Caught herself on her wrist. She called me, I took her to the ER, they did x-rays and everything. She's *supposed* to be wearing that brace until she sees the orthopedist."

Last night…

"Was Marco there?" My voice cut the air like a knife.

"No."

"Yes."

They replied simultaneously, then Reese turned and glared at Smith. "Traitor," she whispered.

I caught Reese's chin between my thumb and forefinger and lifted it until she was forced to meet my gaze. "Would you be willing to show me your last texts from him?"

Her eyes widened, and her lips trembled. I barely heard her reply. "He was there."

"Was this his fault?"

"Yes."

"No."

They spoke in unison again. I wanted to find Marco and use him as a punching bag, bury my fists in him until this rage inside me was sated.

"Where was this?" My hands clenched repeatedly by my sides. "The bleachers? Or the back stairs by the food stations?"

Reese wrinkled her brows, as if she didn't understand why that mattered. "The bleachers. The South ones."

I filed away the information for later. "And were you going to tell me?" My tone was dangerously soft.

Reese squared her shoulders, dropping her arm from its protective cradle. She took a step forward, so close I could've bent down and kissed her, and answered in the same tone I'd just used. "And who would I have told? My snare captain? The one who told me NADs should do whatever a vet tells them to? Or the guy I've been sleeping with? The one who's lied to me this whole time about his brother?"

CHAPTER 32

Reese

"**W**HAT HAPPENED TO YOU?" ELI POINTED AT THE brace on my arm.

"I tripped on the stairs." I kept my voice light and shrugged. "But the doctor said I'll be good as new in a week or two."

He looked to the doorway behind me expectantly, and I followed his gaze.

When the opening remained empty, I twisted back around, my eyebrows raised in silent question. "Are you waiting on somebody else?"

"I thought maybe you were bringing Laird with you today. You know, for our double date with Amelia." His whole face drooped behind his thick glasses.

"Oh." I'd forgotten all about it. I'd meant to coordinate a time with Laird, but then things kept snowballing this last week, and it slipped my mind. "I'm sorry, buddy. It's my fault. I didn't schedule a day with Laird."

"I mentioned it to him too," he said morosely, picking at the blanket over his legs. "He knew."

"He had this big project…" I trailed off when Eli tightened his lips and looked away, out the window. I knew that feeling, like everyone in the outside world forgot about you while you were stuck in a hospital room for treatment. No excuse would ever make it okay.

"Let me see if one of the nurses are free. You know they'll only let me take one of you with me down there."

"Yeah. Whatever." He pulled his iPad closer and started playing some game with a yellow octopus that I hadn't seen before.

Lingering for a minute as I watched the beanie slip over his forehead, I felt a pang in my chest. Being a kid with cancer sucked. And I sucked for forgetting the one thing he'd been looking forward to for over a week now.

Martha, my favorite nurse, was working today, but she shook her head apologetically when I asked if she could spare someone to help me take Eli and Amelia down to Starbucks. "We're short staffed today, I had two girls call in sick. Sorry, Reese, you know I have a soft spot for Eli, and I'd help you if I could."

"I understand," I assured her, hating that my last-ditch effort had failed.

But when I retraced my steps to Eli's room, Laird was sitting in my spot next to his bed, pointing and laughing at something on the iPad.

I sucked in a breath, wondering if I could beat a hasty retreat before either one of them looked up and saw me. I could come back later, much later, after Laird was gone.

"Reese!" Eli's excited squeal told me I was out of luck. "Look who's here!"

"Yay!" If my cheer fell a little flat, Laird was the only one who noticed, his eyes dimming and his jaw tightening as he studied me where I stood propped against the doorway, rubbing the foamy hand sanitizer between my palms.

"Give me a second, and I'll check to see if Amelia's ready."

But her room was empty, and the note on her whiteboard said she was scheduled for physical therapy right now.

My legs felt leaden as I re-entered Eli's room with the bad news.

"She's in PT, and I have to leave for biology lab before she gets back." I grimaced as I relayed the bad news. "I could still take you down to get a cake pop if you wanted?"

"We both could go with you," Laird offered, but his words seemed forced.

Eli, picking up on Laird's tone, swiveled his head between us. "What's up with you two? You're acting weird."

"Nothing," I muttered.

"Adult stuff."

Eli scrunched his face up. "Like, mushy things? I thought you were going to peacock her, man? What happened? Do you not know how to use your damn feathers right?"

My hand flew to my mouth to cover my shock, and I eyed Laird across the room, trying to hide how much I wanted to hear his answer.

He tugged on his shirt collar as if it was suddenly too tight and shifted in the chair. A hint of color tinted the angle of his cheekbones. "Eli, I hate to be the one to break it to you," Laird's voice was strained, but his eyes were on me, not Eli, as he spoke, "but sometimes peacocking doesn't fix things. Sometimes peacocking gets in the way of the other things you should be doing, like having a hard conversation about shitty stuff before it's too damn late to repair the damage. Even if the peacocking was amazing. Even if it was the best peacocking you've ever done."

Dear sweet miraculous Jesus who never peacocked in His holy life.

Why were we talking about this in front of a kid? My face burned even as my nipples turned hard at his words. Thankfully, my hoodie hid the evidence from underage eyes, although Laird smirked faintly when I shifted my stance, rubbing my thighs together in the process.

The peacocking was amazing. The best peacocking he'd ever done. Yeah, I'd agree with him on that.

But *peacocking* had never been the issue. The problem was, at the most basic level, we hadn't trusted each other.

He didn't tell me about Garrett, and, if I was being fair, I kept Marco's harassment a secret from him too.

Our foundation was cracked, and no amount of peacocking, no matter how spectacular the feathers, could fix it.

Eli looked at me suspiciously. "He's talking about kissing, right? He's saying that you're a good kisser?"

"She was the best, buddy."

"You weren't bad yourself," I admitted grudgingly.

This was beyond inappropriate. "Eli..." I paused, not sure what exactly I planned to say. "I'm sorry. Sometimes adulting sucks and there just aren't any good answers. Sometimes, you gotta play it safe."

He screwed up his face in concentration, lifting his chin in the air as if the answers were somewhere between the rows of fluorescent lights. "But sometimes playing it safe is bullshit." Eli said the words like a judge delivering a verdict. "It's like cancer. Sometimes, you have to kill all the cells, the good ones *and* the bad ones, and start over again from scratch. And that's the part that hurts the worst, the time when you just want to fucking give up because of all the pain, but you can't. You have to be strong because you know once you're on the other side, it'll be even better than it was before. And you can be happy again. And… and peacock and stuff."

"Oh, Eli." My voice broke, and I swiped at my face to bat away a tear. "Sometimes it's just not that simple."

I couldn't look at Laird, couldn't let him see how much I wanted us to give Eli's advice a try.

He's just a kid. He doesn't know how complicated this shit is.

"Whatever. Y'all can handle your drama on your own time. This is about me right now."

I giggled despite myself at Eli's ego, and sniffled.

"I heard the doctors talking to mom the other day. I think I'm getting discharged soon."

"That's great!" Laird's voice sounded like gravel over sandpaper, and he cleared his throat. "Do you know when?"

"Next week maybe? I don't know, but I promised Amelia a date. And I can't do that once I get home, so y'all need to figure your shit out. Whatever issues you've got, they're cockblocking my peacocking, if you get my drift."

I barely held back my laugh.

"You'll get your date, Eli," Laird said.

"Promise," I added.

CHAPTER 33

Reese

Smith: Where are you?

Me: Home. Back in Morgantown.

Smith: You left early for Thanksgiving break?

Me: Laird wouldn't let me come to the game because of my wrist, so yeah, I left Friday.

Smith: What happened btwn you two?

Me: What do you mean?

Smith: Marco's gone. Laird did something, and now Marco's gone.

Smith: Like gone gone.

Smith: Expelled.

Me: WHAT?!

Me: What about the game today?

Smith: Justin's in for you and Heath's in for Marco.

Me: What about the snare duel?

Smith: I dunno.

Me: Is he okay?

Smith: Who? Laird? Marco?

Me: I don't give a fuck about Marco.

Smith: But you do about Laird?

Smith: Hello?

Smith: You still there?

Smith: No.

Smith: He looks like shit.

Me: How did he get Marco expelled?

Smith: I don't know. He's not saying. Maybe you should ask him.

But I didn't.

Later that day, I watched the game online.

There was no snare duel.

Laird played a solo, the shadows under his eyes visible even on my laptop when the camera zoomed in.

Four days later, I got a text from him.

But not the one I expected.

Laird: Eli's dead.

CHAPTER 34

Reese

"I DON'T UNDERSTAND WHAT'S GOTTEN INTO YOU." MY mother fiddled with the hem of her sensible white shirt while she stood in the doorway of my bedroom, watching me scour the internet for a flight back to Alabama that afternoon while simultaneously flinging clothes and toiletries haphazardly into my suitcase. "Your behavior has been so erratic this week. First, you showed up unannounced on Friday, after *skipping your classes*"— she said it in the same horrified tone one would use when describing a terrorist attack—"and now you up and decide to go back early. Thanksgiving is tomorrow, Reese. Do you know how many people will be at the airport today? Do you know how many germs and viruses will be there?"

Ahhh, now we were getting to the root of her fears. My health.

"I know, Mom. The germs, the viruses, the diseases, oh

my!" My dry sarcasm went right over her head.

"Exactly! And we still need to go over all your scholarship paperwork for next semester too. Who is this guy you're so worried about? You've never mentioned a guy to me in your calls before." Her practical shoes tapped over the hardwood floors—carpet wasn't sanitary—as she approached.

"He's…" I wasn't sure what label to stick on my current situation with Laird. "It's complicated."

But my gut screamed that Laird needed me. That whatever else had transpired between us, he was hurting and needed someone—needed *me*—by his side. And I knew he'd never ask outright. It wasn't in his nature.

Laird was the guy in charge, the one who handled things, who shouldered the heavy lifting. He'd try to bury the grief, pretend it wasn't there, that it didn't matter.

He needed permission to grieve. To let it out so the pain didn't fester.

My heart broke at the image of him in his townhouse alone, facing the loss of someone I knew he'd looked at as another younger brother.

Regret, sharp-edged and swift, flooded me when I realized that the Starbucks double date Eli had wanted so badly never happened.

I'd failed him too.

I blinked back tears.

She touched my bruised wrist softly. "Is this part of the complication? I know you don't want to talk about it, but your dad knows a lawyer he could call if—"

"No!" I cut her off harshly. "He had nothing to do with this. I told you, I fell."

And that was all she'd ever know about the whole Marco situation. If she knew about the other hazing, she'd probably have flown down to Alabama months ago and insisted on accompanying me to practice, or whatever else she could come up with in my worst helicopter-parenting nightmare.

"But this guy you're rushing back to, he took you to the hospital?"

She'd lit up like a Christmas tree when she found out real doctors had laid their hands on me and pronounced me only mildly injured. Nothing excited her more than a good report on my overall health from a licensed medical professional.

"No." I shook my head as I clicked through the website to purchase the plane ticket. My flight left in three hours. "That was a different guy."

"But a kid died? I don't understand all this. This *other* guy who needs you so badly—was it his child? His sibling?"

"No, Eli was—" I broke off again. She didn't know I volunteered. As much as she loved for me to go to the doctor, she didn't like me being near hospitals. Too many sick people. Too many *germs.* "He was special. He had leukemia."

"Oh, honey." She turned away, her hand to her mouth. Mom preferred to live in a world where cancer never won, where kids didn't die from things beyond their control. Her voice wavered. "How did you meet him?"

"Make-a-Wish." The lie came easily. "He wanted to be in a football halftime show. He liked drums."

Mom sniffed, nodding. "But, you have to leave *now*?"

I double-checked the clock. "In an hour." That would still leave me enough time to get through security.

She sighed, her forehead creased with permanent worry lines. "Let me at least go over the paperwork with you then."

By the time she returned with a stack of papers punctuated with colored sticky notes, my bag was packed and by the door, ready to go.

I'd won a total of nine scholarships during my junior and senior years of high school. There were a lot of people willing to throw money at cancer survivors pursuing higher education. Lucky me.

"Most of these are straight forward." She pointed at the first one, where precise yellow highlighter marked the pertinent information and the Post-It that summarized in flawless script the actions I needed to take. "The merit-based ones just need a copy of your transcript, but some need additional documentation."

I glanced over the first few neatly stapled packets. My mom had even included stamped, addressed envelopes for me to mail the forms back with.

A pang of guilt for leaving early spread through my chest.

Mom might show it in weird, overprotective ways, but she loved me.

I sat on the edge of the bed and patted the spot next to me. "Walk me through them, please."

Her face brightened as she settled next to me, the dead cancer kid forgotten.

I listened attentively as she went through the first five sets of papers. Three of the scholarships didn't require any action mid-year. The only one left to discuss looked to be the most complicated, based on the thick stack of print outs.

"And then there's this one." She tapped the page, and the bold font at the top caught my attention.

I'd filled out so many forms and written so many essays back in high school that the different awards had all blurred together in my head. I'd known escaping my parents' clinging reach depended on creating distance, so I'd applied for dozens and dozens of prizes, the specifics of each long since forgotten.

But the name of this particular award sounded familiar, now that I was seeing it in black and white.

The Garrett Bronson Memorial Scholarship.

My mind tripped and stuttered over the name.

"For this one, you need to submit not only your transcript showing you maintained a 3.0 GPA, but you need one of your professors to…"

I tuned out the rest of her words.

Garrett Bronson.

G stands for Garrett, my brother.

Laird's family was literally paying for my education.

Did he know?

Dear sweet heavenly Father who forgave those who profited from other's misfortunes.

If Garrett hadn't died, I wouldn't be at Rodner.

I wouldn't have met Laird.

I wouldn't have fallen in love for the first time.

How messed up was it that I owed all the good things in the last few months to Laird's biggest loss?

Guilt simmered low and hot in my gut.

And I felt a renewed urgency to get to his side, to tell him I understood why he didn't bring up Garrett's passing, to let him know he wasn't alone.

I snatched the papers from my mom and stuffed them haphazardly in my bookbag, ignoring her gasp of dismay when the edges crinkled and bent. "Thanks. I'll take care of it," I said distractedly.

Despair at the broken situation between Laird and myself squeezed my chest, making each beat of my heart feel dull and heavy.

I needed to get back to Alabama immediately.

There was a green-eyed drummer who needed me.

CHAPTER 35

Laird

THE WHISKEY—EXPENSIVE AND NEARLY AS OLD AS me—was Dad's favorite brand. I stared at the unopened bottle on my coffee table, a glass tumbler next to it ready to go.

It'd worked for him—drinking away the pain. Why wouldn't it work for me too?

Yet the seal had remained intact for the last sixteen hours, while I slowly became one with the couch cushions.

The problem was, I couldn't decide who to forget about first.

Everyone had left me.

Garrett.

My parents.

Reese.

Now Eli.

And I got it.

I deserved it.

I'd failed them all.

I couldn't save Garrett.

I wasn't enough for my parents—not without my brother.

I failed to protect Reese from Marco hurting her right under my nose, and didn't deserve her even if she could forgive me.

Which she wouldn't.

And Eli.

Motherfucking Eli.

He'd looked at me with those big, worshipful eyes the same way Garrett used to.

Like I could save him, so he could grow up to be a miniature version of me one day.

And he'd died too, a bad reaction to what was supposed to be his last chemo treatment before he was released.

Oscar whined and nudged me with his nose until he'd wiggled his head into my lap. I hadn't bothered to put a shirt on after my shower, and his nose was cold against my side. He snuffled, staring at me with his soulful hound dog eyes, his ears spread wide like a superhero cape.

The only one who still loved me.

I rubbed his head absently, trying to summon the energy to lean forward and open the whiskey.

But it almost seemed too nice, too elegant to waste on a useless asshole like me.

I picked up my phone, scrolled to the text thread from Reese.

She hadn't responded, and I hadn't expected her to, but my fingers itched to reach out to her. To beg her for—for what exactly?

I didn't even know. I just knew everything was better

with her.

I was better with her.

My head throbbed and my mouth was gross and dry. I tipped my head back on the couch, studying a crack on the ceiling, the way it veered to the left of the fan before splintering into smaller cracks, like a tree branch.

The lights were off, and the sky had shifted to shades of purple, but I didn't mind the dark.

Nothing worth seeing anyway.

I should probably get up and feed Oscar at some point though.

Maybe in a few minutes.

My head pounded louder, two thumps, a pause, then two more thumps. The same rhythm I'd told Reese to use during Shark Day.

I glanced at my phone again. I could call her, let it go to voicemail, and just listen to the sound of her voice. If I didn't leave a message, she might not even realize I'd called. No harm, no foul, right?

More pounding.

Oscar jumped off the couch and headed for the kitchen.

Et tu, Brute?

I swore, if I listened hard enough, I could almost hear her saying my name.

I pinched my eyes closed.

Fuck. I was hallucinating now.

Oscar whined at the front door, his paw scratching against the wood plaintively.

"Laird!"

"Reese," I muttered to myself. "Damn, I'm so sorry." My hand clutched my phone until my knuckles paled.

"Laird!" The voice was louder this time, and Oscar barked sharply.

I opened my eyes slowly, wondering if I was dreaming.

My feet were unsteady as I stumbled to the door, my fingers clumsy as I twisted the lock.

The door opened a crack, and I stepped back, leaning against the wall for support.

"Reese?" I croaked, half wondering if I'd conjured her up.

Dark brown hair appeared first, tied in a messy bun, then those familiar long, tanned legs. She slipped inside, her expression solemn as she studied me in the darkened hallway.

Oscar danced around her legs, tail thumping like an out-of-control metronome, and demanded her attention. She stooped down to give his head a quick pat.

"What are you doing here?" My voice was monotone, empty.

Reese bit her lip, uncertainty lingering in her eyes. "Do you want me to go?"

"I—" I swallowed hard against the lump in my throat.

And then I moved, so fast I couldn't second-guess the decision, wrapping her in my arms and burying my face in her neck.

Fuck, she felt good.

Her arms slipped around my waist, her fingers brushing against the bare skin of my back, and I shuddered at the warmth of her pressed against me.

For long minutes, I didn't budge, just clutched her to me as if she was the only lifeline keeping me afloat, breathing in her familiar cherry scent.

I nuzzled into the curve of her shoulder, wanting to somehow get closer, to find that elusive comfort that only she seemed able to give me.

"Laird," she whispered, loosening her grip and trying to

pull away.

I didn't let her, instead taking a step forward and backing her against the wall, so she had nowhere to escape.

"Please." My voice cracked, and I shuddered when she squeezed her arms around me again. "Just let me hold you for a little longer. Let me pretend this is real."

Her body softened in my embrace, and I burrowed closer, until she was wrapped around me like a fucking koala bear. I couldn't handle there being any distance between us.

I just needed someone—no, I just needed *her*—to hold onto.

Time passed. Minutes, hours, eons. I didn't know. But gradually, my muscles relaxed and my chest loosened enough that it didn't feel like I was suffocating any longer.

I could breathe again.

"Laird." Her voice was barely audible. "I'm so sorry about Eli."

I turned my face so I spoke against the delicate skin of her neck, my eyes closed tightly. "It's not fair."

"No. It's not."

Reluctantly, I eased away from her. I didn't let her go. I kept my fingers curled around her hips, but I gave her some space.

Her fingers skimmed up the plane of my chest, causing me to suck in a sharp breath, then she cupped my face and brushed her thumbs along my cheekbones. Through the darkness, she squinted up at me.

"You look like hell."

I dipped my head in acknowledgement, then captured one of her hands in my own, lifting it and pressing a kiss to her palm.

"You look beautiful."

She glanced down at her oversized Rodner sweatshirt

and cutoff denim shorts, cheap flip flops on her feet.

I caught her chin, tilting her face back up. "You always look beautiful."

She sighed, then took my hand and led me toward the couch.

When we reached the wall with the light switch, she paused and reached for it, but I nudged her forward, shaking my head.

"Leave it off."

She sat on the cushion next to mine, but it was too far away. Hooking her under the knees, I scooped her into my lap, setting her down sideways across my thighs, and breathed a sigh of relief when she didn't fight it.

I looped my arms loosely around her waist, and when she shifted to run her fingers through my hair, I could almost pretend that nothing bad had happened.

That Eli had been discharged home instead of to the morgue, that Reese's wrist wasn't still wrapped in a brace, that my own hand didn't ache from the revenge I'd exacted on Marco's face two days ago.

That things were right between us, instead of heavy with unsaid words.

"Are you okay?"

"No." Maybe it made me a pussy to admit it, but lying had fucked things up between us once. I'd never lie to this girl again, by omission or otherwise.

"Do you want to talk about it?"

"No." I saw her start to speak again, her eyebrows pulled down tight in a frown, so I amended my answer. "Not yet. I just... *fuck*. I just want to stay here in the dark with you and forget about all the bad stuff. Can we do that? Just a little longer?"

Her eyes searched mine in the dim glow of the

moonlight filtering through the blinds. I held her gaze, let her see all the naked pain that I felt inside.

When she nodded, it felt better than winning the lottery.

I sunk back into the couch cushions, content just to have her here with me.

To not be *alone*.

Her nails scraped against my scalp, and I closed my eyes, turning into her touch and groaning softly.

She continued her ministrations, smoothing her hands over my head over and over, until slowly, achingly slowly, my nerve endings began to tingle from the attention.

When her nails dragged through my short strands again, I stifled a moan, but couldn't stop my dick from stirring to life beneath her lap.

It was wrong, so fucking wrong, to be aroused at a time like this, but she was warm, and in my lap, and touching the edge of my face and the tender skin at the nape of my neck like she still cared deep down inside. Like despite all the wreckage of my life in the last week, a tiny part of her still belonged to me.

She traced around the edge of my ear, and I pressed my lips together at the sweet torment, trying to tamp down the sensation. But when she shifted in my lap, it was too much for my dick. He pulsed against the sweet curve of her ass, and from the way she stilled her motions, it hadn't gone unnoticed by her.

Reese was only trying to comfort me, not turn me on, and I was fucking twisted to be getting off on it.

"Laird?"

My hips bucked at the husky sound of my name coming from her full lips as they hovered just out of reach.

"I'm sorry." I sounded strained. "This isn't what you came for, I know that, and I'm sorry. But you'll never feel anything but right in my arms, and my stupid dick is just a little bit confused right now."

Reese wiggled again, and I bit back a curse, my hands clamping down on her hips to hold her still.

"That's not helping," I bit out.

My hard length throbbed between us, and I willed it to calm down.

And I thought I just might win the battle until she raised up and turned so she was full on straddling me, her knees tucked along-side my hips, and her hands resting on my shoulders for balance.

I groaned when I felt the heat of her through her shorts.

She licked her lips, leaving them a little shiny in the moonglow.

"Let's forget, Laird. Like you said. Let's just stay in the dark and forget a little longer."

And then before I could draw another breath, she reached down and whipped her sweatshirt off.

CHAPTER 36

Reese

H E STARED AT THE BLACK LACE PUSHING UP MY breasts, then slowly lifted his eyes to mine.

"You need to be sure," he said each word deliberately. "You need to be sure, because I can't resist you on my best day, and this... this is far from my best day."

His hands dug into my hips, like he was holding himself back from touching me until I gave him the word.

In a single deft move, I reached down and cupped his hard dick, stroking it softly in my hand.

"Fucking hell, Reese." He growled, and I barely had time to lock my legs around his waist before he carried me the short distance to his bedroom.

After yanking the blankets off, he laid me carefully in the center of the bed, then hovered over me, his hands on either side of my head and his knees bracketing my thighs.

"This isn't going to be some sweet, gentle lovemaking,

Reese. I need you too much. I need to feel you squeezing every long, hard inch of me deep inside you until that's the only thing I fucking feel. Until my universe begins and ends between your thighs. Until I fucking feel alive again." He dragged one finger down my throat, through the valley of my cleavage, until it curled into the dip of my bra. Then he raised an eyebrow, as if offering me one last chance to change my mind.

"Waiting for an invitation again?" I plucked the hair tie from my bun and shook my head, letting my hair fall wildly around me.

His eyes darkened to emerald green, and he leaned down to capture my mouth, his hands working together to tear my bra off at the same time.

The kiss was raw, all teeth, tongue, and reckless angles. He fisted the hair at the back of my head, holding me in place as he attacked my mouth with a desperation that brought tears to my eyes and a rush of dampness between my legs.

He took everything I had to offer and demanded more, claiming my lips over and over, until I was drunk on his taste. Until the imprint of his mouth was seared on mine.

Somewhere along the way, the rest of my clothes disappeared, my attention distracted by the scratch of his stubble along my cheek and the hot promises he whispered in my ear.

"You're fucking soaked for me, aren't you, Reese? If I touched you right now—"

His finger traced an achingly slow path up my seam, delving into the heat at my core.

"It's your fault," I panted. "I need—"

I bucked my hips, trying to keep his finger in my slick channel.

"You need *me*." And it sounded like a vow.

Then his mouth was right there, those clever lips closing around my clit and sucking hard, while he pumped his hand inside me, adding a second finger, then a third.

Even though he'd warned me, I didn't know pleasure could build this fast, this steep, this quick.

His free hand pushed my thighs up and out, spreading me wider for his erotic assault.

Bolt after bolt of electricity shot down my spine, and I raised my hips higher for more, more, *more* of his demanding touch.

I opened my mouth, but I couldn't speak. One of my hands fisted the sheet near my hip, and the other clawed at his shoulder, pushing him away, pulling him closer, trying to prolong the inevitable and chase the explosion all at once.

And when he curled those beautiful, talented fingers of his, finding that special spot along my front wall, things like gravity and death and truth seemed so insignificant. So tiny in comparison to the sonic boom of pleasure he'd just unleashed on me.

I was still blinking in a languorous daze when he entered me in one hard push, burying himself to the root.

My eyes shot to his, my parted lips hanging open soundlessly, as he set a punishing rhythm above me.

"My mom left a year after Garrett died. Physically, she left I mean. Emotionally, she died when he did."

His hand grabbed my thigh, lifted it around his waist, and my boobs jiggled between us from the force of his thrusts.

"My dad blamed me. For everything. For Garrett's death. For Mom leaving. For business deals that fell through and shitty weather and the mailman being late. I'll never be good enough, never compare to the legend of Garrett, the golden son who died too young."

Laird rotated his hips on the downstroke, rubbing his pubic bone against my sensitive clit.

It was hard to focus on his words, to absorb the horror of his childhood in the midst of the hot tension that was already building between my thighs again.

"And Marco. That fucking prick *hurt* you. He hurt you and I didn't even know because you're so fucking strong, so fucking stubborn and I get that, Jesus Christ *knows* I get that, but to find out later? After the fact? It'd hurt less to get shot, Reese."

He dipped his hand between our slick bodies, circled his thumb on that perfect spot so softly. The contrast between the gentleness of his hand and the ferocity of his cock made me rake my nails down his back until he arched and groaned and drove into me even harder, even faster. I reveled in his response, that I made him as crazy as he made me.

"I spent hours going through the security tapes. I found the first time he tripped you on the curb during band camp. Yeah, I watched the tapes back that far. And I found the one from the night in the stadium. Watched him stare at you on the ground, crumpled and bleeding. Watched him pat your head and then walk away. Watched the video of him leaving out of the tunnel, not even looking back."

He pinched my clit suddenly, and the euphoria erupted again, more intense this time, if that was possible.

But he didn't stop. He buried himself in me over and over, relentlessly, refusing to let go.

Tears sprang to my eyes as I realized he was punishing himself, refusing to let himself come until he finished confessing to me.

My mouth was dry, but I reached up to cup his face, to

bend my fingers behind his neck and force his tormented gaze to mine.

He pressed his cheek into my palm, but never slowed.

My thighs ached as he pressed closer, thrust harder, his motions becoming more erratic.

"I turned the videos in. To the band director, to the athletic director, to the dean of the whole fucking school. I sent copies to anyone I thought might help me. They expelled him for breaking the moral and ethical code of Rodner University. And after he got the news that he'd destroyed his future, I broke his fucking pretty boy nose."

I gasped, and Laird pulled my other thigh around his waist, until I locked my ankles behind his back. With each drive of his hips, he lifted both of us off the mattress.

"And… and Eli." His eyes were damp, but I couldn't tell if it was sweat or tears or both or maybe just my eyes watering so badly that he looked blurry. "I was going to be alone on Thanksgiving, you know? Dad hates me, Mom left, Garrett's dead, you were gone. I went to see Eli, to see what time he was eating so I could come and keep him company tomorrow. And his room was fucking empty, Reese. Martha was there putting fresh sheets on the bed, and I thought maybe he'd been discharged early, but then she told me he fucking died. Some fluke reaction to the same chemo he'd gone through a dozen other times. He died and I never even said goodbye. Never told him I loved him. Never got to—"

His voice broke off, and he shook his head before burying his face in the crook of my shoulder.

"I'm sorry, Reese. I'm so fucking sorry. I failed you, failed everyone. I'm so damn sorry…"

I tangled one hand in his hair, and wrapped the other around his back, crying from his pain, wanting to absorb it into myself and take it away from him.

He sucked my earlobe, his breath hot and fast against my neck, and his hips changed tactics, switched to short, quick drives, his ass flexing beneath my heels, his pelvis doing a drumroll on my clit.

Finally, finally I found my voice.

"*Laird.*"

I chanted his name, whispered it against his forehead, shouted it at the moon, felt it vibrate through every cell of my body.

And when my body tightened up again, impossibly finding another release, he finally let go, pulling out and pumping his cock furiously with his fist until he erupted in hot spurts on my stomach, marking me as his.

CHAPTER 37

Laird

REESE WAS QUIET.

She was quiet while I started the shower.

While I lathered her hair, soaped her perfect curves, and rinsed the suds down the drain.

While I scrubbed myself quickly, keeping her under the warm spray, being careful not to bump the kaleidoscope of bruises on her wrist.

But when she went to twist the knob to turn the water off, I stopped her, snagging her hand and turning her to face me.

"Talk to me. Did I hurt you? Was I too rough earlier?"

She blinked in surprise, tiny beads of water clinging to her lashes. "No. Not in the bed."

But the way she qualified her answer gave me pause.

"Before? About Garrett?"

I leaned back against the tile wall, and caught her waist,

tugging her forward to stand between my legs. Despite the reservation in her words, she wasn't pulling away, and I couldn't seem to stop myself from taking every opportunity to touch her in some way. To feel the silk of her skin against me.

My thumbs rubbed soothing patterns over the soft points of her hips.

She nodded, that little furrow appearing between her brows. "It wasn't just that you hadn't told me. It's that everyone else already knew that day. I felt humiliated when Marco mocked me, and you just ran off and left me to fend for myself." Reese crossed her arms over her chest, forcing some unwanted distance between us. "And then, when you didn't want to talk afterward…" She trailed off and dipped her chin.

"Then?" I prompted, bending my knees to catch her eyes.

She shrugged one shoulder. "It just felt like you didn't care. Like I wasn't a priority."

Her words hit like buckshot, the impact sharp and widespread, leaving me reeling.

"Reese, no." I shook my head to deny her words, my fingers digging into her skin. "*Never.*"

Her gaze flitted between my eyes, and I pleaded with her silently to believe me, to trust me even though I'd let her down. Long moments passed, and then she bit her lip, giving me a slight nod.

Loosening her protective stance, she traced the inked G on my chest with a featherlight touch, and sighed wistfully. "I wish I could've met him."

"I do, too." A lump formed in my throat, making it hard to swallow. "He would've liked you. The two of you would've ganged up on me."

She gave me a sad smile. "Yeah?"

I nodded, drawing her closer, needing to feel her solidness against me if we were going to talk about him like this. Squeezing my eyes closed, I rested my forehead on hers. "I could take you to his grave." I waited for the familiar wave of anguish that hit whenever I said that word—*grave*. "If you want? I think… I think I'd like that. No one's ever gone with me before."

"No one?" Her voice sharpened with disbelief.

"Not since the funeral."

A sound of disapproval hummed from her throat, then she slid her arms around my waist, and for a long moment, we just held each other. "I'd be honored."

The hot water sprayed against our legs, and steam billowed around us. It'd be easy to pretend the rest of the world didn't exist outside the foggy bathroom, to stay in here forever.

"I have to ask you—it's been making me crazy. Did you know? Have you been lying to me about the scholarship too?" Her words were hesitant, unsure.

"What scholarship?" I tilted my head.

"The one for your brother. The Garrett Bronson scholarship."

I paused, trying to understand her question. "What about it?"

She tapped her fingertips on my lower back, but I'm not even sure she realized she was doing it.

"I'm this year's winner."

"You are?" My brows shot up.

"You didn't know? Really?" Her beautiful brown eyes narrowed up at me. "Your brother's name is on the award and you didn't know?"

"No. I mean, you're right, it is his name, but…" I trailed off for a minute, trying to wrap my head around this other new connection between us. "The money is withdrawn from my account automatically. I used to pick the winners, read all the essays and pore over the applications, but it just got too hard after a while, hearing about these people who'd done all the things that Garrett would never get a chance to do." The back of my eyes burned, and I blinked furiously. "So now some official for the school chooses instead."

Reese pressed her lips to my tattoo, the heat from her mouth hotter than the steam around us. "I thought maybe you'd been lying to me about that this whole time too. I didn't make the connection until I went home this weekend and saw the paperwork again."

"I'm sorry I hurt you. And I'm not saying it won't happen again, because, fuck knows, everything good in my life seems to disappear, but I promise I won't lie to you. And I promise to always answer any questions you have. Past, present, future—anything you want to know, just ask."

I dipped my head and ran my nose up the side of her neck, nuzzling into her, wanting no wasted space between us.

"I know I fucked up. I didn't realize it at the time, because I was too caught up in my own shit, but I let you down, and that's not okay." I tasted the sensitive spot beneath her ear, felt her shudder in my embrace. "Reese, you make me want to be a better fucking man. Someone you'd be proud to hold hands with in public, to let the world know I was yours."

It stung that she didn't see me that way. Not yet. But I'd fucking earn it if she'd let me.

"Laird…" My stupid heart tripped over itself when I heard my name. I was so lost to this girl, and I couldn't come up with a single good reason for keeping it inside any longer.

At least if we crashed and burned, I'd have given it my all, no regrets.

I thought of Eli, how sometimes we didn't have time for second chances, and if we were lucky enough to get them, it'd be stupid as fuck to waste the opportunity.

And I wasn't stupid.

I tipped her chin up, until I knew my face was the only thing she could see. I didn't want her to miss a single word of my confession, even if it came too late to make a difference. "I love you, Reese Holland. Because you're feisty and opinionated and so damn strong—the strongest woman I've ever met. Because you make me smile every time I see you. Because you challenge me. Because your heart is so big and giving. Because you're so damn stubborn. Because your courage humbles me." I ran my finger over her lower lip. "Because I can't stop fucking thinking about you, and I don't want to *ever* stop thinking about you. I want to spend every day finding new ways to make you happy, to have your back while you chase your dreams, and to worship your body the way it deserves. I want to make you proud of me, to be worthy of standing by your side."

I don't think I'd said those words—*I love you*—since Garrett had died.

I trembled when her hands skimmed up my back until they were locked behind my neck. I'd never felt more raw or vulnerable than I did in that moment, waiting for her response.

"I love you too, Laird."

Her voice was thick and shaky, and I crushed her to me, until no drops of water could fit between us, scared I didn't hear her right, that my mind was playing tricks on me.

"Say it again," I demanded, my lips right at her ear. "I need to hear it again."

"I love you, Laird."

I hoisted her into my arms, spinning her so her back was

against the shower wall, and peppered her with kisses. Her cheek, her jaw, her throat, her delicate collarbone. I wanted to press my lips to every inch of her skin.

"Again."

"I love you. And I'm not good at this either. Everyone in my life has always looked at me like I was broken, or fragile, or needed protection. I'm not used to asking for help. I'm used fighting for the right to carve my own path. That's why I didn't tell you about Marco. I didn't mean to push you away. I… I've never had a guy who wanted to help raise me up before. Who wanted to see me reach new heights, instead of stand in his shadow. I've never met a guy like you before, who knows what I need before I can even say it. Who's taught me new things about myself, and inspired me to dream bigger and brighter. And fuck my stupid ideas about no one knowing about us. Life's too short to worry about other people's opinions. I think we know that more than anyone."

We did.

I turned the shower off, and grabbed a pair of towels for us. Being careful of her arm, I dried her off, wishing it was as easy to wipe away the pain of the last two weeks.

I found my softest t-shirt and tugged it over her head, her face clean and smooth as she smiled up at me. The furrow between her brows was gone, and so was the wariness that had been in her eyes when she first showed up.

Progress. I'd take it.

But then her stomach growled, and I winced. "I'm already failing at this boyfriend stuff. Are you hungry? I never asked you. And I know I skipped dinner."

She licked her lips, and her brown eyes sparkled as she pulled the towel from around my waist.

"Later. Some things are more important than food."

And then she dropped to her knees.

CHAPTER 38

Reese

I KNOCKED ON THE DOOR SOFTLY, NOT SURE IF SHE WAS sleeping or just looking out the window. Her head was turned away from me on the pillow. "Amelia?"

She twisted my direction, her eyes red and swollen.

"They're burying Eli right now, aren't they? Mom said I can't go. My white count is too low for all the germs."

I eased into the room, lowered the bedrail on one side, and perched next to her. Her small hand was cold in mine, the blue veins stark beneath her pale skin. She didn't have nail polish on because they'd want to be able to get a quick pulse ox on her finger if necessary. I knew from experience.

I made a mental note to bring some manicure stuff next time. They'd let me paint her toes.

"Soon. I'll be there. I thought I'd see if I could sneak him some drumsticks for the journey."

She smiled, faintly, but it was there. "He'd like that."

"I thought so too." I winked at her and fixed the edge of her hospital gown where it'd curled up. "Two weeks ago, I'd promised him that I'd take you two down to Starbucks for cake pops. And I want to apologize for missing the opportunity. But I brought you two cake pops. I thought you could have his too."

Her eyes welled with fresh tears as she took the cellophane bag from me. "You got me the pink one! It's my favorite."

I leaned in closer, and whispered, "That's what he told me."

"You know, don't tell my mom, but he was my secret boyfriend. Except, now he's gone. What does that mean? Is he still my boyfriend forever? Does this mean we broke up? I don't want to break up with him. I liked him. He told me I was pretty, and played cards with me, and made me smile. He told me some crazy story about peacocks last time."

My heart swelled and broke for her, and I searched for the right words to help. Spying a sheet of paper on the wheeled table next to her bed, I grabbed it and dug a pen out of my purse.

Writing in big, blocky letters, I spelled out her name on the page.

A M E L I A.

"See." I pointed to the letters. "That's you. But if you look closely, right in the middle of your name are the letters E-L-I." I drew a loop around them. "That's Eli. He's with you everywhere you go. You carry him with you in your name."

She traced the letters I'd circled. "That way I'll never forget him, right?"

"That way you'll never forget him," I confirmed, then hugged her to my side and kissed the top of her head. "Whenever you get sad and miss him, just remember he's with you, okay? And have a great big adventure that you can tell him about the next time you see him. I think he'd like that."

"I can do that." She sounded uncertain, but I hoped it'd give her something to look forward to. A broken heart was tragic at any age. "Can you take something to the funeral for me? Since I can't go?"

"Of course. I'd be happy to."

"I cut up some Uno cards and made a peacock with them in the craft room. It's over there on the windowsill."

I retrieved it and tucked it carefully in my purse while she watched. "It's beautiful, Amelia."

"You won't forget?"

"I won't forget."

CHAPTER 39

Laird

"**S**NARES, THIS IS OUR LAST REGULAR SEASON GAME, and as your captain, I want to thank y'all for your hard work and dedication the last few months." We were in the equipment room, where I'd asked everyone to report fifteen minutes earlier than normal. "Overall, this was an incredible season. I know we had some shit go down last week with Marco, but it never showed at practice or on the field. You were all professionals 'til the end, and I appreciate that."

I paused as people murmured their agreements and fist bumped each other.

"As y'all know, this is my final halftime show. I have to hang up my drumsticks and join the real world after this, which sucks ass. And last week, I played a solo during the snare break. But here's the thing. I don't want to play a solo this week. I don't want to play a snare duel either."

A few of the upper classmen looked at each other in confusion, but I kept Reese in my peripheral vision. I wanted to see her reaction to this next part.

"So… what are you doing?" Bubba finally asked.

"I want to play a duet. With Reese. Because I fucking love her, and I can't think of a better way to end my last football season than her by my side, playing for forty thousand screaming Rodner fans."

Around me, the rest of the line whooped and hollered, pounding me on the shoulders in congratulations. Beyond their genuine happiness for me, I'd told them about the shit Marco had pulled on her before last week's game, facts Smith was able to corroborate. They'd all been understandably disgusted at Marco's actions and even more disturbed that he'd specifically targeted a girl. I knew some of the guys with girlfriends and sisters took it especially hard that he'd physically hurt her, and they hadn't known to intervene.

Well.

I didn't tell them everything.

I didn't mention the private visit I'd paid to him where I'd delivered my special parting gift of a free rhinoplasty. Some things a man just had to handle on his own.

I snuck a peek at Reese.

With her hand over her mouth and her pretty eyes wide with shock, she tried to shake her head no. To refuse me.

And it went against everything I stood for to force a woman to do anything without her consent.

But I wasn't opposed to a little persuasion.

"It should be Bubba," she objected, pointing at the behemoth on my other side. "He's a senior too."

"Darlin'," Bubba drawled, adjusting the lapels of his uniform. "I know I've spent the last four years with him, but I don't think his feelings for me are quite the same. I'm pretty sure your guy there wants *you* standing by his side for his last game, not me. Besides, with this face of mine, I'd attract all the attention and no one would even look twice at him." He winked and stepped back, as if formally ceding the spot to her.

"Reese." I used my authoritative voice, the deep tone that forced people to pay attention. "I'm telling you as your captain to accept the field placement you've been assigned."

I grinned when her spine straightened with a snap, and her eyes sparked with that fire I loved so much.

Then I softened my voice and lifted my hand out to her. "And I'm asking as your boyfriend if you'd stand by my side tonight, in front of everyone."

She paused, rolling her eyes and acting reluctant to take my hand, but I saw the smile edging the corner of her mouth. "What happened to no special treatment?"

I tugged her to my side, and wrapped a possessive arm around her waist. "I hear what you're saying, but do you *really* want me to repeat that thing I did with my tongue this morning—the one where you got all religious for a moment—with the rest of these guys? 'Cause I'd rather save that just for you." I swung my head around. "No offense, Bubba."

He put his hands up and retreated another step. "Yeah, I'm good over here. In the tongue-free zone."

I looked back at her, where her irresistible grin had broken free and spread wide across her face.

She shook her head at me, her cheeks pink. "You're—"

"Insatiable? For you, absolutely."

And then I leaned down and captured her mouth, wrapping my arms fully around her, ignoring the catcalls and cheers from our audience. I didn't stop until I'd given her a little reminder of what my tongue had done between her thighs earlier, slipping inside for a quick taste when she moaned.

When we broke apart, I kept her in front of me, using her as a barrier to hide the evidence of my raging arousal, even though I'm sure every guy there saw right through my ploy. I didn't care though.

Let them be jealous.

Even though we'd barely left my bedroom for the last three days, I couldn't get enough of her.

It was like hearing those three magical words, that she loved me, had ripped free the last of my inhibitions. No more hiding and sneaking around.

I wanted everyone to know that she was mine.

After the preshow festivities ended and we were situated in the stands for the first half of the game, Reese and I decided to keep the duet simple. It'd be a riff off the cadence we'd both been teaching Eli in the hospital. It felt right to continue to honor his memory today, especially since he'd been such a big Rodner fan.

And when the time came, she performed flawlessly next to me, our drumsticks in perfect unison, our timing impeccable. I was so damn proud of her.

As we finished out the show, I scanned the stadium, taking in the view from the field under the floodlights one last time.

It felt slightly larger than life, being a part of a production like this, knowing everyone was watching you, knowing it was one of those performances where everything just clicked and flowed effortlessly.

My pulse raced at the same tempo as my drumsticks, the adrenaline thrumming in my veins, mixing with the roar of the crowd.

I was going to miss this.

As we marched off the field, the drumline pounding out the popular fight song while the audience cheered, I saw him.

My hands kept playing on autopilot, but I twisted my head for a second glance.

It was my dad. In the stands. On his feet and clapping, looking right at me.

I'm not sure he'd ever seen me play before.

Not in person.

But when the game ended, and the fans emptied the stadium to continue the celebration of another win somewhere else, I couldn't find him.

Not that I expected to.

Still, it was a nice gesture on his part.

After a pit stop at Sammy's, where I doubled our usual order, ignoring Reese's protests and telling her that I intended to help her work up an appetite, we headed back to my townhouse and changed into comfy clothes.

When the doorbell rang fifteen minutes later, I feigned confusion.

"Can you answer it? I'm feeding Oscar." I held up his dog food bowl as proof.

"Are we expecting someone?" Reese glanced down at her gym shorts and t-shirt, and patted her messy bun self-consciously.

She looked beautiful.

I just shrugged, since I'd promised myself I'd never lie to her again.

Reese cracked the door slowly and peeked outside, before suddenly yanking it all the way open.

"Mom? Dad? What are y'all doing here?"

Her mom fluttered around Reese, touching her arm, her cheek, smoothing a stray lock of hair off her forehead. Her dad wiped his feet fastidiously before entering.

"We got a call," her mom said, "from that young man you had to rush back here to see. He told me he felt bad we'd missed Thanksgiving with you, and flew us down, set us up with box tickets—it's so much cleaner up there—then said to swing by for a late dinner. He even booked us a hotel. So here we are."

She wrapped her daughter in a hug, then studied me over Reese's shoulder.

"He's very good looking," her mom stage-whispered. "And so thoughtful."

Reese laughed. "Among other things."

She untangled herself from her mom's embrace, hugged her dad, then joined me in the kitchen, where I was putting the subs and chips on actual plates instead of just serving them on their wrappers like we normally did. I figured I'd serve them up fancy since it was Thanksgiving dinner and all. When I was organizing this surprise, I'd considered ordering a turkey and all the fixings from Publix, but changed my mind.

The subs were her favorite, and she was my favorite. It was that simple.

Her parents were washing their hands in the bathroom, out of sight, but I still wasn't expecting her to launch herself at me the way she did.

I barely caught her as she wrapped her legs around my waist, then pressed her mouth to mine for a hot, but brief kiss.

"Have I told you today that I love you?"

"Not in the last hour, at least." I stole another kiss.

"Tragic. How can I make it up to you?"

I whispered a couple dirty suggestions in her ear that had her squirming against me until we heard her parents approaching, and I reluctantly had to let her go.

"Later," she whispered. "All of those things. At least twice."

It was the best Thanksgiving dinner I'd ever had.

Especially dessert.

EPILOGUE

Reese

"**R**EMEMBER THAT STUPID QUIZ YOU GAVE ME THE first time you came over here?"

We were sprawled in a satisfied heap on his bed on a lazy springtime Saturday morning, our limbs tangled together, my head pillowed on his chest.

"Vaguely."

"Look it up. Ask me again. I'm pretty sure I'd pass this time."

I squinted up at him. "Like… now?"

"Yes." He swatted my ass and handed me my phone from the nightstand.

Humoring him, I opened up my browser and typed RELATIONSHIP QUIZ, and scrolled down until I saw the familiar Cosmo quiz. It would be kind of interesting to know how his answers had changed from before.

"Okay, ready?" I squirmed, trying to find a more

comfortable position. "Question one, her idea of a perfect date is A. Getting dressed up and—"

"I don't need multiple choices," he interrupted.

I poked my tongue in the side of my cheek. "That's kind of how these things work."

"You'll know if I pass, won't you?"

"I guess," I conceded.

"All right. Your perfect date. Something that challenges you. Something outdoors. Something that gives you a chance to show a bunch of guys you can hold your own. And then a giant picnic afterward, naked, right here in this bed."

I paused, contemplating his answer. "Not bad."

"Maybe something like the Tough Mudder 5K obstacle course I signed us up for next weekend."

"I—wait, you did what?"

"Planned our perfect date." He dropped a kiss on the top of my head, and I could hear the smile in the cocky, pleased tone of his voice. "Next question."

"Oh my God, really? I've always wanted to do one of those!"

"And next week, you will. You're going to conquer it, and then you're going to help me deal with my wounded pride when your time is better than mine by letting me conquer you that night. All night. Until my fragile male ego is fully restored. Keep reading."

A little dazed, because that actually *did* sound like a perfect date, I read, "Question two. She hates it when her man…"

"Tells her what to do. Unless we're in the bedroom, where she not-so-secretly loves it."

I tipped my head to the side in thought. "Valid. Question three. When it comes to your friends…"

"She prefers I disappear with them when that time of

the month rolls around, so she can deprive me of her extra swollen, extra sensitive boobs, which I think is just bullshit, but I love her, so I'll go with it."

Another bullseye for him, although I giggled at the exaggerated pout curving his lips.

"Question four. You want to go to the big party on Saturday but she isn't feeling well. You—"

"Call Smith to come deal with your moody ass."

My shocked gaze flew to his, my mouth dropping open a little in disapproval.

He smirked. "Just kidding. You know I live for the times when you actually let me pamper you the way you deserve."

I flushed. My insistence on my independence was a long-standing source of frustration for him, although, to his credit, he always supported what I wanted to do, even if I wouldn't allow him to help me most of the time.

"Moving on. Question five. When it comes to living together…"

"The sooner the better, considering I don't think you've spent more than half a dozen nights at your dorm since New Year's."

My heart fluttered. He'd hinted at that before, but I'd worried he'd start to feel trapped.

"Yeah?"

"Of course. Haven't I made it obvious by now how much I like waking up next to you? Have you already forgotten the last three hours?" He shrugged, the movement making his chest rise and fall beneath me. "Plus, Oscar pouts when you're not here. You know how I feel about having a sad wiener."

"There's *nothing* worse than a sad wiener," I mocked him, rolling my eyes.

"There's really not. Good thing you know how to keep

mine so happy." And he flexed his hips, showing me just how happy I made his.

"My ideal anniversary gift is…"

"Sausage. Lots and lots of sausage."

"I'm starting to sense a trend with your answers here, Laird."

He stretched, his sculpted muscles bunching and shifting, and I stopped myself from running a palm over the ridges of his abdomen.

"Not my fault you can't get enough of me. Keeping you happy is damn near a full-time job. Not that I'm complaining. I'd happily clock forty hours a week between those long legs of yours."

I blushed, and felt a familiar tingle start between my thighs.

"Question six. Does she—"

"You know what? Let's save the rest for another time. I've got a multiple-choice question of my own to ask you."

"Oh yeah? What's that?"

"How do you want to come in the next twenty minutes? A. In the shower. B. Against the wall. C. In the bed. D. All of the above." His voice was low and husky, the sound vibrating through my chest.

I licked my lips, dropped my phone on the bed and turned over so I could see him.

"Have I mentioned how much I love your penchant for being an overachiever?" I threw one thigh over his hips, straddling him. "Start the clock."

ACKNOWLEDGEMENTS

Honestly, I don't even know where to start. I'm lucky enough to have a huge tribe of amazing people who supported me during the course of this book, and writing a few lines in the back will never be enough to thank them.

To my husband, for understanding the need to chase my dreams, and watching our boys so I could.

To my bestie, Erin Noelle. Not only could I not do this without you, I wouldn't want to. I can't wait to see you in Vegas and celebrate properly! Thanks for keeping me sane and reminding me I could do this. I love you!

To the most patient PA a girl could ever wish for, Melissa Panio-Petersen. I don't know how you put up with me and my craziness, but I hope we keep it up for another dozen years at least. I love our late-night chats, your gorgeous graphics, and the way you keep me organized. I'd be lost without you.

To my brilliant betas who called me out when I took a wrong turn and selflessly spend hours helping me perfect the details of this story. Y'all are the real MVPs. Lex Martin, Kata Cuic, Hazel James, Melissa Panio-Petersen, Jordan Bates, Emily Snow, Yessi Smith, Ashley Christin, Alison Evans-Maxwell, Lindsey Rodner, Michelle Grad, Allison East – you guys rock and have my endless thanks.

To Erin Noelle and Jennifer Van Wyk for editing and fixing all my goofs.

Thank you to Hang Le for creating an absolutely beautiful cover to go along with this story. I have no doubt some of you grabbed this book without even reading the blurb because of it. Hopefully, the inside lived up to the outside.

Thank you to Stacey Blake at Champagne Formats for swooping in Superman-style to get my files the right size! Thank you to Erica Alexander for saving the day with some crazy last-minute formatting for the ARCs! I can't wait to see the paperback in person!

To Kata Cuic, Julie Deaton, and Ellie McLove for squeezing me in for proofing – I swear I'll schedule things better in the future!

To my author buddies who gave me the biggest compliment ever, and said they wanted to read Drumline – y'all humble me. Tijan – your encouragement over lunch that day meant a lot to me. Sara Ney – your insane enthusiasm the last few weeks has motivated me. Time to trade ARCs! Kandi Steiner and Brittainy Cherry, Sierra Simone, Ahren Sanders, RC Boldt, Meghan March, Aly Martinez, ME Carter, Mariah Dietz, and everyone else who listened to me babble about this story, thank y'all.

To my readers in The Wreck – omg, you guys make every single day brighter for me. I hope I made you proud!

To every blogger who helps the spread the word about stories they love – never doubt that you're making a difference. You are.

To all the readers who spent a couple hours with Laird and Reese, thank you! Thank you, thank you, thank you. And if you went above and beyond and left a review or told your friends about Drumline—that support is priceless. Keep being awesome!

ABOUT THE AUTHOR

USA Today Bestseller Stacy Kestwick is a Southern girl who firmly believes mornings should be outlawed. Her perfect day would include puppies, carbohydrates, and lounging on a hammock with a good book. No adulting, cleaning, or bacon allowed.

Find me at:

www.stacykestwick.com

www.facebook.com/stacykestwickauthor

www.facebook.com/groups/StacyKestwicksTheWreck

www.stacykestwick.com/mailing-list-sign-up

www.twitter.com/stacykestwick

www.instagram.com/stacykestwick

www.goodreads.com/stacykestwick

ALSO BY
STACY KESTWICK

Wet

Soaked

Made in the USA
Monee, IL
20 February 2022

91520309R00197